TANGLED CHARMS

CHARM HAVEN MYSTERIES
BOOK TWO

TABATHA GRAY

Copyright © 2023 by Clue LLC

All rights reserved.

No part of this book may be reproduced in any form or by any electronic or mechanical means, including information storage and retrieval systems, without written permission from the author, except for the use of brief quotations in a book review.

Author site: www.tabathagray.com

Editing by Victory Editing

This book was written and is set in the traditional land of the first people of Seattle, the Duwamish People past and present. We honor with gratitude the land itself and the Duwamish Tribe.

AUTHOR'S NOTE

As you read, you can get exclusive messages from Charm Haven sent right to your email. It's like having an insider friend filling you in on all the gossip.

If you picked up your book through my website, tabathagray.com, the bonuses will start arriving in your inbox just a day or so after your purchase.

And if you bought your book elsewhere, no worries at all! You can still get the read-along experience by visiting tabathagray.com/chbonus. Enjoy!

PROLOGUE

By the witch-flame's dying gasp
a tale unfolds of virtue spent.
A soul unsoiled by darkness past
shall dangle o'er the fiery pit.
A dagger drawn. A deed undone.
A love unsaid. A war unwon.
A lie that has been told and told again will ravel.
A wounded heart in silence battles
love, and lovely things resents,
and reaps what vengeance it can sow
in letters sealed but never sent.

1

I stood on Gran's porch and looked past the stranger in tweed. Beyond the lush clover, buzzing flowers, and plum trees heavy with dark sweet fruit, the ground dropped away and the honeysuckle air stretched out to a clear blue promise.

The letter, clenched in my right hand, was a promise, too. One I didn't need to look at. The envelope's soft paper had the kind of handmade roughness you paid for. My Uncle Max must have paid his attorneys well.

He wanted the house, of course. I should have known when we refused his offer that he wouldn't take no for an answer. But the house had chosen my sister and me. Even as we stood on the porch looking out, I felt it behind us like a slumbering giant breathing softly as it dreamed.

Our first step would be to meet with our lawyer, Hector Morales, to see if there was any substance to Uncle Max's threat. Our second step—

"Well? Do you deny it?" A woman's crisp voice plucked me down from the wild blue yonder. It came from the stranger. The reporter. Dana Something-Or-Other. She looked familiar, but I couldn't place her. "The explosion wasn't caused by a gas leak, was it?"

She was a thirty-something brunette with her hair tied back and a tweed blazer that had British aspirations. Serious. Smart. Professional. But there was something about her posture, maybe the way she stooped to hide her height, that gave away her humanity like a stray hair.

Memory flashed, and I knew where I'd seen her. A TV news segment about my bookstore. The kind of talking head blurb they film on scene at every car wreck, robbery, and murder. Those vultures had arrived just after the firefighters and swarmed like flies, while I sat on the curb and rocked myself and shivered under a crinkly foil blanket.

"Why are you here?" I asked. I knew the answer, of course. She was here for fresh meat for her viewers. For ratings and clicks and a pat on the back from a boss as nihilistic as she was.

"You are Holly Nightingale, aren't you?" She eyed me for three heartbeats, then glanced at Hazel.

"You came all the way from Seattle to interview the woman whose bookstore exploded?"

"There were several discrepancies in the police report. For instance—"

"I don't care."

"But I have reason to believe that officials are lying about—"

"Does that look like my problem?"

"It's all of our problem if we don't—"

She started going on about journalism with a capital J, but the words flew past me. I had a queasy feeling in my stomach and an itch in my brain. Something about her didn't make sense. It hit me. "Where's your crew?"

She looked up from her speech. "My crew?"

"TV journalists always have a van following them around, don't they? A guy with a camera?"

"Usually, yes—"

"How do you expect to show the viewers how devastated I am without a camera?"

"I was just hoping to get a statement from you about—"

"I'll give you a statement. In the past week, my life has been turned upside down, spun around, and hung up to dry. I have a lawsuit to deal with and a house to save, and I don't have the time or the patience to be your human-interest story."

My sister, beside me, glowed in her yellow sundress, but she looked worried. She bit her bottom lip and flashed me a weak smile. She'd been quiet since yesterday, when she'd nearly become the first witch in a few hundred years to be burned at the stake by the Inquisition. I couldn't blame her. She needed time and space to recover. She needed protection. Good thing I'd come through unscathed.

I put my hand on Hazel's back and started toward the open door. "Let's go inside."

"Wait! You're right!" Her desperate voice might have grabbed me. I turned.

"I don't have my crew." She looked at the ground. "I don't have a crew anymore. And I'm not here officially. I tried to get my editor to assign me to the story. The city's covering up something big. But he doesn't care about anything but what the corporate office tells him. He sent me to shoot another accident just north of Issaquah. A lumber truck blindsided a minivan full of retirees and sent them tumbling down a hill."

"That sounds awful," Hazel said. She was always so empathetic, even when she should have been thinking about herself.

"Have you ever seen land that's been logged?" Dana asked. "The stumps stick up from the ground like spikes. They tore the van to bits. First the body panels, then the engine, and finally… Rob and I set up at the top of the hill just as a breeze pushed up from below. It smelled like gasoline and Vicks VapoRub. I threw up twice and broke down crying five times before I called my editor and told him I couldn't film the segment. He fired me."

"That… does sound awful," I said, dammit. "But if the TV station fired you, why do you want to interview me?"

"The city's been working hard to cover up some aspects of the explosion. I want to know why."

I snuffed out a laugh. "I'm not sure you'd believe us if we told you."

"Try me."

And besides, I wasn't sure I wanted to tell her. It was all so fresh. So raw. I felt like the van that rolled down the hill. I needed time to gather my pieces and weld them back together. I needed to deal with the lawsuit—wait. Something tickled the back of my mind.

Hazel and I were being sued by our uncle over the house. Gran left it to us, not him. An inheritance squabble. The most normal thing in the world.

But Uncle Max was one of the richest men in the country. He could spend millions on the best lawyers in the world. I wasn't even sure we had money to pay Hector Morales. If we were going to save the house, we had to be smart about it. Most of all, we had to know why. Why did he want the house?

Who better to find out than a maverick reporter who wanted to hold powerful people accountable?

Talking to her would be a risk. She might not believe us. She might decide that I was crazy, or that I'd committed insurance fraud, or done something to Caleb. After all, the world still thought he was missing in the explosion. Only a handful of people knew him as the psycho he was, leading a double life as Grand Inquisitor or whatever.

I peered at Dana. Her soliloquy had sloughed off some of her broadcast perfection and in the big blooming garden she seemed painfully alone.

I turned to my sister. "What do you think, Hazel? Should we invite her in for tea?"

"That sounds"—she looked at Dana in a way I couldn't decipher—"lovely."

We filed into the foyer, where the morning light made the white lace curtains glow. We took a left toward the kitchen. I slid Max's letter in my back pocket, found the kettle, filled it with water and set it on the cream enamel stove of the old design that was lit by magical fire.

A steeper shaped like a crescent moon sat in the cabinet by a collection of six glass jars filled with dark, curled tea leaves and labeled with a spidery hand: JASMINE, OOLONG, PEPPERMINT... I grabbed the oolong and filled the steeper. When the kettle screamed, I took it hot and sizzling from the stove and poured steaming water into a chipped blue teapot. I carried it and three mugs over to the small breakfast table where Hazel and Dana leaned toward each other conspiratorially.

Holly clapped her hands and shot back in her chair. "... and then I said, 'I guess we both took the scenic route!'"

They burst out laughing. I smiled too, because Hazel was becoming herself again. I saw the old effortless ease flooding back in like a tide. Was I wrong to judge Dana so harshly?

Hazel took a mug from me. "I was just telling Dana about a hike I took in Borneo. Turns out she's been there too. From the sound of it we both had the same shady tour guide."

I sat and poured tea for myself and lifted the mug to my mouth. It was too hot to drink, but it smelled amazing, like flowers and fruit and earth.

"So let's get down to business," Dana said.

I savored the feeling of steam on my face, then lowered my cup to the table. "What if I could help you hold one of the richest men in the world accountable?"

"Not where I expected this to go. But, who?"

"Our uncle... Maxwell Amp."

She almost spit out her tea. "Your uncle is Maxwell Amp? *The* Maxwell Amp?"

I nodded. "He has a dark secret in his past that caused him to leave Charm Haven. I don't know what it is, but Gran —his mother—alluded to it in her will. When she left us this house, he tried to buy it. When we said no he sued us. There's something here he wants. Or maybe something he wants to cover up."

Dana looked around the cozy kitchen, as if seeing it with new eyes. "But you don't know for certain."

"No."

"He might want the house for sentimental reasons."

"Perhaps."

"But if there was some meat on that bone, it could get me back in the game." She swallowed and I'd never seen someone so hungry. "It's an interesting offer."

"Will you help us?"

"Will you finally answer my question?"

"Sure. Why not?" I sipped my tea and felt its warmth spread through my body. "You were right. The explosion at my bookstore wasn't caused by a gas leak."

She leaned in. "So what was it? Chemical spill? A drug lab? Neighbors told me the wildest stories. A few claimed they had seen an elderly woman fleeing the scene on a broom. Of course that suggests psychotropic chemicals being released—"

"She was a witch."

Dana shook her head and squinted. "Excuse me?"

TANGLED CHARMS | 9

"I know it's hard to believe, but the elderly woman. Her name was Maleia, our great-aunt. She was a witch."

Dana glanced at Hazel, who shrugged.

"Maleia set the bomb in my bookstore. She was working with my evil ex-fiancé, who had been ordered to seduce me by the Inquisition."

"Like… the Spanish Inquisition?"

"They wanted to bait me back here to fulfill a prophecy and bring magic back to Charm Haven. But they wanted to steal it and destroy it because they hate magic but the bird reached me in time and we flew on a broom and fixed it!"

Dana cocked her head to the side and frowned. "And do you know how to reach this Maleia for comment?"

"Not unless you can raise the dead."

Dana let out an enormous sigh, closed her eyes and shook her head. "Ten years in the business and you'd think I'd know how to sniff out a liar." She stood and the chair squealed back behind her. "Do you seriously expect me to believe that your evil stepmother blew up your store and flew away on a broom?"

"Great-aunt, but, yeah."

"It's the truth," Hazel said.

"Have you even *been* to Borneo? Or was that your idea of a joke too? I can understand not wanting to talk to the press, but you don't have to be such… such… jerks about it!"

My heart leaped into my throat. If Dana left now, who would help us dig up dirt on Uncle Max? "I can prove it."

She laughed. "Are you going to take me on a broom ride?"

I couldn't. The broom had been confiscated by the police as evidence. But I didn't need it. What had Gran's ghost told me? I'm the thirteenth daughter. I don't need to *learn* magic. I *am magic*.

Last night I had almost drowned in white-hot power. I had rescued my sister from the bonfire, pulled her to the ground with only a thought and a twitch of my fingers. I'd summoned the broom and woven a magical barrier that both saved the people of Charm Haven and returned the magic their families gave up long ago.

Surely, surely I had enough magic left for sparks, to dim the lights, to convince a skeptical journalist.

I closed my eyes and reached for the place above my heart where the magic had entered me. But what had been full before was empty. I searched but I was a cupboard full of cobwebs.

I clenched my teeth and willed the magic to appear, but I might have been wishing on a shooting star for all the good it did me.

Why? Why couldn't things work just for once? How was I going to—I opened my eyes and saw Dana's slack-jawed face illuminated like a paper lantern. She stared at Hazel's outstretched hand, which held an ethereal orchid softly glowing white. It flickered out and Dana brought her gaze up to Hazel's face and they locked eyes.

"How did you do that?" Dana reached out and took Hazel's hand, examined the empty palm, then flipped it over.

"Magic," Hazel said, nervous, blushing. That wasn't like her at all.

Dana's mouth opened but she didn't speak. I could almost see her entire worldview rearranging itself on the spot.

I coughed and they turned to me. "Now, will you help us?"

It was a man's voice, behind me, who replied. "Help you with what, exactly?"

2

*D*eputy Sprout stood in the doorway. The top of his black-and-tan police cap grazed the doorframe, but you could have fit two of him side by side. I suspected if I gave him a good shake, his head would have rattled around in the hat like a bean inside a maraca.

His tan uniform billowed around him, cinched at the neck by a tight collar that squeezed his bulging Adam's apple, and at the waist by a thick black belt with a waxed leather holster and a cherry-handled pistol made of dark blued steel.

He gave the room a slow inspection and nodded like the cozy kitchen was just as sordid and depraved as he'd imagined.

I remembered the smell of stale coffee and floor polish from the police station, the morning Maleia died. I'd sat on a hard steel chair, in the morning chill, wearing only leggings and the oversized Morrissey tee I slept in. I shivered.

Hazel had rescued me then. Burst in with our lawyer, Hector, and whisked me to freedom. But she was the one who needed protecting now.

I squared my shoulders and looked Deputy Sprout in the face. "Don't you need a warrant to barge into people's homes?"

The deputy shrugged. "Door was open."

"What do you want?"

"I'm not here to arrest you, if that's what you're worried for."

"Then what? Shouldn't you be out there rounding up the inquisitors?"

"Already did, though your boyfriend got away."

"He's not my boyfriend. He's a sociopath."

Sprout's hard soles clapped the kitchen's tile floor as he walked to the breakfast table, slid out a chair, sat and kicked his feet up and flashed his teeth at the three of us standing. He steepled his fingers then let out a weary sigh. "Quite a mess you've caused."

"I don't know what you're talking about."

"Of course you don't. It's rare to find real civic spirit these days. Nobody thinks much beyond their own gratification."

"...he says with his dirty shoes on my breakfast table."

"Let me ask you, Holly, have you ever considered what it must be like to be an officer of the law on a small, remote island such as Charm Haven? Have you ever stopped to think about all the flavors of rivalry that could flare into hatred when so many unique individuals are bottled up in such tight quarters for centuries?"

I'd grown up here. Sometimes folks didn't get along, but hatred? "It's a dramatic way of putting it."

"In a big city you can arrest troublemakers, ship them off to the county lockup and forget they ever existed. But out here? We're on our own. An island full of eccentrics and troublemakers, with feuds going back centuries. If I locked them all up, there'd be nobody left."

"That must be very sad for you."

TANGLED CHARMS | 13

"My job is more about maintaining balance, equilibrium, stasis. The founding families might hate each other, but if they're equally matched, neither of them can do much about it. Or, I should say, they couldn't."

"I'm still not seeing the point."

His gaze might have cut me. "The point, Holly Nightingale, is that you and your sister have upset the balance. Your little stunt last night—"

"Our stunt? We saved the town from being *murdered* by the Inquisition!"

"And in the process, you release a wild, chaotic energy into a place that had simmered down and settled into a quiet, grudging coexistence."

"We *returned magic* to Charm Haven! You should be thanking us!"

"Is that right? This morning I got a call from Judie Thomlanson. Said a miniature snowstorm had appeared out of nowhere and frozen her prize begonias. Just after that Michael Thorn reported that one of his beehives had sprouted legs and run toward the Crone's Wood."

The way the deputy stared at me told me it was a bad idea to laugh. I coughed. "And what do you want us to do about it?"

"Fix it."

"You can't give us orders."

"I'm informing you what has to be done."

"And if I refuse? Are you going to arrest us? Throw us in jail?"

"Sweetie, if the founding families start feuding again, with the power that you so irresponsibly distributed, things will get bad around here pretty fast. And you two, the Nightingale sisters are sitting at the top of the hill. If things get out of hand, there might not be enough of you left to arrest."

I narrowed my eyes and swallowed a growl. How dare he

sneak into my house, put his dirty feet on my table, and make up stories to threaten us. I'd seen how incompetent Deputy Sprout was first hand. He hadn't come close to finding Maleia's killer. He was too busy trying to pin it on me!

A blinding flash of white-hot pain streaked behind my eyes. I winced and rubbed my temples.

It was laughable, really. Charm haven wasn't a flaming tinderbox. It was a sleepy little village at the edge of the world. The town square might have been from a Hallmark movie: tea shop, bakery, grocery run by my hunky ex.

The world around me had thickened somehow, like it had all gone underwater. The pain came again and stayed, not a flash, but a laser drilling a hole in the front of my skull.

Only a petty tyrant like Deputy Sprout would think it was a bad thing for us to return magic to everyone. I mean, there was a prophecy for crying out loud!

And he *still* had his feet on my table! A clod of dirt on the side of his heel dangled just above the table cloth. He shifted and it fell.

My vision narrowed to a pinprick. The pain whistled in my ears.

The teapot, on the table, exploded.

Shards of wet ceramic pelted my face, hailed against the wall and clinked to the floor. My headache faded. The world was normal again. I grinned at the soaked deputy. "I don't believe you."

He used his sleeve to wipe tea from his face, then picked a pea-sized shard of ceramic out of his ear and peered at it like a bullet at a crime scene. "It would seem you just proved my point."

"Even if the founding families are snapping at each other's throats, I'm not responsible for them."

"Your last name *is* Nightingale, isn't it?"

"I don't care about the Thorn beehive or the Thomlanson begonias."

"As easy as that? And I suppose you'll just waltz back to Seattle and leave me to clean up your mess."

I glanced at Hazel. She and Dana were whispering to each other like schoolgirls. It was good to see her getting over yesterday's trauma, but I wasn't naive enough to think that you ever really got over something like that. She needed to take care of herself, not get caught up in small-town politics. And after I failed her yesterday…

Mom and Dad were gone. Hazel only had me to look out for her. And what had I done? I'd let her get captured by the Inquisition.

I wouldn't put her in danger again. Not for Charm Haven. Not for the world. "My answer is no."

But the deputy looked past me, at Dana. She had taken off her blazer and was picking bits of ceramic from it.

"Who's your friend?" His tone was a little too casual.

"You want to talk with me?" Dana said, looking up. "Why?"

Deputy Sprout swung his left foot then his right off the breakfast table. He leaned forward, pressed his hands against his knees, and stood. "Place like this you get used to seeing the same faces. I don't believe I've seen yours before."

"I came in this morning on the ferry."

"You staying with your friends here?"

"I wasn't certain if I would overnight at the inn, or take the ferry back to the mainland later today."

"When you got off the ferry, did you walk straight here?"

"I had a cup of tea at the shop. I wasn't sure where I would find Holly. I spoke with a strange man with an umbrella and an old-fashioned black suit. He gave me directions to this house and I came here. Now why are you giving me the third degree?"

16 | TABATHA GRAY

"I think you'd better come with me to the station."

Dana laughed. "No way in hell am I going to speak to you without an attorney."

"If you don't want to come voluntarily, I can always arrest you."

This was nuts! He couldn't barge into my house without a warrant, interrogate my guest, then threaten to arrest them. I felt a hand on my shoulder and turned to see that Dana had put on her jacket.

"It's okay Holly," she said. "I'll go. Just find me a lawyer." She started toward the door, followed by the deputy.

"Why are you arresting her?" I called after them. "What are the charges?"

Deputy Sprout turned around and flashed a twinkling smile. "Blackmail."

I stared at the empty doorway and heard the muffled click of the front door closing. I stared for a dozen breaths, then turned back to the table, pulled out my chair and sat on something spiny and wet.

Right. The teapot.

The tea in the chair felt warm as it soaked into my jeans. A moment later it felt like nothing at all. Hazel sat too, with a faded, faraway look. "You don't think Dana committed blackmail, do you?"

We hadn't known her long, but unless everything about her was a lie I couldn't see it. She wanted to hold powerful people accountable. If she had dirt on someone, she would share it with the public. I shook my head. "I don't think she did."

"Then why would he arrest her? Her answers must have incriminated her somehow."

"Deputy Sprout is truly awful at his job. Do you still have Hector's phone number?"

Hazel shook her head. "It's in my pack back at the inn."

"It's better that we go in person, anyway. We can bring Uncle Max's letter and see if that lawsuit holds water while we're there."

3

ON THE OUTSKIRTS OF CHARM HAVEN

The beehive looked like any other beehive. It was made of two cedar boxes, naturally finished, stacked one atop the other. At the bottom was a base with a ledge where bees landed and took off. At the top was a lid shaped like a small gabled roof.

Bees lived in the lower box, and the upper box was where they built out honeycomb to cells, deposited the nectar of countless wildflowers, and fanned it with their buzzing wings until it thickened to sticky, golden honey.

All of this was very normal for a beehive. And yet, the beehive didn't feel normal. Not normal at all, it thought, as it walked through the tall grass, leaving a trail of bent and broken stalks behind it.

The world had been still for most of the beehive's life. It had spent a hundred years (although such concepts are entirely foreign to it) growing from a sapling to a tall tree in a modest copse by a river. Those had been wonderful years.

TANGLED CHARMS | 19

Then the fast-moving things, which he would later learn were called people, had come. They had used iron to separate its trunk from its roots, had floated the trunk in a river to an awful place where they had used iron once more to split the trunk into long narrow pieces, and to sculpt its lovely natural curves into sickening straightness and horrific flatness. After this violation, more of the people had come, and assembled the pieces into its current unnatural shape, and filled it with buzzing things that moved even faster than the people. There, it had sat for many years, until it had almost forgotten what it was like to be a tree by the river. But now the memories flooded back.

The beehive, being made of cedar, didn't understand the finer points of existential dread. It wasn't smart enough to have an identity crisis. And as it had no nerves, it couldn't have a nervous breakdown.

But it did have an impression, made suddenly urgent, that things were not now as they had once been. That made it furious.

The hive stopped and peered between the blades of the grass, feeling them scrape along its smooth wooden face. Just ahead, there was a sound like running water from an oddly shaped piece of iron sitting on a small puddle made of stone. Behind it sat an enormous pile of wood that had been cut and rearranged into an even stranger shape, covered with thorny vines.

The shape had many holes. Through one the beehive saw one of the fast creatures known as people.

The person was softer-looking than the woodcutters had been. It looked at its reflection. It reached up and removed the bark-colored pelt from its top box and replaced it with a different pelt the color of straw.

Seeing this creature made the beehive feel a sort of pressure. At first, he thought the bees had started fanning particularly hard. But he soon realized this sensation was something different. It was new.

The beehive had just experienced its first *idea*.

It would find the people who had separated its trunk from its roots. Who had changed its curves to straightness, its roughness to smoothness. It would find them, then it would make them reverse the process. And if they didn't... well, there were always the bees.

4

We walked down the hill into town, toward the Morales law firm. The remnants of last night's celebration still littered Charm Haven Square. Summer blooms, slightly wilted, hung from every lamppost. Matching ramps bracketed a pile of fine ash, all that was left of the Litha bonfire after it blazed with magic and shot us whooping into the air and floated us safely down.

In the midnight fire glow it had seemed that everything was mended. We'd saved the town, fulfilled the prophecy and defeated the Inquisition once and for all. You'd think that would bring Hazel and me together. But something had changed between us. Talking to her felt strange and stilted, like a singer stopping before the last note of a scale: Do Re Me Fa So La Ti…

Then again, maybe I was overthinking it. We'd both had a shock. Anyone would need time to recover. And hadn't she perked up once we invited Dana in for tea?

I glanced at Hazel from the corner of my eye. She had that faraway look that was so out of place on her. "Don't worry," I said, "Hector will fix all of this. He'll pop over to the police station and rescue Dana just like he rescued me yesterday."

"I hope so…"

I waited for her to finish. Waited. Nothing? Well then, it was time for me to bring out the big guns. I cleared my throat. "I might be crazy, but did you and Dana have, like, a moment?"

"I don't know."

"You were both laughing."

"She's funny."

"Is that all?"

"I was thinking… there might still be time to get my room back at the house share in Bali."

I froze and stared at Hazel, who kept walking for a few paces then turned around. My face felt hot and my head was full of buzzing flies. It took a dozen heartbeats for her words to sink in. She wasn't leaving, was she?

She flashed a weak smile then looked at the ground. "I just think it might be time for me to go, you know?"

"Like, right now?"

"Of course not! I want to make sure Dana's okay, maybe stop by the pub and say goodbye to Luna and Silas and the others. And I still want to spend the night in Gran's house, now that it's all fixed up. I've only really seen the kitchen and I know you were excited to show it to me."

"Then when?"

"It's summer, the high season in Bali. House shares fill up really fast. I'll need to get there quickly."

"When!" I didn't mean to bark the word.

"I'll catch the ferry out in the morning."

This couldn't be happening. She couldn't be leaving me when there was still so much unsettled. I was the thirteenth daughter of a family of witches. Wasn't there anything I could do to make her stay?

"What about magic? We're just beginning to learn about our powers."

"Powers? You mean this?" She held out her hand with a ball of white light that vanished when she closed her fist around it. More than I could do. She shook her head. "It's a nice party trick, but I'm not going to upend my life for it. You didn't expect me to stay here forever, did you?"

"But we haven't even dug through Gran's library. It's full of books about our family history!"

"That was always your thing. We left here when I was little. I didn't really know Gran. I'm not as attached to this place as you are."

"You said it felt like home!"

"It did! But—"

"And we've only been here for two days but you've already made friends with half the town."

"I thought I would die, Holly!" It rushed out so jagged I sucked in a breath. "They tied me up and threw me on the ground. They made me watch them build a pyre. They told me over and over how glorious it would be to see me burn. They told each other that the world would be such a better place without me in it."

"Oh. Oh my God." I knew they captured her. It was my fault, after all. I never stopped to think how afraid she must have been. I wanted to rush to her, to hug her, but there might have been a wall between us.

Her mouth was a quivering line, and tears pooled in the bottom of her eyes. "I'm not like you are. I'm not strong."

What was she talking about?

"After they disappeared. You started a bookstore. You found a building and fixed it up, made connections with publishers, learned about business."

"None of that makes me strong."

"When I was on the road I'd check your website, just to

see what you were doing. You constantly had readings and signings and book clubs. You made something that was precious to people. You built a community from nothing, like a chosen family."

My vision went blurry. Why did she have to remind me of everything I lost in the explosion? "The bookstore is how I dealt with Mom and Dad disappearing. If I was working I didn't have to think about it. Work was an escape for me."

"Well I just ran."

"You were living, traveling the way most people only dream about. I've seen you. People love you! All you need is a couple of minutes sharing a taxi with someone and you'll leave on a first-name basis with promises to keep in touch."

"I lose friends just as quickly. That's what you don't see. Still, Dana reminded me of how nice it is to meet somebody completely new, someone who hasn't heard all your stories, who doesn't have any idea who you are, who you can't disappoint."

"Who are you disappointing?"

"I'm like the world's biggest disappointment! Mom and Dad never wanted me to go to pastry school. You never wanted me to travel! You gave me lecture after lecture about not wasting the insurance money, like I was a child."

I was only looking out for her! I bit the words back. "I... shouldn't have done that. It was your money. If you wanted to spend it traveling that wasn't my business."

She laughed but it died in her throat. "That's the joke of it all. I never spent a dime. If I spent it, then they were really gone. I made a separate account at the bank, deposited the check, and never looked at it again."

"But how did you afford—"

"Hostels are cheap."

"What about your house in Bali?"

TANGLED CHARMS | 25

"Not a house. A *house share*. I shared a house with six other people."

"Even that must cost something."

"You'd be surprised how easy it is to get under-the-table work in a tourist town when you speak English and are a cute girl in your twenties." The way she said it, you'd think being a cute girl in your twenties was just about the worst thing that could happen to somebody. "I sat there all day watching them build my pyre and I started to think, what if they're right?"

"Hazel."

"If they killed me, would anyone care? Would my friends overseas even know? If they found out would they grieve? Maybe for a minute or two, but they always expected me to leave."

"Then why do you want to leave me here?"

"I… don't know how to stay."

She looked up at me and her pooled tears breached. Even crying, she glowed in her yellow sundress. How could she be so beautiful and carry so much shame? Wasn't there some way to make her see how wrong she was?

"You have a gift," I said. "The other day when you were making those magical scones for Tilly was the happiest, most focused, most in your element I've ever seen you."

She smiled sadly. "They're scones. Even the best scone in the world is—"

"Mediocre. I know. But the ones you made were fantastic, remember? The best thing we'd ever eaten."

"They were all right."

"They were magic! Admit it, you have a gift, and you can't convince me otherwise. You took that crazy recipe of Tilly's into an unfamiliar kitchen and made a hundred impossibly delicious scones in just a few hours."

She shrugged. "It was kind of fun. Especially the part where you got covered in flour."

"I'm sorry for not trusting you."

"You were only trying to step in for Mom and Dad."

"I shouldn't have made assumptions. And, Hazel, if you had died, I wouldn't have just been sad for a few minutes."

"Really?"

"It would have ruined my whole day."

She snorted a laugh. "You mean it? Your entire day?"

"It would have been the worst day of my life."

"But you would have gotten over it."

"I mean, life is for the living. But it would have bugged me for weeks. Maybe a month or two."

She smiled and the morning sun streaked her damp cheeks with gold. "That's the nicest thing anyone's ever said to me."

She held her arms open and the wall crumbled. I rushed to her and held her as she trembled. As if by warmth and pressure I could keep her close forever. As if they could show her she was never a disappointment. As if they could promise that nothing bad would ever happen again.

5

I walked past the long conference table with its leather chairs and looked through the blinds to the cobblestone street below. It was empty except for the black iron lamp post where, lifetimes ago, I'd lifted my chin toward Lucas and let him kiss me. The magic of youth and hope and a wide-open future.

There were other kinds of magic, back then, too. Tilly had her herbs. Gran preserved the old ways. Maleia bartered her soul for scraps of power. None of them were anything like the stories where Augustus Nightingale cleared the land and founded the city with only whispered words and sigils. That magic had allowed a ragtag group of refugees to build a haven at the edge of the world. Now it was back. How could it not be a blessing?

Homesickness blossomed, slow and bruising, as if my memories were more of a place than a time. As if they came from a gauzy homeland I could never sail back to, full of friends I'd never see again.

"Holly. Hazel. This is a pleasant surprise." The voice shook me from my thoughts.

Hector Morales, attorney at law, wore a crisp navy suit with a red silk tie. His deeply tanned face was perfectly shaven and his slick black hair was combed straight back above piercing, hawklike eyes. I wouldn't want to go up against this man in any sort of battle, legal or otherwise. He glanced at his gold watch, then looked up and flashed a thousand-dollar smile. "I only have a minute. I'm supposed to be taking some documents over for Tilly to sign. What do you have for me?"

I sat next to Hazel, who absentmindedly picked at the varnish underneath the edge of the large walnut table. "Uncle Max is suing us." I slid the expensive coarse envelope over to Hector.

He unfolded the letter and read it, then shook his head and heaved a sigh. "I was afraid this would happen. You surprised him when you turned down his offer. Titans of industry aren't used to being told no."

"But he wasn't interested in the house until Gran died. Wasn't there something in her will about a struggle, or a problem Uncle Max had?"

"Yes. I must have read it a dozen times, trying to decipher its meaning. 'If love were enough to pay your debts, I would have paid them ten times over.'"

"Does he have a case? Gran left the house to us, not him."

"Not at all." He slid the letter back to me. "He accuses you of abusing your grandmother, and forcing her to alter her will. It will be simple enough to show in probate that you hadn't seen your grandmother for years. No, this would never hold up in a court of law."

A tightness in my chest released, and I let out a deep breath. "So we don't have to worry about it?"

"If we lived in a just world, and you had infinite resources, no."

So much for deep breathing. "What about in the real world?"

"Some lawsuits aren't meant to be won. They're meant to apply pressure. To cause the defendant to waste resources on the battle. Even if Mr. Amp's lawsuit does fail, he can keep it going for years."

"How do we fight it?"

"Come by the office this afternoon and we'll work out a strategy. Now, I need to get these documents over to Tilly."

"There's something else we need. Deputy Sprout just burst into our kitchen and arrested a journalist, Dana Radcliff, for blackmail."

He furrowed his brow and shook his head. "I haven't heard of any ongoing blackmail investigations. This is a small town. News travels fast and gossip even faster. This is a fresh case. Very fresh."

"Can you help her? We'll take those documents to Tilly," I said, glancing at Hazel. "We'll deliver them and get them signed and brought back to you. I know that you can't make any promises about Dana but she's out here all alone and we're the only people who can help."

"Works for me. Here you go. The places she needs to initial and sign are marked with tabs. Make sure she gets the date right."

"Got it."

We filed down the stairs and out the door and said goodbye to Hector. Hazel and I passed Lucas's grocery store, which was closed, past the bronze sculpture of our ancestor Augustus, and Luna's Inn & Pub.

"I wonder what the documents are for," Hazel said. "Tilly's lived here all her life. She must already have a house. With all the plants at her tea shop she must own that building too."

"Maybe it's estate stuff? She's old enough to be retiring

30 | TABATHA GRAY

soon." The bakery was already empty because nobody in Lin's family wanted to take it on when she retired. Did Tilly have anyone to run the tea shop?

"Stop." Hazel stuck her arm out to hold me back. She stared hard at the tea shop, then glanced at me, confused. "Sorry. I could have sworn I saw something move. Maybe I'm imagining things."

Nobody would ever call the tea shop ordinary, but it looked the same as it always did. Windows displayed rows of small, orange, green, and maroon boxes, and a tea set of white-and-blue porcelain. The shop's front was woven through with chestnut-brown branches sprouting green. The branches twisted up and held a sign in place: GREENLEAF TEA. Much farther up, I saw the green fringe of Tilly's rooftop garden where she grew herbs.

The front door creaked as I pushed it open. A wave of the most delicious aromas rolled over us. Peppermint and cinnamon and cardamom. Spices I couldn't name. Underneath it all was a clean, fresh smell, like the forest after it rains.

The ceiling was covered with woody vines as big around as my finger. Small green leaves sprouted from the branches, along with milky-white orbs that glowed and served as lighting. The vines wound their way down the ceiling, past the overstuffed, mismatched armchairs and the antique wood and marble tables filed with chattering customers, to the counter, which (despite holding a register and a mostly empty pastry display case) also resembled a tree stump.

All of this, except for the crowd, was exactly as it had been two days ago when Tilly welcomed us to town after our long ferry ride. But one other thing had changed. One very important thing.

The plants were moving. Not only that. They were moving with purpose.

TANGLED CHARMS | 31

I watched a honeysuckle vine detach from the wall behind the counter, wind its tip around the handle of a blue ceramic teapot, and carry it over to a large shelf with jars of curled black tea leaves, cinnamon sticks, star anise and other spices. It opened a jar, flicked some tea into the pot, then opened another, and another and when it was satisfied, it brought the pot under the hot water dispenser.

It dipped a little as the teapot filled with steaming water, but the vine held tight, then it whisked it over to a table full of vacantly laughing ladies with salt-and-pepper hair. It traded their empty pot, took it to the sink and scrubbed it, as two other vines started up new pots of Tilly's special calming blend, which in her words, would take the fight out of a polecat.

"I guess Tilly's putting the magic to good use," Hazel said.

"Where is she?"

"Probably in the back taking a nap. It's what I'd do if I had a bunch of magical plants doing my job for me."

The vines didn't stop us from pushing past them, through the saloon doors, and into the tea shop's back room.

I wanted to sneeze but couldn't. It was like smelling everything that had ever existed all at once, and add on top of it an overwhelming green, prickly pollen smell. I felt dizzy, looked around for a window to open, but there wasn't one, just walls filled with hexagonal cubbies filled with glass-bottomed jars. And on the other side of the room, a small kitchenette, where a pair of ivy vines thick as my thumb were drowning Tilly in the kitchen sink.

…were drowning Tilly in the kitchen sink?

Hazel reacted quicker than I did. She rushed to Tilly and yanked her head out of the water, but the vines twisted around Hazel's wrists. Waxy green leaves rustled as they bound my sister and pulled her toward the water. I rushed to help but stopped. You couldn't fight these things hand to hand, but I had an idea.

Yesterday, I'd seen Tilly use a bread knife to slice open a scone for taste testing. When she was done she'd place it... There, I found it.

I dropped Hector's papers, grabbed the knife, and lunged toward the viny tentacles at the wall where they were thickest. The knife's serrated edge bit into the woody vine. One tendril squealed and went limp. The other tried to loop back and attack me. Hazel bear-hugged it. Used her body weight to hold it. My knife cut the vine. The plant slackened. Hazel and Tilly toppled to the floor together.

Tilly grinned ear to ear as she picked herself up. "Glorious!" Her eyes bulged white above black mascara streaks. Water dripped from her hair and face and darkened her white linen dress. I took one step back.

"It tried to kill you." Hazel said.

"We were just having a little dance, Robert and me."

"Robert?" I asked.

"Plant!" She slapped her knee and laughed so hard she started wheezing. The vine wasn't the only thing acting strange in this shop. "I was just taking the old fingers for a spin. A little spell I heard in a nursery rhyme when I was a girl. Back then it was just stories and rhymes and herbs can work wonders under a new moon but magic? The real abracadabra stuff? Pfft. Except I remembered a spell from the nursery. Wiggle your nose and clap three times and what do you know? Quicker'n you can weave snakes into a basket the shop comes alive and starts serving folks."

"Weave snakes into..."

"It's a miracle is what it is! No more cleaning. No more washing up. No making tea for chatty old women with clucky tongues. It's enough to make me want to keep the place!"

"This is dangerous, Tilly. It tried to kill you!"

"Dangerous schmangerous!"

Was she drunk? Maybe magic was more than a blessing. Maybe it was more complicated than I thought. Tilly wasn't acting herself. She didn't even care her spell backfired and tried to kill her.

Well, if Tilly was incapacitated, that meant it was up to me and Hazel to protect her. Hazel must have had the same idea, because she was looking at me, concerned.

In the other room, something shattered. A teapot? It happened again. Definitely a teapot, and a full one. That was when the screaming started.

6

Forty years old, you'd think I'd know something about life. By now I was supposed to be well established in a career. To be on the ball from eight to five, and after, whisking my well-scrubbed children between karate and soccer practice.

The world was supposed to make sense by now. And when it didn't, I was supposed to make sense of it. At forty you're the adult in the room. That's the idea that was sold to me.

Whoever did the selling had clearly never stood in a doorway looking at a jungle of thick, whipping, rustling, disgustingly alive vines as they tried to murder a tea shop full of customers.

A stout man in a white polo shirt and chinos rushed past the snapping vines, flung the creaking front door open and ran into daylight. His friend, taller in tennis white, followed, but green runners caught his ankle. They slowed him like honey, then molasses, then stopped him entirely. They lifted him off the ground and brought a teapot up to his mouth and forced it in. He struggled and spat, but the vine crashed him through the large front window, then whisked him up and away.

The salt-and-pepper ladies dangled above their empty table, only their heads sticking out of leafy green cocoons. Their heads tilted back and they each had a teapot with their lips wrapped around the spout. They sucked on them like babies nursing.

Why weren't they fighting? Were the vines that strong? I looked at the bread knife in my hand. I scanned the room for a place to attack and caught Tilly, still loopy from her bush with death, smiling like a proud mother.

There was no good place to attack in that jungle of vines. As soon as the knife bit into one, another would spiral around my ankles and wrists and soon I'd be out the window.

The window? "Where is it taking them?" I said.

"Must be the roof." Hazel's words flashed like lightning in the dark.

"The rooftop garden! That's where the vines must have been planted, before Tilly brought them to life. To kill a plant you have to pull it at the root. If we could get up there…"

"Do we have to kill them?" Hazel asked.

"We have to save these people!"

"But they're living things."

"Only because of magic."

"If magic made the plants this way, could we use magic to turn them back?"

Leave it to my sister to feel sorry for foliage. Still, she had a point. Magic caused this mess. It might be able to clean it up too.

"Okay, we'll try." Easy enough to say, but how?

I closed my eyes and listed to my heart pound in the darkness. I was a fool. The only magic I'd done since last night, was to break a teapot and soak Deputy Sprout with

36 | TABATHA GRAY

oolong. You'd think with the Nightingale name and a prophesy, I'd have some sort of power. At this point I'd settle for rabbits out of hats. Pick a card, any card. Instead, I was Cinderella after the ball, back in rags, my carriage a pumpkin.

Light flashed red through my eyelids. I opened them.

A tendril of thin white light extended from Hazel's outstretched hand. It moved toward the thrashing vines, and spiraled around the nearest shoot. It wrapped the fuzzy bright green stalks with searing light, and up the stems to waxy dark leaves. Where the light wrapped them, they relaxed like an ordinary plant.

"It's working!" I said. She didn't reply, but a bead of sweat rolled off her brow and tatted onto the wooden floor. The magic took a lot out of her.

Suddenly, a clutch of leafy tentacles lunged past Hazel's light, pruned the cured leaves and branches from itself, and threw them to the ground. A buzzing, shiny black fluid dripped from the plant's wounds. The liquid jumped like an electric arc to Hazel's magic and dissolved in it like blood in water, turning the light dark crimson. It moved toward her.

"It's coming!" I shouted but Hazel didn't seem to notice.

"You have to stop it!" I shook her but she felt limp and swayed like a doll. I slapped her once across the cheek and reeled like I'd slapped myself. I felt sick to my stomach.

The red infection whipped around the spiraled light. It shot across the room toward us, had almost reached us when Hazel's magic vanished and she stumbled back.

"I… connected with the plant. I felt it."

"You were healing it, but you caught something's attention." Vines lashed toward us. We must have caught their attention as well. I grabbed Tilly by one arm. "Follow me."

Tilly didn't want to come, but Hazel took her other arm and we dragged her through her shop's back room, past the

TANGLED CHARMS | 37

sink where she'd nearly died, to the small stairwell leading up.

Getting Tilly up the first few steps was tough, but she must have figured out our plan because she tugged free from us and sprinted ahead. She rushed past the door to the second-floor apartment and climbed another flight, opened the door and stepped out onto the rooftop garden.

I squinted in the blue-sky glare. Shaded my eyes with my hand. Charm Haven Square was down there somewhere, but I couldn't see it over the enormous forest-green rosemary shrubs and gigantic blue-green sage bushes. To my right a trellis supported at least a hundred small potted plants hanging from it by hooks.

A thud came from beyond the rosemary. Another thud and a scraping sound. Tilly ran toward it. I followed. Ran into her. Stumbled back. Looked up.

Oh.

Oh, my.

A dozen people hung suspended in the air, swaddled in vines, slowly undulating over the garden. All hung docile, suckling on blue-and-white ceramic teapots.

The thick woody vines creaked as one of them broke away, moved to an empty garden bed, swept away the rich black loam and laid the man in tennis whites like a sleeping baby and covered him with dirt. My stomach twisted. The vine hadn't put him to bed. It had buried him. The man wasn't like a baby. He was a seed, or worse, compost.

Off to the side, I spotted the point where the base of a throbbing torso-sized vine rooted into the soil. I pointed at it and glanced at Hazel, who held up a small, serrated steak knife. She must have grabbed it on our trip through the kitchen. I raised my bread knife in a wordless salute and charged.

I swung my weapon like an axe, and heard it thwack into

38 | TABATHA GRAY

the thick, bright green trunk. But it had gone in only a millimeter or so. This job would take some elbow grease.

I leaned in and sawed at the woody vine, but didn't make any progress. I pressed my left hand into the back of the knife to drive it deeper, but that thick dark electric sap oozed from where I'd nicked the plant. It touched the metal of the knife and boiled white steam that smelled like raw asparagus. I gagged and clenched my stomach muscles to stop myself from throwing up. I stumbled back and looked at my knife. Half of the blade's edge fell away like ash.

Hazel joined me, green in the face. Holding the bladeless handle of a steak knife. She dropped it. "What now?" She asked. "Should we run and get help?"

"From who?"

"I don't know… the crones?"

"It would take hours to find them."

Past the uncut trunks, the vine buried one of the laughing salt-and-pepper ladies. Could they breathe under there? Not long enough for us to run for help.

Tilly's eyes bulged over mascara cheeks. She stared at the murderous scene like it was the most blissful thing in the world.

Wasn't that odd? I knew she was acting funny, but people often act funny after a brush with death. And her brush had been exceptionally weird. But even that couldn't explain why she was beaming at the plant. Like it was doing exactly what she wanted. What had she called it? *Glorious.*

"It's her." I said it as the horror dawned on me. "She might have cast the spell accidentally like she said, but it's not over. The spell is still working. Flowing through her. That's why she's acting so weird! That's why she's not herself!"

"But how—"

I wheeled on Tilly and looked her in the face. "You have to stop it."

TANGLED CHARMS | 39

She looked right through me.

"You have to stop the spell, Tilly! Your plants are hurting people! They're burying your customers alive!"

A gurgling, cooing noise rose from the back of her throat. I slapped her, and winced. "Tilly!"

"If the magic's flowing through her, maybe taking her away from the plant will make it stop." Hazel said.

"We can't know that will work. What if it doesn't stop? We can't leave all these people to be buried alive. Could we knock her out?"

"I don't want to hurt her."

"I don't mean hitting her. Look at those people," I pointed at the swaddled ladies. "They're not fighting back because they can't. They're intoxicated."

"From the tea?"

"When we first arrived I saw them making pots of Tilly's special calming blend, but they were adding extra ingredients. With all the herbs that Tilly has in this shop, they must have found one that would sedate people."

"To keep them from fighting. It makes sense, but how are we going to get ahold of any of that tea?"

"Here. Take this." I handed her my knife. Part of the edge was gone, but at least it still had a blade. "Next to the place they buried that guy, see there's a vine holding that teapot he drank from."

"I see it. Looks thin enough to cut."

"On three, we'll rush it. I'll grab the teapot. You cut the vine holding it."

"Got it."

"One. Two. Three." I sprinted toward the teapot, jumping over runners that whipped at my feet, dodging twiggy boughs of rosemary that leaned into the path. We arrived together and I grabbed the pot. "Now!"

Hazel swung the knife in a wide arc and sliced clean

through the thin vine. It screamed and the teapot's weight fell into my hands. Another vine coiled around my wrist. Hazel chopped it. It screamed. I ran to Tilly, holding the teapot out in front of me like a chalice.

Behind me, Hazel screamed and I heard metal hitting stone. I turned and saw her lifted off the ground. The hand that held the knife was empty.

"Tilly, drink this." No reply. Damn. How do you get a grown woman to drink when she doesn't want to? But she wasn't acting like an adult. Maybe, just maybe…

"Here comes the airplane, neeeeeeeerw."

Nothing.

Fine.

We were doing it the hard way.

I grabbed her nose. She was too spaced-out to fight me. When she opened her mouth to breathe I shoved the teapot spout in and tipped it back. She coughed, but swallowed.

I caught a whiff of the tea and gagged. Lavender. Vanilla. Almond, sickeningly strong, and mixed with a gagging odor I could only describe as green. My head swam and I caught myself from falling. I whipped my head to the side like a swimmer doing the breath stroke and sucked enough clean air to stay upright.

Tilly was relaxing. She lost an inch of height. Had she been standing on tiptoes? She took another swallow and nearly collapsed. I drew a breath, held it, and moved beside her for support.

The vines were wobbling and the still-unburied victims dipped in the air and jerked upright. Then, in an instant, they fell to the roof. The vines, like so many lengths of rope, collapsed. The people who the plant had buried sat up and coughed black loam. And Hazel, jumped up and helped them.

Tilly turned to me. Her linen peasant dress, dark with water and stained chlorophyll green, hung around her like a sack. Her eyes no longer bulged, she rubbed them like she'd just awakened from a dream. "Holly Nightingale? What on heaven's earth are you doing here?"

So that was how one handled a jungle of thick, whipping, rustling, disgustingly alive vines as they tried to murder a tea shop full of customers. Good to know.

7

---

y nose was almost used to the everything-all-at-once smell in Tilly's back room. It still felt like I'd inhaled a porcupine, but at least I wasn't sneezing.

I walked over to the table where I'd found the bread knife earlier. I could have sworn I'd dropped Hector's papers here. Had someone moved them? Kicked them in the rush upstairs?

Hazel was still up there, in Tilly's apartment, helping everyone clean up, making them warm chamomile to clear their heads.

Maybe I should have been up there too, but I'd promised Hector I'd deliver the papers. And while a magical-plant attack would be a pretty good excuse, I felt a nagging, tugging anxiety that wouldn't go away until I kept my word.

I spotted the corner of a letter, the one from Uncle Max's lawyers, sticking out from under a bookshelf. I went and grabbed it, peeked under the bottom shelf and found Hector's manila envelope. The letter went in the back pocket of my jeans. I inspected the envelope full of documents. They seemed to be unharmed. Hazel's question came back to me:

What were they? I shook my head. None of my business is what they were.

There was another reason I'd come down here. The people. The way they looked at me made me nervous. They stared, mouths agape, like I was a character in a movie not an ordinary person. After all, they'd seen me last night, piloting a broom above the thronging Litha festival. And here I was again to rescue them.

I didn't want to be a character in a movie. Two days ago when we arrived, I felt like a lost lamb rejoining the flock. And the way Luna and Tilly and Lucas and Vincent and all the others welcomed us, made me think I'd found a place where maybe, for once in my life, I belonged.

But you couldn't really belong when people saw you as apart and above. When they stared at you, and thanked you, and envied you and probably resented you. I mean, I had my own prophecy, for crying out loud!

I heard a bitter cackle, and it took me a moment to realize it had croaked from my own throat. I had my own prophecy, and yet, when our lives were on the line, I couldn't summon the tiniest spark of magic to save us.

Not like Hazel.

She had barely had time to explore her powers, and yet she'd summoned a glowing flower for Dana. She'd woven a rope out of light and hurled it at the too-alive plant, and stilled it, at least until it fought back. Magic flowed to Hazel as easily as people did, as easily as she moved through the world.

It made perfect sense. She was the only woman I'd ever known who looked put together in a kaftan. I was the one who made lists and plans and dogged them until every box was checked. It made perfect sense that magic would choose her instead of me. I winced as something tender deep inside me tore.

44 | TABATHA GRAY

Maybe I wouldn't ever belong. Maybe people and magic would never flow to me. But still…

Wasn't I the woman who charged into a nightmare forest to rescue my sister? Didn't I prevent a mass murder at the festival? Hadn't I just defeated that little shop of horrors on the roof?

It wasn't magic. But it wasn't nothing.

In only a few days we'd faced more threats than we had in a lifetime. I would have loved to think we'd passed through the storm, but the world didn't work like that. My psycho ex, Caleb, was still on the loose. The Inquisition would regroup. Spells would misfire. New threats would arise.

If Hazel was the special one, so be it. I would be the one to keep her safe. But how could I convince her to stay? She wasn't interested in family history, Gran's house, or magic.

She'd seemed happy working at the bakery. It was for sale, but probably not affordable, even with Mom and Dad's life insurance.

There was Dana. They'd only met, but Hazel had come to life swapping travel stories. Now Dana was in jail and who knows when she'd get out. Wait. Back in the kitchen. Right before she got arrested. Hadn't Dana mentioned she'd come here to Tilly's and drunk a cup of tea? Why had that aroused the deputy's suspicions?

"This room's messier than a rabbit in a pig pen," Tilly said, walking down the creaky steps. She had changed clothes and now wore loose gray culottes with a simple white blouse and a lilac linen duster. The mascara was gone, and she seemed older than before, though I liked it better than her crazy I've-seen-the-Messiah-and-it's-a-carnivorous-shrub look.

"Your mother would be so proud to see the women you and your sister have grown up to be. I owe you a debt."

"Anyone would have jumped in to help. We just came to

TANGLED CHARMS | 45

deliver these documents from Hector." I handed her the envelope.

"Thanks. I was waiting on these." Her hands trembled as she slid a thumbnail under one side of the brass clasp and bent it up, then did the other and removed about a dozen sheets of crisp white paper with the Morales logo along the top in blue. "I suppose I have to sell the place now. My plants tried to kill half my best customers, and the others will know about it by dinner. It's just so damned embarrassing."

"I didn't know the tea shop was for sale."

"Didn't you hear? No, of course not, you haven't been in town a week. A company's making offers to a lot of the old timers here on the square. Anwir Holdings, something-or-other. See it yourself." She held up the document. It was a bill of sale between Tilly Greenleaf and this Anwir company. So corporate, so out of place in Charm Haven. "Doesn't matter because the price is right. They low-balled me at first, but yesterday, just before I closed up for the night I got a new offer. Double."

"You're taking it?" It seemed wrong. Like making home after being lost at sea, and finding a moving van in the driveway.

"An offer this good doesn't come along too often. Never, in fact. Of course, Lin told them to shove it where the sun don't shine. You know her. She's up there talking to your sister now."

"The same Lin who owns the bakery?"

"The one and only."

If she was talking to Hazel… A gauzy vision filled my sight, of Hazel baking in the back while I handled the business and tended a line of happy customers. It was a nice thought, but I had other business. I cleared my throat. "Tilly, this morning, did you happen to notice a stranger in your shop? A tall woman in tweed?"

"Why, yes, I remember her. Heavy coat for the season. I thought to myself, soon as the fog burns off she's going to be sweating something fierce. Had good manners though, and tipped well. Can't be that much wrong with a person who tips well, is what I say."

"Did anything unusual happen while she was here?"

"No magic, if that's what you mean. It was a slow morning up until I got my bright idea."

"The deputy seems to think that her visit here has something to do with a blackmail case."

"Really? Only heard of that in movies."

"He seemed serious."

"Sprout has an imagination, though, doesn't he? Word gets around too quick in this town for people to have many secrets." She looked away. "I didn't expect that spell to be so strong. I was only paying half attention when I fired it. And I hadn't thought of that nursery rhyme in must be forty years. But I found myself humming it and making shapes in the air with my fingers. I tried to stop, really. Held out for a good five minutes, but there was an itch behind my eyes that wouldn't go away until I said the right words, made the right motions."

My memory flashed back to the dark electric fluid that had moved with intent and stained Hazel's magic with crimson. "Has that ever happened before?"

She shook her head. "I suppose my herbs are a kind of magic, but making plants come to life? Wouldn't know where to start."

It was a mystery, but I had to stay focused. "Tell me about the woman in tweed."

"She ordered a cup of orange spice. That's more of a fall tea, you understand, though I suppose it matches her getup. She sat by the window. Shop was empty except for Vincent

TANGLED CHARMS | 47

who dropped by to let me know my scones made a lot of fans over on Brimstone."

"Did she talk him?" I could have sworn Dana said she did.

"Can't say. With so few people in the shop I like to go in the back so they don't feel I'm spying on them."

I groaned. I knew what I had to do and didn't like it, but before I could think about it too hard, the stairs creaked and a herd of salt-and-pepper ladies stampeded down. There were six of them, hair wet, faces scrubbed, clothes smeared with black dirt and slashed with green. The first of them, a battleship of a woman with glittering jewelry, spotted Tilly and wheeled around.

"You'll be made to answer for this, Matilda."

"Hattie, I'm so—"

"Hattie is what my friends call me. You may call me Mrs. Henrietta Thorn."

"You've got to believe me, all this was one big accident. I didn't mean—"

"You used magic to attempt the murder of not only myself, but members of the Sinclair and Woodruff families as well. I had thought you were different from the other Green-leafs. I was wrong."

"It was all a mistake." Tilly sounded desperate.

"It goes without saying that you are no longer invited to tonight's fete. I do not want you ruining things with Maximilian. And for that matter, you're disinvited from all fetes, moving forward, in perpetuity. Are we clear?"

Henrietta sniffed and grimaced. I guess she wasn't used to the everything-all-at-once smell in Tilly's back room. She scrunched up her face and wiggled her lips around to scratch the porcupine itch. She gasped, sucked in a breath, reared back like a horse and sneezed. She looked up, glanced in my direction and paused, confused, until recognition flashed in her eyes. Suddenly, she stood taller, her brow lifted, and her pink, rubber-band lips stretched into a wide smile.

"You are a Nightingale? Which one are you?"

"Holly."

"Little Holly! All grown up!" She walked over to me and for a second I thought she might pinch my cheeks, but she stopped a few feet away and stared, her mouth a little open. "The last time I saw you, you were in pigtails, dear, running around that great old house of Stella's. Your grandmother and I used to be great friends. She was a mentor to me, an older sister in many ways. It simply devastated me when, in the last years of her life, she turned inward. It's past time that the Nightingale and Thorn families resume our historically friendly relations, don't you think? I would be honored if you would join us tonight for a small celebratory dinner which my family holds every year on the day following Litha."

I glanced at Tilly. Was this the fete she'd just been disinvited from? Was it the sort of event I wanted any part of? Was there a way out? "I can't say yes or no until I talk to my sister—"

"The girl upstairs? I thought she looked familiar, but it wasn't until I saw you, dear, that I made the family connection. You have Stella's eyes. You must tell your sister that I apologize for not introducing myself. She's welcome too, of course. We always have plenty of room at our table for *friends*."

8

Tilly's tea shop, soon to be a vacant building owned by Anwir Holdings, was behind us. We'd turned down one of the small side streets radiating from the square and walked until the shops gave way to tall row houses built close together. It was Vincent's neighborhood. He had talked to Dana at the tea shop. Maybe he had information that could free her.

On the other side of the street a woman with a stroller stared, mouth a little open. The look. Or maybe it was my clothes.

Even though I'd avoided most of the too-alive vines, my swampy jeans had green chlorophyll streaks lashing the thighs. The knees were black with dirt. I had no memory of kneeling.

Hazel's yellow sundress didn't show a speck of black or green. It had been good for her to help those people. She seemed happy, contented, taking in the summer morning, the charming row houses, the passersby. She didn't notice or care about women in strollers with their mouths a little open. On such a nice day, how could you worry about anything? Even when you'd just fought a herbaceous nightmare.

Even when you'd just made the worst decision of your life.

"I can't believe you said no," I shook my head. "You're a baker! It's a bakery! All the equipment ready to go. A beautiful building. A beautiful town. A seller with a sweetheart deal. And you wouldn't even need a loan! You have the money sitting in a bank account!"

That earned me a sharp look. "I told you I'm leaving tomorrow. Besides, you know I can't spend it."

"The money's yours."

"I only have it because Mom and Dad died. It's... blood money."

I'd known she had feelings, but *blood money*? Come on. It was a life insurance payout, not payment for a mob hit. "Mom and Dad loved us. They wanted to make sure we were taken care of."

"I'm an adult."

"You weren't back then. They took out the policy when we were kids, after we left Charm Haven. They were on their own for the first time in their lives, and didn't want us to be helpless if anything happened to them."

"Did they expect something bad to happen?"

"And it wasn't only *their* love." I looked away and stiffened. I'd never told her the full story about the insurance. I was the oldest. It was my job to throw myself on that grenade. To protect my kid sister. Make sure she finished school. I might have let it slip after graduation, but she'd hopped the light rail to SeaTac and was halfway round the world before I had a chance.

"Did they expect it?"

"Do you think life insurance companies are happy to pay for missing persons? Who might be in the Bahamas

TANGLED CHARMS | 51

drinking rum punch on the beach? I fought for years to get that money. I was on the phone with them every day. I read that damned policy, and the FBI report, and the flight logs over and over until they were all I could think of, all I dreamed about, until I could recite them backward and forward and in the end I made them pay, but God it was hard."

Hazel looked at me like I just broke her heart. "Why did you do it then?"

"Because the bastards owed it to Mom and Dad. If the insurance didn't pay it would be like a big middle finger to them, to us, to everything we might have been. If insurance didn't pay they were saying our family was worthless. I couldn't stand it."

"I... didn't know."

"The money's yours. Use it."

We walked and a warm breeze pushed on our backs, blowing stray hairs into wispy halos. The air smelled like the ocean, like it had that day when I'd planted myself on the ferry's bow and stared through the fog, and imagined I was coming home.

We reached Vincent's house and climbed the stairs I'd run down screaming. I could still feel the smooth, warm sandstone on my bare feet. The jarring thud of my heels impacting pavement. The salty, garlicky aftertaste of lunch. The panic, followed by embarrassment. What a disaster.

"He likes you, you know." Hazel's words were like a flower picked from the side of the road by a small child and given solemnly as a gift.

Could she be right? No. "You're delusional."

"I saw the way he *gazed* at you when you met."

"Are you seriously trying to set me up with a *vampire*?"

"Half your bookstore was filled with books about people dating vampires."

"Those are books. Fiction. Besides, even if he were interested, it doesn't matter. I'm done."

"Done?"

"With men. With dating. With love. Done. Done. Done."

"That's a little dramatic."

"Was it dramatic when Caleb turned out to be a religious psychopath? When he faked a years-long relationship with me, just to steal our family's magic? Was it dramatic when he blew up everything that mattered? Can you understand why I'm not itching to dive headfirst back into the dating pool?"

I looked at Vincent's heavy wooden door and everything inside me balled into a fist. It wasn't just the embarrassment of running away. Because she was right. He *had* gazed at me. I'd felt something, and for a moment thought he did too. When he'd leaned in to look at my necklace, I'd thought he might— "I can't," I said, backing down the steps like a coward. "You talk with him. Be sure to ask him what he and Dana spoke about, and if he saw her with anyone else, and— oh—and what he knows about the blackmail case."

"Holly?" Was that pity in her voice? Maybe I *was* pitiful.

"I'll walk around the block and meet you here and we can debrief. Or maybe I'll go check on Dana."

"Holly Nightingale, you'll do no such thing!"

I stared at my sister, wondering who she'd become.

"You are not going to run. You are not going to hide. You are going to stay here while I knock on the door. When Vincent answers, you will smile and act like a normal human being."

"How do I do that?"

"You are going to be your charming self."

"Never met her."

"Because even if you're not ready to get back in the water after Caleb won the grand prize at the jerk contest, it will do you good to practice. Do you hear me?"

"You're being—"

"I said, do you hear me!" She didn't sound like relaxed, breezy Hazel. It sounded like our mom, resurrected and pissed about it.

"Yes... ma'am?"

"That's more like it!" Her yellow sundress blazed against the dark-stained wood. She grabbed the large brass door knocker, swung it back and stopped. She leaned in, for some reason, peered at the thing, then turned to me. "Holly, get up here."

I approached cautiously. Maybe in the afterlife Mom had found out the real reason her favorite earrings had gone missing back when I was in fifth grade. Or maybe Hazel had unknown depths. She wore an odd expression, her head cocked to the side, her lips pursed a little.

"What is this?" She asked.

"It's a door knocker." What else could it be? It was made of black iron, a heavy shape all curves and crescents, probably forged in a primordial forest, left out in the weather for centuries, then restored and polished to a shine by an expert blacksmith.

"I know it's a door knocker, but what does it look like to you?"

It was an abstract shape, but now that she drew my attention to it, it was clear enough. "It's a bat."

"And you had *no* idea he was a vampire?" She stared at me stone-faced, hard-eyed. "He has a bat doorknocker, and gas porch light, and red drapes, and pointy windows and you had *no* idea?"

I felt a pressure rise from my chest. "He has fuzzy bat slippers, too."

We looked at each other, expressionless, for three heartbeats then cracked into laughter, doubled-over jelly-legged laughter pouring out onto the smooth red sandstone, scrubbing it like rain.

"I thought… he was rich… and eccentric!" I said.

"Oh.. Holly!" Tears streaked her cheeks. She wiped them away, smiling.

"Fine!" I shoved her like we were kids. "Get out of my way. I'll do it. But don't be weird. Remember, we're here to help Dana, not get my groove back."

The brass door knocker was cold. I lifted it, let it slam into the strike plate like a judge's gavel. The wind brought the sound of seagulls and children laughing. Nothing. I lifted the knocker again and let it fall, then stood back and peered at the windows. Not a movement. Not a sound…

… except for the footsteps behind us.

9

SOMEWHERE IN THE NORTH PACIFIC

*C*aleb Robinson knuckled the helm of the thirty-foot Zodiac and stared into the fog. Behind him, twin two-fifties raged like a swarm of angry hornets, thrusting the boat over swell after swell, sending salt mist up to soak the black robes of the men of his order.

There were fewer of them leaving than had arrived. The others were left to the east, with the lights of Charm Haven, to be drowned by the rising sun.

Nicholas, the abomination, had been sacrificed at no real loss. Quite the opposite. The vampire's presence had been yet another stain on the order's sanctity. He had been judged and found wanting and his death checked a rather unpleasant task off Caleb Robinson's list.

The real difficulty came from Brother Albinus, not sacrificed, but captured. He would know, of course, where his duty lay. Through the door that is never locked. The final, glorious sacrament that the Lord our God has given us to reveal strength even in weakness, victory even in defeat.

Brother Albinus would know of the door, of course. Whether he was strong enough to open it was another matter entirely. Caleb Robinson would have to ensure he found the strength. He smiled.

Victory was not merely assured. It was already theirs. How could it not be when they were the sword of righteousness? When they were the Lord's will manifest?

To suggest that the Almighty could be defeated by mortal hands was not only blasphemy, but absurd. If the sword hand was stayed, it was because the Lord wished to strike a different blow.

Caleb Robinson inhaled sharply and received the word of God.

It came as an image, a memory, a weakness he had seen that could be attacked. If he and his order acted quickly, Charm Haven would be aflame before Father Superior had cause to doubt their devotion. He crossed himself and said a prayer of thanks as the fog cleared and the trawler was revealed.

The ship was a sleek gunmetal miracle, 120 feet long and the height of a three-story building, topped with a rotating weather station and a bank of dish antennae. Its sea anchor was deployed and its props were disengaged so it wasn't any trouble to bring the Zodiac astern.

When the boat's rigid, inflated hull impacted the ship's docking point, the brother sitting at the bow stood and looped a small rope around a stainless steel cleat. Soon the brothers were filing up the steps to the trawler's main deck, except for one, pushing against the flow.

"Brother Robinson! Brother Robinson!" He sounded nervous. Then again, this was Brother Avery, and he always sounded nervous. He had learned, of course, that victory was already theirs. Each member of the order had it chiseled into his soul on the Mountain. But where Caleb Robinson's soul was granite, Brother Avery's was clay, easily impressed and the impression easily overwritten.

Caleb Robinson held up a hand for silence. "Brother, I have received the word of God."

"Praise be! But I must tell you—"

"Surely you don't think, Brother Avery, that what you have to say is more urgent than the will of our Lord?"

"Of course not, Brother, but—"

"For you see, the path forward has been revealed to me. A way to bathe that wretched island in cleansing flame."

"Glory! Father Superior will be overjoyed."

Caleb Robinson coughed. He regarded Brother Avery carefully. "Have you had communication with Father Superior?"

"Yes!"

Caleb Robinson drew his hand back to strike, but stayed. Violence was his holy sacrament, but he could not defile it by acting in anger. When he spoke, his voice was low and hard. "I instructed the order to maintain radio silence. Who contacted him?"

"No one!" Brother Avery said, eyeing the hand.

"Do not toy with me! I am awash with holy fire and won't be denied. Who contacted him?"

"I swear it! We followed your orders! Father Superior arrived by helicopter last night. We would have contacted you, to warn you but you ordered us silent. He's waiting for you on the bridge."

"The bridge?" Caleb Robinson couldn't hide the note of panic in his voice. "Shit."

10

 $\mathcal{I}$ stood on the red sandstone landing in front of Vincent's heavy wooden door and tried not to panic at the sound of footsteps. They had to be his.

It was one thing for Hazel to tell me to act normal. Just look at her, glowing in that sundress. It was another for me in jeans, dirty at the knees, with chlorophyll lashing the thighs.

It was easy for her to say, "be your charming self" when *she* hadn't been the one to almost kiss a man then run out screaming. Where's the right spot in the greeting card aisle for that one, huh? Where do I find a card to say sorry for, you know, all of this, gesturing vaguely at myself?

I screwed on my tightest smile and turned to face the music, but instead of Vincent, saw a mass of pink and brown jogging toward us. It took me a second to recognize Luna, her pink hair bobbing above three brown paper grocery bags. She reached the bottom of the stairs and looked up at us, eyes bulging.

"Oh my God you guys, did you hear? Tilly went crazy and

TANGLED CHARMS | 59

tried to poison everybody and dragged them up to the roof and tried to throw them off the ledge!"

"I—"

"And— Oh, how are you doing, guys? You were literally flying! And there was a bomb? Are you going to stay? I promise it's really not like this all the time. Only since you showed up—not that you caused it or anything—oh I should just shut up now before I dig myself a bigger hole, shouldn't I?" She flashed me a nervous, hopeful smile. I have never identified more with another human being.

"That makes two of us," I said.

Luna glanced at me quizzically. She tried not to stare, but I caught her eyes darting to my filthy jeans. "What did I miss?"

"Where do I start?"

"You two want lunch?"

I glanced back at Vincent's house. It seemed as if nobody was home. And now that she mentioned it, my stomach did feel kind of sharp. My breakfast, a blueberry bagel with plain cream cheese, had faded to a memory and a sour taste in my mouth. Hazel was hungry too, and Vincent was nowhere to be found, so lunch seemed like a good option. Anything to get us out of the noontime sun.

Hazel and I each took one of Luna's grocery bags and we headed toward the pub. As we walked, I found myself stealing glances at Luna. She was anxious and her pink hair was frizzy and she tripped over her words and she was loud and messy and utterly, utterly alive.

Nothing like the dead-eyed boy I'd known in high school. The one who talked so slow and quiet you could barely hear him. The one who never smiled, but seemed to float through life like a raft on a dead lake, neither happy or sad, just... nothing.

Somewhere, sometime, when I was studying for finals, or

organizing book groups, or buying groceries, that ghost of a boy had built a chrysalis, climbed inside, and emerged as Luna. If you'd told me about it I might have thought it was impossible, but here she was, living proof, of what exactly? That life wins? That people become who they were meant to be? Or maybe Luna didn't have to prove anything to anyone. Maybe she was just Luna, herself, and that was the point.

I switched my grocery bag to the other arm and stretched. I didn't recognize the logo on the side. Luna said it was from a store on the edge of town. The festival crowds had cleaned the pub out of napkins and a few other things. She usually bought that kind of stuff from Lucas's grocery, but it had been closed all morning, without a note or anything.

By the time we reached the pub, we'd convinced Luna that Tilly wasn't a murderer. She seemed relieved.

The pub was mostly empty. Silas, looking like a rumpled old dad in his golf hat and gray vest sipped on a stout and listened intently to another man I didn't recognize. Neither of them noticed us arrive. I was surprised to see him drinking at noon, especially after last night when he'd charged into the Crone's Wood half-corked. Maybe he had a tolerance. Or maybe he had a problem. Hard to tell.

"Hey Judie," Luna said to the woman working behind the bar. "I got all the stuff. Thanks again for covering for me. I know it's like the least bad thing he did, but Nick really left me in a bind when he decided to go all evil on everybody."

"No problem. I'm up for more hours if you've got them," Judie said. She was younger than all of us, even Hazel, mid-twenties I guess. She was thin, with short dark hair and the hard eyeliner that was popular in the nineties, and that some influencers were trying to bring back.

"Yes! Yes! I'm drowning!" Luna said. She turned to us. "So what are you having? We've got anything you want as long as

TANGLED CHARMS | 61

it's fish and chips. The crowd cleaned us out yesterday, and Lucas is missing in action."

"I guess—"

"Fish and chips it is!" Luna said, before disappearing into the back.

"Fish and chips!" I said to Hazel. We both laughed. Then again, if I ran a pub and an inn with barely any help, I'd be frazzled too.

I walked over to the copper bar, where a bank of six tall stools were slid underneath. The legs squeaked on the ground as I pulled one out and climbed up and rested my weight on the padded leather seat. It deflated slowly, like a basketball with a hole in it.

The air around the bar smelled like maraschino cherries, and malted grain. The sourness in my mouth continued. Judie, the bartender with the hard eyeliner busied herself on the other side of the bar, polishing glasses, giving us space.

I put my elbows up on the copper bar and leaned my face into my hands. It was the first real break I'd gotten all day. We'd woken first thing, grabbed a bite, and headed up to Gran's house to explore. Only Dana was there, and we got roped into this mess. The coolness of the copper seeped into me through my elbows. It was polished to an orange-red shine, but the surface was patinaed with darker spots, ghosts of condensation flung from ice-cold cocktail shakers long ago.

From the back I heard the muted crackle of oil, and a moment later smelled the briny aroma of frying fish. I glanced at Hazel who had her eyes closed and looked like she might lift off from the ground and float back to the kitchen like a cartoon dog on Sunday morning.

"If Vincent's not home, I wonder where we'll find him?" I said.

Hazel opened her eyes and shook her head slowly, as if waking from a dream. "His office maybe?"

"Do you know where it is?"

She shook her head again, this time to say no.

"Excuse me, um, Judie?" I said to the bartender.

She looked up from her polishing.

"Do you know where the mayor's office is?"

"Like, city hall? It's over on the west side of the square. Across from the statue of the old guy."

"Augustus Nightingale?"

"That's it."

I'd walked by that statue at least a dozen times in the past few days but hadn't notice anything resembling a city hall. Was she putting me on? She finished polishing one glass, and hung it upside down on the rack, then grabbed another and went to work. Didn't seem to be laughing under her breath. Why would she?

Before I could ponder that question, the kitchen doors popped open and Luna emerged with four red plastic baskets filled with golden brown fish and shoestring fries. She gave one to Judie then brought the rest around and sat with us on the customer side of the bar.

"Be careful," she said. "It's hot."

I picked up one of the thick fillets and broke the crispy crust open. A stream of heaven-scented steam came out and my stomach growled at me, daring me not to chow down, but I'd been burned too many times to listen. I set the fillet to the side and grabbed one of the thin fries, popping it in my mouth. Oh. Wow. Crispy. Salty. The soft potatoes inside had peppery savory flavor that lit up parts of my brain I didn't know were dark. I popped another.

Hazel hadn't waited. Her fillet had a large bite taken out of it and her eyes were wide as she sucked in and blew out puffs of air, to try to cool the scalding fish in her mouth.

TANGLED CHARMS | 63

"Told you it was hot," Luna said.

"It's… delicious!" Hazel managed, finally chewing and swallowing the bite. "Crispy crust. Flaky inside."

"Old family recipe." Luna smiled. "Fresh caught local."

"You know, I worried for a minute it would be frozen fish fingers from the store."

"I'm already in enough hot water with my ancestors," Luna said, laughing.

Her ancestors. That got me thinking. She was a Sinclair. Hadn't I heard that name recently? I remembered.

"Speaking of your family, one of them was at Tilly's during the, you know, murder-plant thing."

"Really?" She held a fry, about to put it in her mouth but stopped. "Who?"

"I don't know. I've been away from town so long I don't recognize anyone, but this snobby lady, Henrietta, um, Thorn, dropped the name. They're safe though. Nobody got hurt, except Tilly's feelings. Henrietta really raked her over the coals."

"I can imagine," Luna said. "Henrietta Thorn once sent a burger back five times because it wasn't the exact shade of pink she had in mind. I ended up giving her a raw patty and a spatula and told her to cook the thing herself!"

I laughed and took a bite of my fish. Perfect. Warm and crispy and flaky and filling and everything I wanted. "She seemed pretty upset about the ruckus. She even disinvited Tilly from her dinner party tonight."

"She what?" Luna stared at me like I'd sprouted a second head.

At the other end of the bar, a glass fell to the floor and shattered.

11

I swallowed the bite of fried fish and stared at Judie. Her dark eyeliner made it seem like her eyes were bulging. That the shattered glass had triggered some deep, cosmic horror, so out of place in a pub that smelled like maraschino cherries. My mouth was salty and dry. I wanted a drink, but now wasn't a good time to ask.

Luna was halfway around the bar before I realized she was no longer sitting beside me. She ran in the back and emerged with a dustpan and broom.

"I'm... so sorry," Judie began, but Luna cut her off saying there was no need to worry, that glasses break all the time, that you should see how many glasses she'd broken since she bought the place, and besides, anyone would be surprised hearing that about Tilly...

My throat was screaming for something wet. I took another bite of the golden brown fish, crispy on the outside, flaky in the middle. It helped for a second, then made things worse. I ate a fry. Bad move. My mouth felt like it might shrivel up and blow away on a stiff desert wind.

TANGLED CHARMS | 65

I cleared my throat. "Hey, could I get something to drink?"

"Oh, yes, I mean, I can't believe I forgot to offer you anything," Luna said, from the working side of the bar. "We're out of the hard stuff, except for that beer Silas drinks. If you ask me that stuff's so dark it'd be better as motor oil than for lunch."

"Sparkling water for me, thanks," Hazel said.

"A cola please... and can you put a cherry in it?" I felt a little childish. I wasn't sure why I'd asked. I usually order sparking water, like Hazel, but something about this place, maybe the smell of maraschinos, maybe the way the copper bar gleamed under the hanging stained glass lamps, brought up a memory.

It must have been on the mainland, during a vacation, or on one of Dad's work trips. I'd been seven or eight, and he'd had a meeting of some sort with an enormous man in a too-small suit, and for some reason I was there, I don't know why.

It was a bar, copper like this one, but much more luxurious. The room had felt cool and dark, and the metal of the bar, and the burgundy upholstery, and the green leather seats gleamed with colors so pure they might have been jewels gleaming in a pitch-black cave.

The bar had been empty except for Dad and me and the enormous man in the small suit, and the bartender, his white blousy sleeves puffing out of his slick black vest, cinched with garters.

I'd felt so grown-up when Dad let me sit at the bar, instead of hiding me in a booth with my crayons and unicorn coloring book.

I'd felt even more mature when the bartender had asked me what I was having. When I didn't know how to answer, he suggested a cherry cola, which turned out to be heaven.

Now another one arrived in front of me. I grabbed it and took a sip. It was so sweet I wanted to cry.

I smiled at Luna. "Thanks."

"Crazy news though," she said, fixing her own drink, something pink and fizzy.

"I don't understand why it's so crazy," I said.

"I keep forgetting that you haven't been around. A lot can change in twenty-five years."

"It's just a dinner party."

"No," Luna said. "It's not just a dinner party. It's Henrietta Thorn's annual fete. She's literally the chair of the city council. Her fete is the one time a year where members of all seven founding families come together to hobnob and eat canapés and pretend that they don't hate each other, or her."

"Sounds awful."

"But everybody still goes. They don't have any other choice. Nothing gets done in this town without Henrietta Thorn giving the say-so, at least for now. And the fete is the one time each year where people scheme and plot to get in her good favor."

"Isn't Vincent supposed to run the town? He's the mayor."

"How do you think Vincent got elected? He never could have without Henrietta's help. He's a mainlander."

"How long has he lived here?"

"Only twenty years or so." Luna was back on our side of the bar now, digging into her fish and chips.

I laughed. "Only."

"Look," she said while chewing, "it's crazy, but that's how things are. The place is named Charm Haven, right? And everybody's people came here as immigrants, fleeing some kind of trouble, right? For the most part it's welcoming. It's kind of our thing. But the founding families have always had a stranglehold on power."

"It doesn't seem fair," Hazel said.

TANGLED CHARMS | 67

"It doesn't." I agreed.

"It isn't fair, but Henrietta's sister, Lucretia, was even worse. Still, as far as I can remember, neither of them ever disinvited a member of a founding family. Especially one like Tilly who's the last of her line. The Thorns are pretty mad at the Thomlansons right now, but I'd bet my life they'll both be at the fete."

The sheriff had mentioned a feud. Something about a beehive eating the begonias. And as apparently serious as that was, it hadn't gotten them disinvited. The snub to Tilly was even worse than I imagined. How unfair and arbitrary and just, bogus.

Luna popped a fry. "What are you going to do?"

"Not go to the dinner party, that's for sure."

Luna coughed and grabbed her drink. The ice rattled as she gulped it and set it down.

"She invited you?"

"Well, yeah."

"You have to go."

"I don't have to do anything." The words shot out before I knew I said them. If there's one thing I hate it's being backed into a corner.

"G'dammit, Silas! You can't be asking me that." The man's voice filled up the mostly empty room. All four of us looked over at the table in the far corner.

Silas was bent low, his eyes shaded by his golf hat, talking in tones too quiet to hear. But from his eyes and the way he thrust his head forward I got the impression he was spitting words at his companion, a taller man with ruddy cheeks who leaned back as if he wanted nothing to do with the conversation.

"But you have to go!" Luna said. "I mean, nobody has to do anything if you think about it but, oh, how can I put this? If you want to have any kind of life in Charm Haven then

68 | TABATHA GRAY

you should really, seriously, absolutely, think about going, and then when you're done thinking, hold your nose and go anyway. Some people around here are trying to change that. Some of the business owners I mean. None of us thinks it's really fair that she should have so much power. They're trying to get her voted off the council, but who knows if that will work out. For now things stand as they stand."

"I told you, Silas, the money's too good! If I'd of known you brought me here to lecture me, I never would have come!" He stood and kicked back his chair and it squealed.

I faced Luna. "And if I don't go, what will happen?"

"Nothing," she said, "at least not at first. But sooner or later, you'll need a building permit, or a loan, or construction materials, or a gardener, or a pet sitter."

"And she runs all of those things?"

"If you get on her bad side, she can sure keep them from running."

Another squeal of a chair and Silas stood, grabbing the tall man's arm. "I'm begging you Hank, reconsider."

"It is what it is," the tall man, apparently Hank, said. "You can't stop progress."

I swung back to Luna. "So I'm supposed to go to some fancy party and grovel at the feet of some snooty old lady so she won't ruin my life?"

"More or less. But it's not groveling, not really, it's just being polite. Look, this is a small town. The only way to get by is to play ball. She invited you to dinner. The food will be good. Go. Make an appearance. Sneak out after dessert. That's what my family does."

"So you'll be attending this fete?"

She laughed. "Oh hell no. My mom and Henrietta are peas in a pod and neither of them want me within a mile of their wheeling and dealing."

The tall man, Hank huffed past us. The bell above the

TANGLED CHARMS | 69

door chimed and a gust of ocean-smelling wind blew past before the door closed. Silas, rosy cheeked and rough, dragged himself over to the bar and leaned against the polished railing.

"Another pint," he said, placing his glass on the copper. It was empty except for a few drops reddish-brown liquid and white leggy streaks on the side of the glass.

"How about some water?" Luna said, nodding to Judie.

"My own people betray me, betray all of us! And after everything we've been through. After we dove into the woods and fought the enemy. Brought magic back to Charm Haven. Even now they plot to ruin us, and for what?" He eyed me like he expected an answer.

"Um, what?"

"Lucre. Filthy lucre."

"Does this have to do with the real estate people?" Luna asked.

"Anwir Holdings?" I asked, remembering Tilly's bill of sale.

"Anwir. An old Welsh word meaning liar." He turned his head and looked at each of us, making sure it sank in. "Well, the devil's a liar, miss, and I'll be damned if this ain't from him. And to sink the boat, they're fighting like cats 'n dogs. I thought to restore the McIntosh magic would be the end of our troubles, but it looks like it was only the beginning."

That got my attention. "What kind of problems is the magic causing?"

"You give a man an axe and he ain't Paul Bunyan, but to listen to them you'd think their little fireballs and will-o'-the-wisps made them Merlin incarnate, the Goddess's gift to magic. Gone to their heads, it has."

Okay, so no too-alive plants. That was good, I guess.

"It's kicking up old problems," he said, "matters long settled, Daddy's pocket watch, the family silver, and fights where there weren't none before. A name on a piece of paper gives one the right to sell family land, to pocket the funds, to leave the rest of us with nothing. I was a fool—not a fool to help you, miss, but to think that happier days had come."

"Quite a mess you've caused." The deputy's words rang in my ears.

I was starting to feel a warm kind of queasy rising from the bottom of my stomach. Guilt? I didn't have much to feel guilty about. I hadn't exactly meant to dust the town with magic. It was a side effect of saving them from being blown to bits by the Inquisition's hidden bomb. It had just kind of... happened.

Maybe Deputy Sprout wasn't entirely, completely, off base. Maybe the influx of magic was causing problems. But what did he expect me to do about it?

12

HOLDING CELL #3, BELOW CITY HALL, CHARM HAVEN

*B*rother Albinus looked out the small, rectangular window, set in the wall just below the ceiling. The window's glazing was covered on the interior with scuffed Plexiglas and blocked on the exterior with black-painted metal bars.

A sidewalk lay just past the window, and he had counted ninety-eight pairs of ankles walk by since he had been pushed into the cell and heard the steel door clank shut. And such a wide variety of ankles they had been. Skinny and fat. Hairy and smooth. Bare and clothed. Some were quite shapely, and aroused certain... feelings.

Was it a sin to look at them? Brother Robinson would say it was. Yet, it was acceptable for Brother Robinson to have relations with the opposite sex, a witch no less, in the pursuit of the Lord's will. Was it not the Lord's will also that Brother

Albinus be in this cell, with nowhere to look but out, and nothing out but ankles?

It was not a sin, he concluded, or at least not one that would send him to the pit.

Killing, too, was a sin, and one the order did not hesitate to commit. He had asked once, at the Mountain, why this was so. It had been explained to him that victory was already theirs. The actions taken to achieve it had already been taken. Therefore, the order wasn't killing with their pyres and curved swords. It was more akin to bookkeeping.

When they had explained it, it made sense to Brother Albinus. But now, on his own, surrounded by ankles, he found it hard to remember why.

He was not strong. He knew this. He turned to the small metal stool bolted to the floor. On it was a hard compressed capsule, the size of a pea. A pill, which would open the final door. The last refuge of the righteous. The sacrament God had given them to find victory through defeat, everlasting life through death. He had hidden it, as he had been taught. But he was not strong.

Had he his robes, he might have found strength. But they had stripped him, given him a gray sort of jogging outfit that made him feel naked even as part of him found it ironically amusing. Did they expect him to run?

Why would he? His cell was not uncomfortable. With a bed, stool, table, his own toilet, room to pace and a window, it was frankly nicer than his cell at the Mountain. The view was better. And the people, while they had shoved him into the cell, had not hit him once.

It was quite confusing. These were witches, Satan's spawn. They drank the blood of children and feasted on the entrails of holy men. And yet, Brother Albinus had seen twenty-two child-sized ankles pass by, all in good health.

Eight had been skipping. Four sported shoes that flashed colorful lights with each step.

He had not seen any ankles of holy men, true, but Brother Albinus, a member of the order was holy, and no one had come after his entrails, as of yet.

Perhaps there had been some mistake. Perhaps they had landed on the wrong island. Or perhaps the order was working with outdated information, and the descendants of monsters weren't monsters themselves.

Brother Albinus decided to wait and see.

13

A small brown bird landed on the outstretched bronze hand of Augustus Nightingale. It shook as it pecked at the seed, sending small brown specks of it tumbling through the ocean-smelling air to land in our path and be crunched underfoot.

It had been a similar bird who sang to me in the forest late last night, whose song had loosed wild magic into an unsuspecting world. Was this the same bird? I couldn't tell.

It was still hot but my jeans weren't swampy. I'd traded them for a clean pair after lunch. Our clothes still being in the inn above the pub, in the rooms Hector Morales rented for us, when we first came to down two days ago. After everything we'd gone through, it felt more like two months.

I still had the queasy feeling in the pit of my stomach. That I had done something wrong, no matter how accidentally. It was unfair for the deputy to blame the crazy events around town on me. But I did feel at least a little responsible for the flare-ups of strange power that had caused Tilly's plants to come alive, and set Silas's family at odds.

But what could I do? Magic didn't listen to me. I'd been

trying and failing all day to summon the slightest spark of it. I didn't know where to begin. Maybe if we hadn't lost touch with Gran, she might have taught me, might have given me advice on how to use it, but she was gone and Hazel was my only family now. Uncle Max didn't count.

Maybe after we freed Dana, I could take some time and dig through Gran's library. It was full of magical books. Maybe one of them could help.

But now? Vincent, the mayor, was at city hall. He had information that could help us free Dana.

Hazel and I were headed there now, following the directions Judie had given us. Right across from the statue of the old guy, Augustus. Except I didn't see any city hall, only the police station, the one I'd been dragged to after Maleia died. It was a plain redbrick building that, despite having three stories, still managed to seem squat. Maybe it was the scaffolding that stretched along the right side of the building. The mortar between the bricks there was a slightly different color. A worker in white painter's coveralls busied himself with his tools.

I glanced at my sister. A breeze rustled the hem of her yellow dress while the noontime sun drew tiny pinpricks of sweat on her forehead.

"Where do you think it is?" I asked.

"It's a small town," she said, looking at the police station. "A lot of small towns have all the city stuff in one place."

"But isn't a city hall supposed to be more impressive? Where's the clock tower?"

"Maybe it got struck by lightning."

I laughed. As we got closer to the squat building, I noticed a detail that had escaped me that early morning. Most of the police stations I'd seen had a real don't-mess-with-me vibe. Every single one of them had a big sign with the word

76 | TABATHA GRAY

POLICE in a bold sans-serif font, all uppercase, preferably chrome.

This building didn't have any of that, only a small directory, the type made by sliding small white plastic letters onto a stiff backboard and casing it in locked glass. It had room numbers for police, post office, permitting, water, and so on, with about ten more entries, and at the very end: mayor, room 323.

The aluminum and glass door ground against its frame as I pulled it and held it open for Hazel. She wore flats, and I had my sneakers, but they sounded like heels on the echoey hard terrazzo.

The inside was stuffy and warming up. It smelled faintly of floor wax and burned coffee. I had a lump in my throat and my heart sped up a little, remembering how tight the hallway felt when Hector Morales rescued me from the deputy. That door was just ahead and to the right.

I heard another set of echoey footsteps and a woman in horn-rimmed glasses emerged from a door farther down. She held a stack of papers against her chest and pointedly ignored us as she walked toward us, taking a right through the door to the police offices. She didn't look like a cop. She was too much the faded-blonde-bombshell type. An assistant maybe?

"This place gives me the creeps," I said. It wasn't just the police side of things. The building had the kind of worn, dingy feel that old town post offices and Carnegie libraries had. It was as if the thousands of people who passed through them had each left behind a little bit of their soul, left it clinging to the walls like grime from too many hands.

"The sign said the mayor's in 302. Third floor."

"Actually... I want to check on Dana. Why don't you go ahead and we'll meet up after?"

TANGLED CHARMS | 77

"Seriously?"

"It'll be more efficient."

"Hazel, stop it. I know exactly what you're doing."

"What?" She looked around, a purposefully dim expression on her face, like she was that girl at the beginning of the movie, *Legally Blonde*, before you realize that she's the slickest one in the room. "I only want to see if Hector got her released. And if not, to see how she's holding up."

"We'll both go."

"No."

"It'll just take a minute, then we can interview Vincent together," I said.

"You might not have noticed, but Deputy Sprout seems to have a grudge against you."

"He's mad I didn't kill Maleia."

"Whatever it is, I can be more persuasive without having to deal with that." She glanced to the elevator to our right. "Maybe you can be more persuasive too?"

I huffed out an enormous sigh. She did have a point, damn her. The moment I set foot in Deputy Sprout's domain, he was sure to become that little boy playing cops and robbers. He'd been so sure I killed Maleia, and he was mad about being wrong.

And I hadn't forgotten about the way Hazel and Dana had hit it off. Maybe the new acquaintance would be enough to make Hazel postpone her house share in Bali. Even a few days would be something, with Caleb and his inquisitors hiding God knows where.

"Fine," I said. "Go check on her. I can handle Vincent by myself."

She winked. "I bet you can."

"Shut up and go before I change my mind."

She left me feeling like a sucker. I walked over to the

elevator and pressed Up. Deep inside, some mechanism ground to action with a clanking, whining sound that made me wonder for the first time in my life if I'd rather take the stairs. It dinged, and the door clanked open.

The car was lit by a humming green fluorescent. It leached the color from the wood wall panels, like they'd been sawed from the ghosts of trees.

A small black picture frame in the top right corner showed a pink safety certificate. I stepped in to get a closer look and the door scraped closed behind me.

The certificate had been issued in January of this year, so I decided to take a chance and hit the big number three. The topmost in a stack of buttons. At the bottom, a button labeled Basement had a keyhole next to it.

The elevator shuddered. I grabbed the steel railing. A mechanism whirred above me and I felt the acceleration in my legs. They were a little sore from all the hiking I'd done in the past few days.

The door chimed and I stepped out. Still alive.

I bet you can, she'd said. What was that supposed to mean? I told her I was done with men. After seeing Caleb with my best friend, after his misogynist book, after he destroyed my store, and showed up at Charm Haven to steal the one thing I had left? How many times could someone betray you? I needed a break. I was done.

More of that echoey terrazzo led down a dismal corridor, to a door made of dark wood with little brass numbers: 323. The mayor's office.

I grabbed the door handle and froze. It seemed odd barging in to someone's office without knocking, but this was a public building, wasn't it?

If I barged in, it would be super embarrassing. But if I knocked and I wasn't supposed to knock, what would I do if he answered? I could already feel the heat of embarrassment creep up my neck. I was blushing already.

Before I could make up my mind, the door handle turned on its own. Someone was opening it from the inside.

14

POLICE HEADQUARTERS, CHARM HAVEN

A warm breeze rustled Hazel's soft cotton dress against her legs as she walked through the door into police headquarters. The breeze was a blessing because the sunlight streaming through those open windows was heating the place up quickly. And, like most old building in the Pacific Northwest, city hall wasn't air-conditioned.

The room Hazel entered seemed smaller than it had been the other morning, when she'd saved Holly. Some filing cabinets had been shoved up against a gray wall next to a crumbling corkboard. A couple of desks, heavy steel ones, sat in the middle of the room. Each had a rolling chair behind it and a stiff-backed steel and vinyl chair next to it. Just looking at the thing made her neck and shoulders feel even tighter than they already were.

The room was empty. Strange for a police station. The only movement came from the shadows of the workers moving on the scaffold outside. The sunlight cast them larger than life on the terrazzo floor, the desks, the opposite wall, and onto Hazel herself.

There had to be at least one person on hand, didn't there? She had seen a woman, an office-manager type with horn-rimmed glasses, come in this same door carrying a stack of papers. If she wasn't out front, she must be in the back somewhere. Even if she didn't have the authority to let Hazel see Dana, she would know where the deputy had gotten himself to.

Hazel walked past the desks, to a door marked OFFICIALS ONLY and knocked on it. Waited. No answer. She tried the handle. It opened.

"Hello?" she called into the dark hallway. "Anyone there?" She tried a little louder.

She stepped inside and her pulse kicked up, as if she were a criminal stepping into a bank vault. The corridor was darker and cooler but also stuffy. The smell of burned coffee was stronger.

Where were they keeping Dana anyway? She hadn't seen any cells. Judging from the gray doors' black nameplates, this was a hallway of offices.

"Hello?" She tried again. Wherever Dana was, she'd better be okay. Hazel took a tentative step, then another and it became clear that no one was home, or if they were, they were hiding in the offices, lights out, door closed. She kept walking.

Hazel had only dated a handful of women, and she wasn't sure that she had a type. But if she had made a guess, it wouldn't be Dana, wearing tweed in summer, speaking in full sentences like a TV reporter, because she was one.

But there was something about the woman, something that fascinated Hazel. Maybe it was Dana's commitment to truth.

The reporter spoke of truth as if it was solid and tangible

and solemn as the pyramids. She'd abandoned her career for truth, and there was something exciting about that, because Hazel had traveled the world and knew most people jump off when the ride gets bumpy.

Maybe, just maybe, this officials-only hallway wasn't the reason her heart sped up. Hazel reached the end of it, and found a staircase leading down. An ancient metal sign read: HOLDING CELLS.

So that's where they must have Dana, assuming Hector didn't free her. And that's where the office manager must have gone. In such a small town it was no surprise that a secretary would pull double duty as a jailer.

Hazel stood at the top of the stairs. She stuck out her right foot and kept it hanging. It was one thing to wander around an empty police station, looking for assistance. It would be another thing entirely to enter the holding cell area. Who was even down there?

But what would they do if they found her? Arrest her? She would just explain that she was looking for help. It wasn't official procedure to leave the station unlocked and empty. The office manager might be in more hot water than Hazel.

And it wasn't like she was doing anything wrong. Just checking on a friend, that's all. In her years traveling through places where she was a stranger, she'd learned how to pull the clueless tourist routine. Most people bought it, even if Holly didn't.

Now there was a question: what would Holly do?

She'd go down the stairs. Holly always jumped in. She never ran away. She was strong.

Hazel hadn't known about the insurance. She'd been so grief-stricken that she'd blocked out everything but school. Holly had shielded her.

Hazel stepped down one step, then another, all the way

down to a gray door which was unlocked. It opened into a basement hallway, made of white-painted cinder block. She squinted as her eyes adjusted to the glaring blue-tinged sodium light, coming from aluminum hemispheres mounted on the ceiling, among exposed pipes and conduit. It was cool. Her skin felt clammy.

"Hello?" she called. Surely the woman with the papers would be here. There was no other place she could have been. "Dana?" she called out. The only reply was a shuffling noise coming from just ahead. She walked toward it.

HOLDING CELL #1, said the sign by the door. It was empty, and sterile under the sodium light. It had a small window, a cot, a stool, a toilet made of metal, all behind thick iron bars painted with so many coats of enamel gray they seemed to drip with it.

Hazel shuddered. How awful it must feel to be locked in a small room like that, underground, away from sunlight and air and freedom.

Sometimes, in her travels, it had seemed that the world itself wasn't large enough. Cities blended together. No matter where she fled to, she couldn't escape the creeping sameness. One airport was like another. A condo in Mexico City could be swapped with one in the Philippines. And the expat circles she traveled in were populated by a handful of stock characters.

There were the hippie trust-funders, the group the most people thought she belonged to. There were the earnest NGO interns, ready to change the world. There were gap year students, and lecherous old men, and digital nomads. A handful of types, no matter where you went.

This didn't figure the locals. They were more than stock characters, the full-spectrum of humanity, but theirs was a world she could never access. No matter how much she learned the language, studied customs, chatted with friendly people, she was only passing through and everyone knew it.

Hazel walked on, to holding cell 2, which was empty but the cot looked like someone had sat on it.

The stock characters had one advantage. They didn't expect much from you. There were no prophesies about magic, no family baggage, no townsfolk staring at you, mouths a little open, because they saw you fly through the air on a broom with your legendary sister. And despite traveling through plenty of places with State Department advisories, not once had she been kidnapped, tied to a stake and told she deserved to die. Not until she returned home.

Holding Cell 3 was not empty.

Hazel froze and swallowed a gasp. She wished she could quiet her heartbeat, which surely must be loud as a kettle-drum in that cramped place. But the occupant of holding cell 3 gave no sign of having heard it, or the calling she'd done earlier.

The man, pale, a little pudgy, stared out the sliver of a basement window with the intensity of a lifelong Cubs fan at the last game of the world series. He wore baggy gray joggers with a thin sweatshirt of the same material, but she knew, she was absolutely certain he was one of the inquisitors.

Without any warning, he spun around and looked at her, eyes wide with terror, as if he'd been caught *in flagrante*, though he'd only been looking out the window.

"You're her," he said, with a kind of breathy wonder.

Hazel pressed her back against the cold cinder block wall. Its heaviness was a comfort.

He was younger than she imagined any of them could be. Surely not a day over twenty-five. He reminded her of a ham radio geek she'd once met, the kind of specialized enthusiast that would practice hours to become fluent in Morse code, who bragged about bouncing signals off the moon, and contacting people as far as France. All she could think about at that time was how she had a phone in her pocket that could call France in an instant.

The inquisitor stepped toward her and stopped at the bars of his cell. He looked at her with a puzzled expression. They locked eyes then his went down, speeding over her breasts where most men lingered too long, then down the skirt of her yellow sundress, all the way to her bare ankles.

"I've seen 112 pairs of ankles today."

"That's... nice?"

"You're just a person," he said, shaking his head as if this mystified him, as if he'd expected her to have bloody fangs and razor-sharp claws. "You're all just people."

It took a minute for this to sink in, to work its way past Hazel's fight-or-flight, past her confusion, past her disgust, past the memory of last night's fear that still lived in her muscle and bone.

He hadn't known they were people? No, he hadn't.

All at once the tension in her neck and shoulders melted. Her legs which had been pressing her into the cold cinder block relaxed. The fear, the darkness, the pain of that awful experience from something unutterable into a form that could pass through her. This frightened, confused, caged young man had freed her.

She stood straight and managed a sad smile. "You're a person, too."

15

Okay, so the mayor's door was opening. This was not a drill. The door handle was turning. The brown door with shiny brass letters was swinging toward me and I had to get myself under control. Because who comes out of the mayor's office except the mayor, Vincent himself?

How could Hazel do this to me? How could she send me up here all alone to face him with a wink and a nod and a corny joke when she knew I was done with men?

Except it wasn't the tall, handsome, slightly pale mayor.

The woman standing in the doorway was somewhere in her sixties with straight salt-and-pepper hair chopped sharp at her jawline. She was a good head shorter than me, not something I'm used to.

I'd startled her from the way she goggled, then recognition flashed on her face and it twisted into a scowl. She stepped forward and tapped her finger hard against my sternum.

"Ow!" I stumbled back.

"You've got some nerve!" she said, with a raspy voice.

What the hell was she talking about? I'd never seen her

before in my life. Or had I? Could she have been one of the salt-and-pepper ladies at the tea shop? I couldn't say. With all of my attention on the too-alive plants I hadn't studied their faces.

"There might be a misunderstanding," I said, rubbing my breastbone. She sure had bony fingers.

"Misunderstanding nothing! You're ruining your sister's life and you know it."

"Excuse me?"

"Don't think I don't know how older sisters are. I had three of them! None of them wanted me to open my bakery."

"Are you Lin?" I asked.

Could this be the same person who offered Hazel the sweetheart deal she turned down? Tilly had said she told Anwir Holdings to stick their deal where the sun don't shine. I was starting to wonder if she might have said something even worse.

"I made cakes out of my home at first. They say, 'Lin, don't play around. When are you going to get married?' The town likes my cakes so I rent a kitchen. They say, 'It'll never last.' Then it lasts and I buy a bigger kitchen with good equipment. They say, 'Why do you spend so much money?' So let me tell you, I know older sisters. No mistake."

"It's not my fault she said no!" I tried to keep myself from shouting. The door was open and I didn't want to act a fool if Vincent was inside. "I want her to stay. I want her to buy the bakery!"

"You wanted her to buy?" Lin raised an eyebrow and turned her head to stare me down with that single eye. Why did I have the feeling she was about to tell me to walk the plank?

"Yes," I said. "She has the money. It'd be great for her. But she wants to go back to her old life." And right now, I

88 | TABATHA GRAY

couldn't blame her. I still felt the sting of Lin's finger on my sternum.

"You aren't lying?" Her eye bulged at me.

"Why would I lie?"

She held off staring me down and grunted. "Okay. You and me are on the same team."

"Great." The sarcasm dripped off my words, but Lin didn't seem to notice.

She flashed a toothy grin. "Don't worry, we'll get your sister to buy my bakery in no time. I have a plan."

"Holly!" Vincent's buttery-smooth voice filled the space around us. "What a pleasant surprise!"

"Stuff it, Vincent!" Lin said. "I'm not going anywhere until I have a deal with this one. Well?" she looked at me like my flight was about to take off without me.

A deal? What could I say? I was intrigued, but Lin was nuts. I wouldn't agree to any plan of hers without knowing exactly what I was getting into. Besides, I'd spent an hour tracking Vincent. I would not get sidetracked now.

"Lin," I said, using my low, steady, don't-poke-the-bear voice. "I don't know what your plan is, but I'm open to hearing about it. Right now isn't a good time though. Could we pick up our, um, conversation later?"

"Yeah. Don't worry. I'll find you."

How was that supposed to make me not worry? But I screwed on a smile and nodded so enthusiastically anyone looking would have thought I was the unhinged one.

Lin was already walking to the elevator. She pressed the button, it dinged, and she went down. I let out an enormous breath.

"That Lin," Vincent said, "is a real charmer."

"You're telling me."

"She's upset that a mainland company is attempting to purchase properties here in Charm Haven," he said.

"Anwir Holdings?"

"Come into my office and let us talk."

Vincent's office was just an office. No reception area. No secretary out front. It would have been a mistake to enter without knocking. Bullet dodged.

It was a large office, dim and cool. Wall sconces emitted a gentle, flickering light. An ancient-looking wooden desk sat in the room's center, in front of big windows that would have given a wonderful view of the town square, if they hadn't been smothered in burgundy velvet drapes. Next to the windows, a love seat and a chair made a less-formal seating area.

Vincent walked to the desk. There were plenty of papers on it. A Rolodex, the real, physical kind with cards rotating round a central spoke, sat next to a black rotary telephone so shiny it might have just come off the line. There were no computers, or screens of any sort. No telltale electronic whine. No hum of cooling fans.

The only sound came from Vincent and myself, the slight creak of floorboards, the quiet in-and-out motion of breath, both mine and his.

"Sit, please!" He motioned to one of the two chairs in front of his desk.

It was made of solid wood, no cushion, but the wood had been shaped and smoothed in such a way that it was more comfortable than any foam-backed office chair.

Instead of going to his side of the desk, he pulled the other guest chair around and sat in it. I hadn't been so close to him since I ran out screaming.

"Forgive me for my reluctance to speak in the corridor. Recent events have made me paranoid."

"About Anwir?"

"About everything. I can trust you though. You're a member of the Nightingale family."

"Tilly looks like she's going to take them up on their offer. And Silas's family too."

"Lin wants me to put a stop to it," he said. "As if I could snap my fingers."

"Can't you?"

"I wish it were that simple. The thought of strangers owning so much of the town unsettles me. We know nothing about Anwir Holdings. Neither their stakeholders, nor their true purpose."

Their true purpose? Wasn't it the same as every corporation? Profit? Greed? Squeezing blood from turnips except the turnips were people?

"I'm the mayor, not the dictator," He said. "Any change in policy needs to go through the City Counsel. I've drafted an ordinance to set before them for a vote, to limit the number of properties any one entity may own in historic areas, which comprise most of the village. Anyone may draft an ordinance, but only the counsel can make it law."

"It should be easy to get the votes, though, right? I can't imagine anyone would vote against it."

"You would be surprised," he said. "The counsel is a blood sport even in the best of times, but it's grown even more contentious."

"Let me guess: magic."

"Old rivalries have been inflamed to a degree I didn't think possible."

"And in comes Anwir to pick up the pieces."

"You're an astute reader of the political situation," he said. It wasn't exactly what every girl dreams of hearing but I could still feel my cheeks getting hot.

"Thanks for taking my shoes to the house," I said, too embarrassed to look up.

"It was the least I could do. I apologize for startling you. I've lived here so long that sometimes I forget not everyone knows me. Those who know of my kind fear us, often justifiably, but to most of the world we are a myth."

"It's my fault," I said.

"It was the product of an imperfect world."

I dared to glance up. His smile held such kindness I didn't know what to do with it. My throat felt thick.

I coughed, and shook my head. "I wanted to ask you about the woman you talked to at Tilly's this morning. Do you remember her? She was tall, with a tweed jacket. Her name was Dana."

Vincent looked surprised. "Yes, we had a brief conversation in which she asked me directions to your house. I assumed she was a friend of yours."

"Deputy Sprout arrested her for blackmail."

Vincent rolled his eyes and let out an exasperated sigh. "I should never have told the man."

"Told him what?"

"I found this on my front steps this morning before sunrise." He reached over his desk and took a white envelope off the top of a small pile. He handed it to me.

It looked like a greeting card envelope, and sure enough, it contained a birthday card with a cartoon cat holding balloons. Inside, there was a message scribbled in ballpoint: Your secret is not safe with us.

"So you were the blackmail victim."

"I don't know if I am or not," He said. "The envelope isn't addressed to me. It wasn't put through my mail slot. It could have conceivably been intended for someone else, and accidentally dropped during last night's festivities. It might also have been a prank."

"And aren't blackmailers supposed to make demands? Shouldn't it say they know your secret, and if you don't pay them a million dollars, they'll sell it to the tabloids?"

"I informed Deputy Sprout as a courtesy. I didn't expect an arrest, the least of all of a visitor."

I slid the card back into the envelope, and handed it to Vincent. His finger grazed mine and for an electric instant I felt more awake than I've ever been.

The black rotary phone on his desk began to ring, mechanical bells struck by clappers. We locked eyes and he smiled apologetically before standing, walking to the phone and lifting the receiver from its cradle.

I couldn't make out the caller's words, but the outline of their voice held a buzzy, muffled tension.

Vincent nodded. "I see."

The shyness fled from his eyes, replaced by something firmer. Gone was the gentle caricature, the vegan vampire with bat slippers. In his place stood a man of experience, who knew the delights and cruelties of the world. Who had seen humanity in all its beauty and debasement and still, somehow, stood with us.

Vincent hung up the phone and turned to me and I knew with absolute certainty that the being before me was both ancient and immensely powerful. I bit my lip and breathed in sharply.

"There's been a death in the building."

16

SOMEWHERE IN THE NORTH PACIFIC

*C*aleb Robinson stood alone on the bridge, watching through salt-sprayed glass as Father Superior's helicopter vanished into the distance.

The control panel in front of him squawked to life. He lifted the black puck microphone, pressed the button on the side, and spoke the agreed-upon code word.

For a moment, the only noise came from waves lapping on the ship's fiberglass hull, then a burst of static brought a cracking voice: "OKAY OKAY OKAY. ALL GO."

Caleb Robinson spoke the agreed-upon acknowledgment and cradled the microphone. He punched coordinates into the ship's navigation and throttled up the engines.

The meeting with Father Superior had gone better than expected. The order's venerable leader had listened to Caleb Robinson's revelation. He had expanded upon it, ripening it to a glorious whole.

Together, they had made a plan and sent instructions.

Already, wheels within wheels were turning. Soon, all the witches would burn, because they were destined to burn, because they had already burned.

Caleb Robinson smiled and looked out upon a perfect world.

17

ON THE OUTSKIRTS OF CHARM HAVEN

The beehive knew from its own strange shape that people had an unnatural fondness for straight lines and smooth surfaces. It felt certain that if it followed the straight, flat path in front of it, it would encounter the person who had separated its trunk from its roots.

It followed the path until open land gave way to more of the strange person shapes. Some were made of wood. The beehive felt a sort of kinship with them. Others were made of stone or iron or materials that did not exist in the forest. Most of these strange shapes were obscenely straight. Yet one stood out among the rest. Branches of iron sprang from the ground and curved up into shapes that reminded the beehive of the vines that had grown at the edge of the yard, of the trees that had grown in the forest.

The curved branches held large sheets of clear stone. Inside, was a garden filled with plants and flowers. The bees in the hive's lower cavity buzzed with excitement.

There was a person inside the shape. It seemed to be tending the plants, giving them water, arranging them into bundles, generally serving the plants, as it should be.

The person moved with an unusual fluidity, and was making strange sounds as it moved. The sounds and the movement seemed to go together, but the beehive wasn't certain how.

The person tilted its top box back and closed two of the smaller holes. It let out a sound not unlike the bees made when they were excited.

Something in front of the person began to glow. It became brighter and brighter until the beehive could barely see anything else. Then it flashed and sent sparkles all around. They touched the plants and the plants responded by puffing out streams of pollen (the hive knew about pollen from the bees).

This person was not the bad person. The beehive continued its search.

18

I pushed through the grinding city hall doors and squinted in the stinging sunlight, looked up at what should have been a blue sky. It had a haze, almost imperceptible. A reddish tinge, and the air tasted dirty. It could only mean the wind had shifted. The smoke plume of some enormous west-coast summer fire had arrived to engulf us. So much for promises.

Seconds ago, Vincent had told me to leave, and when I'd pushed into the police office held me back. With the deputy so eager to lock people up, it was best not to get on his radar. But my sister was in there! He said no, it wasn't her who died, it was the inquisitor.

As the door had closed I'd caught a glimpse of Deputy Sprout pacing, mumbling to himself, his expressions flickering from joy to puzzlement to despair, like he couldn't figure out if he was in trouble or if this was the best day of his life.

My eyes adjusted to the stinging sunlight and I saw my sister, a slash of yellow across the stone base of Augustus's statue. She leaned against it, one foot cocked back, tossing breadcrumbs to a flock of birds gathered at her feet. Where she got the bread I didn't know, but she seemed different, calmer. That agitated me even more.

"Where were you?" I asked, stomping over.

Her face scrunched up in confusion. "Here. What's going on?"

"You know how they caught one of those black-robed freaks? Well he's dead."

"Dead?" Hazel dropped the half slice of sandwich bread to the ground. A storm of gray wings erupted. The flock of birds pounced, grabbing, tearing the bread to pieces. They were gone an instant later, except for a mangy pigeon, not too bright, who searched the cobbles and waited for more crumbs to fall.

"How did he die?" she asked.

"I don't know. Maybe he had a poison tooth like the Nazis?"

"He apologized."

What was she talking about?

"It was the strangest thing. I went into the police station to see Dana, but no one was there. There was a hallway with some offices, but they all seemed to be empty. I found the holding cells, and went to look for Dana, and found him."

She shook her head and looked at the ground, where the not-too-bright pigeon was pecking at her flats. Gently, she nudged it away until it got the idea and flew off.

"It was kind of a shock, you know. He didn't seem evil, not exactly. Just mixed-up, brainwashed. It surprised him the people here aren't monsters. That I wasn't a monster. He said something about how if we weren't evil then we weren't already dead, then it was a sin to kill us, not just book-keeping."

"I don't get it."

"Me either, but he said it like it was the most profound

TANGLED CHARMS | 99

thought he'd ever had. He was desperate to get in touch with his order so he could warn them."

"What did you say?"

"What could I? I told him I'd pass the message along to the police."

"Did that upset him?"

"He was happy about it."

"Not exactly what I'd expect from someone about to do himself in."

"No."

I almost wish she hadn't told me because a suicide would make sense. Those guys were fanatics, the same you see in any country torn in two by religious people with guns. They probably believed that burning Hazel at the stake would earn them a ticket straight to heaven, with harps and angels and the whole nine yards. Even though they failed, there had to be a consolation prize waiting up there for good little inquisitors who chose to die rather than betray the cause.

But this one was different. He had apologized. It seemed too convenient, and Hazel could be too empathetic, but she wasn't an idiot. If she said he was happy, I had to believe her.

I didn't like it, though.

If it wasn't suicide it was either natural causes or murder, and what were the odds a healthy twenty-something kid would drop dead of natural causes?

Realization hit me. If the inquisitor was murdered, Hazel would be suspect number one. I tensed. Reached out and steadied myself against Augustus. I had the feeling that if I didn't hold absolutely still, that the world would start spinning around me, flashing, bobbing, like wooden horses on a mirrored carousel. After a few seconds, the feeling passed. I sucked in a lungful of dirty air and shivered and forced my voice steady.

"Did you ever find Dana?" I asked.

100 | TABATHA GRAY

Hazel shook her head, but was a thousand miles away. Had she come to the same conclusion?

"No," she finally said. "She wasn't there, but one of the cells, an empty one, seemed like someone just left."

"Then Hector must have rescued her. Let's go to his office and see if she's there."

Hazel glanced nervously at city hall then nodded and we took off toward Hector's. As we walked, she told me more about the empty police offices. About the woman with papers, the open windows, the men on the scaffolding outside.

It would have been child's play for someone pretending to be a construction worker to slip through the window, creep downstairs, and do whatever they liked to the "helpless" inquisitor.

If I was the tinfoil-wearing type, I might have thought it sounded like a setup. Like someone had lured Hazel there to take the fall. Who ever heard of a police station being empty in the middle of the day?

Only it hadn't stayed empty. Not for long. Someone had found the body and called Vincent.

I bit my bottom lip. On that call, Vincent had become—not exactly a different person—but a richer, fuller, deeper version of himself. Or maybe that was just him, once he let the mask fall. It was intriguing, sure, maybe even a little sexy, but Caleb was still out there, living proof I couldn't trust myself when it came to men. If I hadn't been so gullible, if I hadn't let him into my life, I'd still have my bookstore. Hazel wouldn't have been almost murdered. No, I couldn't trust myself. And if anyone was interested in me? That alone was reason to be suspicious.

Not that it mattered. I would be too busy to play footsie anytime soon.

Sooner or later Deputy Sprout would check the closed-circuit tapes that every police station has. He'd see Hazel, opening the staff-only door, going down to the cells. I could only hope there was a camera trained directly on the dead man's cell. That alone would prove she didn't hurt anyone. But Hazel hadn't seen one.

Sprout was liable to arrest Hazel first and ask questions later. I needed to get out in front of it. Find the real killer. That way I'd have something to give the deputy besides my sister.

I was reconsidering his earlier request, too: *Quite a mess you've caused.*

It wouldn't hurt to get on his good side. And my guilt hadn't exactly gone away. The magic I returned to Charm Haven was boiling up into the kind of chaos that would deliver half of the town straight onto Anwir Holding's ledger. I couldn't let that happen.

So, once again, like it or not, I was on the case. I only wished I knew what I was doing.

19

The law offices of Hector Morales were locked up tighter than a casket, so Hazel and I swung by the inn and grabbed our packs to carry them up the hill to Gran's house.

We'd have to start calling it *our* house soon, if Uncle Max didn't get his way and steal it from us with his flimsy lawsuit. But for now, at least, it didn't seem right. Hazel and I hadn't even spent the night there.

My shirt was sweaty under the pack, where the weight pressed it close to my skin. The good news was that my legs only hurt a little. I must have been getting stronger.

The smoke was rolling in. It bit at the back of my throat. When I stopped at the top of the hill, just in front of the big iron gate with its beautiful scrollwork, I looked back. I could barely see Charm Haven Square at all through the reddish-white haze. And the water, which only this morning had glittered like gaudy diamonds in the early sunlight, had disappeared. A deep, bellowing moan sounded from far in the distance. The ferry was arriving.

TANGLED CHARMS | 103

"I wonder if Dana's on it," Hazel said, looking in that direction.

"If I had to spend the morning in a jail cell, lorded over by Deputy Sprout, I'd want to get out of town, ASAP. Go somewhere a little more sane."

"I wouldn't blame her," she said, walking up the flagstone path. "I'm getting pretty tired of bad things happening."

I glanced at my sister. In the haze, her yellow dress was a beacon and I wondered if she knew how beautiful she was. I was tired of bad things happening too. Was she really going to leave?

We took the path through the plum trees, low and gnarled and dripping toward the ground with warm, dark fruit. I had eaten one of them earlier in the morning. I remembered the feeling of my teeth breaking its skin, the sudden surge of sourness, followed by a watery mellow sweet. The memory would have been enough to make me lick my lips, if the air didn't taste so dirty.

Up ahead, like a white egg poking through the grass, was the old weathered softball I'd found when we first visited the house. It had been mine when I was a kid, so serious, practicing pitching drills in Gran's yard, which was much larger than the yard at my parents' house. Kind of strange to think of it sitting out here all these years, stitches slowly rotting in the rain, waiting for me to return.

We followed the flagstones past the plum trees, past the apple trees, around the copse of tall cedars that blocked the house. I'd seen it before, but my heart still caught in my throat.

The house was something out of a fairy tale. A huge Victorian with turrets and a wraparound porch and those cute little scalloped shingles. It had been falling apart, bleak, depressing, but freeing Charm Haven's magic had restored it, gave it a purple paint job with pink trim that was witchy as hell in a girly-pop way. There was even a flag, with the family crest. I loved it. How could I not?

Dana was sitting on the front steps, her tweed jacket folded in her lap. She said something I couldn't hear to Luna, whose pink, shoulder-length hair bobbed as she nodded her head.

Luna locked eyes on us first and stood, waving. "Hey girls! Long time no see. Going camping?"

Camping? It took me a second to remember the packs Hazel and I carried. I slipped mine off and enjoyed the instant coolness as the sweat on my back began to evaporate.

"We were just moving our things," I said. "No point in renting a room when we have a whole house."

"I hope it's okay we're hanging out on your porch," she said. "I promise we're not stalking you or anything."

I wasn't worried about stalking so much as their health, sitting out in the smoky air. The prickling in the back of my throat had changed to a kind of buzzy numbness that couldn't be good.

"What's up?" I asked.

"Well, the lunch rush never materialized so Judie's holding down the bar. I thought why not take the afternoon off? And, well, you got me so curious after we talked about blackmail and magic and everything I thought why not come out and see if I could get myself into some trouble? And who do I find but Dana, here waiting? I mean, I didn't know who she was but now I do."

Dana stood, draping her blazer across her arm. "I owe you both an apology."

"For what?" After all, she'd been the one to get arrested on bogus charges. Charges that a single short conversation with Vincent had cleared up.

"I wanted to apologize for not believing you."

TANGLED CHARMS | 105

Hazel laughed at that one and her eyes sparkled. "Magic being real is a pretty tough pill to swallow."

"And I dumped it on you all at once," I said. "I wouldn't have believed me either. Hey, why don't we all go inside? The air is probably better in there."

They all agreed so I led the way up the porch. The door opened as I approached. It recognized me, as it must have recognized old Augustus—or maybe not, because the style was all wrong. When the founders stole a ship and sailed to Charm Haven Island, the Victorians and their wraparound porches, turrets and cute little shingles were still a few hundred years in the future.

We piled into the foyer, with its glass cases of cursed heirlooms, and its somber portraits. Luna knew the house better than any of us, because she had been close with Gran in the years before she passed. Now, she led us past the library, to a cozy sitting room.

It was a small room with floral wallpaper, just large enough for two turquoise wing-back chairs and a small sofa of the same fabric. A fireplace was built into the wall, with decorative plates on the mantel. Photos too, framed ones. I recognized my mother and turned away before the feelings could rush in.

The air was cooler and cleaner inside the house. Whether it had to do with magic, or closed windows, I didn't particularly care. I breathed deep and cleared my throat, plopping down on one of the chairs. The seat felt weird, like it had actual springs, and I felt paper crumple under my butt. It was the letter from Uncle Max's lawyer dutifully transferred when I changed into fresh jeans.

"This was Stella's favorite room," Luna said.

Hazel sat on the couch next to Dana. "I thought that would have been the library."

"The library was where she worked, but this is where she

liked to bring company, or sit in front of the fire and read. She told me once it was an old-fashioned drawing room, like in the old manor houses in England."

"I thought a drawing room would have more windows," I said, glancing around. There weren't any easels or paint-brushes, either, no paper pads or charcoal.

"I said the same thing. But drawing rooms never had anything to do with drawing. It's short for *withdrawing*. Like if you throw a big dinner party, but you need to catch your breath, you can withdraw to the drawing room."

"It sounds so formal," Dana said.

Hazel scrunched her brow like she did when she was confused. "Why wouldn't you want to stay with your guests?"

That was the difference between Hazel and me. At every party I've ever thrown there's been a moment, about an hour or two in, where I wanted nothing more than to kick everyone out, change into my pj's and eat Chunky Monkey while watching *The Bachelor*. Drawing rooms needed a revival.

Hazel turned to Dana. "What made you believe us?"

Dana laughed, almost snorted. "The exploding teapot, to start with. And the way that Deputy Sprout spoke so nonchalantly about magical feuds, with runaway beehives and frozen petunias in the middle of summer."

"And we haven't even told you about the plants that tried to kill Tilly," I said.

"You know, when you told me there was dirt on Maxwell Amp here, I wasn't sure the story had legs. After all, it was only a family inheritance struggle. It might make decent filler, but only for the celebrity angle. But now you tell me that said inheritance battle is taking place in a town where plants come alive and eat people?"

"You might not be able to report that part," I said.

"Trust me," Luna said. "What happens in Charm Haven

needs to stay in Charm Haven, otherwise people look at you like they're sizing you up for a straitjacket. Ask me how I know."

"Even if the public isn't ready to believe in magic, there's bound to be something here I can spin into a story." Dana had a kind of glow, just like Hazel did the other day when she was baking. Here was a woman doing exactly what she wanted to do.

"There was another reason," Dana said. "A man I spoke with in jail. He called himself Brother Albinus. I'm not certain if that's his real name, but he was deathly afraid of—wait, what did I say?"

She looked between Hazel and me, confused. I guess the temperature in the room did drop a few degrees. It was easy to think of a black-robed cultist biting the dust, but someone named Brother Albinus, who was deathly afraid? It complicated things.

"He's dead," I said.

"But I just saw him," Dana said.

Hazel sighed. "Join the club. I saw him too. Minutes before."

"How did he die?"

"We don't know much about it," I said, "though I've half convinced myself it's murder. I'm worried Hazel's visit is going to put her on the suspect list. I want to gather whatever information I can, to clear her name. First step: finding how he actually died."

"Do you have sources?" Dana asked.

I was about to answer no, but then it clicked. I had one source who knew everything about the case, and had a shiny black rotary phone sitting on his desk.

20

I pulled out my phone and pecked the glass keyboard, tapping it a little too hard with my index finger, feeling the impact through the skin, jarring the bone. I had the strangest feeling, like I was a skeleton tapping on a windowpane. *Open the sash. Let me in.*

I finished typing and hit the search button, but there was no number listed for Vincent Ravenwood, or city hall. There was barely any information about Charm Haven on the web, beyond a few conspiracy videos. Everything about the town was shrouded in fog, only visible if you didn't look too hard. Hazel and I had wandered off the map to a place that, for most of the world, didn't exist.

"I can't find his number," I said. "It's not online."

"Do you have a phone book?" Dana asked.

"A paper one? Do they still make those?"

Luna let out a chuckle. "They do here. And let me tell you that was a weird reverse culture shock. I mean, I grew up here, right? But when I lived in the city I got so used to ordering whatever off the internet."

"Yeah—"

"And when I moved back and bought the Inn & Pub they needed a ton of work which means a ton of materials and I literally almost fainted when I had to call the lumber guys and actually talk to them, because let me tell you that sexism is alive and well in the construction trades."

Moved back? I hadn't known she'd moved away, but before I could think about it too hard, a light clicked on in my head.

"I saw a telephone on the wall in the kitchen," I said. "Maybe there's a phone book too. Let me go see."

I left them in the drawing room, and walked past the library, through a hall to the kitchen doorway.

I didn't know why I froze, only that my heart was drumming and my nerves had turned electric. Something was wrong, but what? The breakfast table looked exactly as it had when we walked in this morning. The old-fashioned stove, a cream-colored hunk of iron, emitted the same low, breathy sound from its always-on burners. The counters were clean. The kettle sat on a trivet, next to the blue teapot.

The blue teapot? Hadn't it exploded? I'd been finding bits of damp ceramic in my hair all morning. But there it sat, the same bulbous teapot, with the same chip missing from its chubby spout. I stared at the thing like it was Freddy Krueger and tried to reason with my amygdala:

This makes perfect sense—no, listen to me—because this house is magic. Good magic. Remember when it saved us from the inquisitors? Went into lockdown mode? It even told us when the coast was clear! So what's the big deal if it cleaned up a teapot—okay, it didn't just clean it up, it put it back together but the point is it's on our side.

And I don't know how to describe it, exactly, but the house *felt* benevolent, like an old family mastiff napping in the corner, eyes shut, but ears pricking up at any strange sound.

Now that I knew what to look for, I found more evidence of the house's magic. The tea mugs, which we'd left on the table, had been washed, and placed upside down on the drying rack by the sink. The jar of dried, black, oolong wasn't on the counter where I left it. It had been placed back in the cabinet next to the jars of peppermint, jasmine and other teas.

I could get used to this.

Don't get me wrong, it was nice that the house could turtle up and save us from sword-wielding lunatics, but seriously, how often did a modern girl have to deal with that kind of threat?

A self-cleaning house, though? If only it came with an enchanted phone book. There wasn't one, not even underneath the off-white wall-mounted telephone with its long curly cable that probably stretched ten feet if you pulled it.

"I don't suppose you have the mayor's number?" I asked the empty room.

There was no reply except the faintest breeze against my cheek. It seemed to be coming from behind me, so I turned just in time to see a slip of paper flutter to the floor.

It was a small sheet of yellow foolscap, filled both sides with Gran's spidery handwriting, a list of names and phone numbers. I only recognized a few of the names: Tilly Greenleaf, Lucas Trembol, and there, the one I was looking for: Vincent Ravenwood. The mayor.

I took the phone off the hook and listened to the dial tone, momentarily clueless, as I tried to remember how to use a landline. Thankfully, it wasn't a rotary. I raised my shoulder, and tucked the receiver under my ear (like I vaguely remembered from the nineties) and punched in the first digit of Vincent's number. A tone blared in my ear. I almost dropped the phone. I'd forgotten they did that. The rest of the numbers went easier, and soon I was listening to the ringing sound, waiting for Vincent to answer, wondering how long before voicemail picked up, if he even had voicemail.

There was a click and a shuffling on the other end of the line. "Office of the mayor," a woman said, her voice like a slow nasal drip.

So this wasn't Vincent's direct line. It made sense that the mayor would have an assistant. I hadn't seen her at his office, but maybe she had her own.

"I'd like to speak with Vincent please."

"Do you have an appointment?"

"Do I need an appointment for a phone call?"

"So sorry, hon, but the mayor isn't just sitting around waiting to take calls from random members of the public."

"I'm not random. Just tell him it's Holly, please."

"Holly? Hmmmmmm, so you're one of the new girls. I saw you last night, doing the broomstick thing. Very impressive. Traditional, which is always underrated I say. You made quite an impression on a lot of people."

"Thanks?"

"Listen to me, hon, you didn't ask for it, but I'm going to give you a word of advice. The mayor's a very busy man. You ever read one of those lawyer novels? The ones where their work is their life and their life is nonexistent? Well, the mayor's like that."

"I don't understand."

"Point is, hon, whatever you're selling, he's not buying."

I caught myself grinding my teeth and forced myself to stop. You catch more flies with a smile in your voice.

"I'm not after anything," I said. "I only wanted to ask a few questions about an… event that happened earlier today."

"Oh, you mean the murder?"

It couldn't be that easy. "Yes?"

"Get in line, hon, because everybody wants to know more

about that. I asked the mayor myself, and—would you believe it?—he brushed me off. After twenty years of working together you think he'd trust me a little! But oh, no, he's acting like he's the CIA or something. But I'll tell you what." Her voice shifted, and suddenly we were conspirators. "You didn't hear this from me, but I talked with Monique down in planning, who heard it from Janet in the comptroller's that it was one of those black robes that got murdered right in his cell."

"No way! You're kidding me." I feigned surprise. I wanted to draw out whatever information she had, not stop her in her tracks. "You're sure it's murder?"

"What else could it be? A man like that. I was looking out my window when they brought in Dr. Green—not that I was spying or anything—but he left maybe five minutes later. Now let me ask you, would he leave so quick if the guy wasn't already dead?"

"Just because he was dead, doesn't mean he was murdered, though."

"What else could it be?"

"Suicide?"

"Oooooh." She drew the word out in a breathy way, like she'd just seen a waiter roll by with a dessert tray. "I hadn't thought of that. How do you think he did it?"

"No idea."

"Don't worry, we'll figure it out. Just let me call Monique and get her to see what Janet thinks."

"But first could you put me through to Vincent?"

"Sorry, hon, he's not here." And with that the line went dead.

"Sorry, hon," I said to myself, and went over to the breakfast table to sit.

Whatever I'm selling, he's not buying? What the hell was that supposed to mean?

So much for drawing her out. I still didn't know who discovered the body, who the woman with the papers was, or how the inquisitor died in the first place. I didn't even get the receptionist's name, not that it mattered. She knew even less than I did, although she let one fact slip. A Dr. Green had examined the body.

The lawyer's letter was stiff in my back pocket so I took it out and placed it on the table and smiled ruefully. I'd give anything go back to a time when my biggest problem was a lawsuit from the richest man in the world.

If I left the letter on the table, would it still be here when I returned? Or would the house have tidied it, sorted and filed it alphabetically under *L* for lawsuit? I guess I'd find out.

21

As I reentered the drawing room, I readied myself to give them the not-so-great news, but my eye caught on that photo on the mantel. It was in an oval frame had the fuzzy look of real silver left too long without a polish. I walked over to it and picked it up.

Mom was younger than I remembered, wearing a long sparkling dress, with a full face of makeup and a smile that stabbed me between the ribs. Had I been alive when the photo was taken? It had the slightly unfocused sepia quality that said maybe not. What was the occasion? A ball? A man's tuxedo sleeve cut into the picture from the right, his hand around Mom's arm. Why was the rest of him cropped out?

I remember back in seventh grade we did a unit on world mythology. A week of that was spent on ancient Greece, and each of us had to write a paper. My deskmate was Jane Hisney. (Plain Jane the mean girls called her because her parents wouldn't let her wear makeup.) She did her paper about the Muses. Lucas did his on the Trojan War. I did mine on the Hydra.

The main thing about the Hydra, the only thing you really

need to know, is that it was a big ugly sea monster with lots of heads. It was almost impossible to kill, because when you cut off one head, two more would pop out and replace them.

I'd come to Charm Haven to answer the question that plagued me all my life. Why did my parents leave? (To protect me and Hazel from the Inquisition.) Why did they die? (See answer #1.) But each question I answered was replaced by two more.

I couldn't remember how they finally killed the Hydra. Seventh grade was longer ago than I cared to admit. The photo was even older still, and its questions would likely never be answered. Maybe at some point you had to move on with your life. I replaced it on the mantel.

Hazel and Dana were still on the turquoise couch, leaning toward one another. Luna had left her wing-backed chair and stood behind them. They were all staring at Dana's phone.

Luna waived me over. "Come here, take a look at this. It's amazing. Dana found the corporate registration for Anwir Holdings, and is trying to trace the owners."

I squeezed in next to Luna and looked over, but either the phone was too small or my eyes weren't what they used to be.

"It's a Delaware LLC," Dana said, "which tells us that this is a corporate play, not someone local."

"Can you look up the owners?" I asked.

"Yes and no," Dana said. "I looked them up but they're not people, they're other corporations, shell companies most likely. I'm still tracking down the details, but not all of them are registered in Delaware, and at least one of them is an overseas entity."

"It's amazing you know how to do all that," I said. And she didn't even need a computer, just her phone.

She shrugged. "It's basic investigative journalism. It's not exactly hard, but it takes time. Give me a few more hours and I'll be able to tell you everything there is to know about Anwir. Everything available to the public that is."

"And if we need to go a little deeper, I might have friends who could help," Luna said. I glanced at her, waiting for more but for once she seemed all out of words. There was that Hydra again. More questions.

"I wasn't able to get hold of Vincent," I said. "We still don't know how the inquisitor died. I think we have to assume that Deputy Sprout has already viewed the security tapes and is kicking himself for not arresting Hazel along with Dana this morning."

That got everyone's attention.

"We do have one lead, though. We know the body was examined by a Dr. Green."

"I know Dr. Green," Luna said. "Everybody does, since he's one of like two doctors on the island."

"Do you think he'd talk to us?" I asked.

"He owes me a favor," Luna said. "I helped him fix up his office computer system a couple of months ago. Turns out network techs are even rarer than doctors out here."

"I'll stay here with Dana," Hazel said. "She's bound to need a research assistant sooner or later, and in the meantime I can look through Gran's library for any books about magic going haywire."

"Good idea," I said. It would be best for my sister to keep a low profile anyway. And if Sprout came around, the house would protect her.

Everything was coming together, quicker and easier than I ever would have imagined. It felt good working as part of a team, except… "Hey, Dana, Luna you know you don't have to do this, right? Somebody's dead, maybe murdered. And the magic thing is a huge unknown, with cosmic forces at play.

And even this Anwir Holdings thing is looking pretty shady. I don't want you jump in without knowing the full risks."

"Are you kidding?" Luna said. "I've been head down working on the Inn & Pub for the past two years. I'm ready for a little adventure. Besides, it's not like the normal world isn't scary, I mean, try going to the bathroom on a road trip, but at least here I have a chance of helping someone, of helping friends."

"I'm in," Dana said, as she pecked her phone. "There's a hell of a story here, and I want to be the one who tells it."

"Good enough, and, thanks," I said, then turned to Luna. "Let's pay the good doctor a visit."

22

r. Green's office was in a part of town I'd only visited once, last night, as I'd hurried through it on my way to the Crone's Wood to save my sister. These weren't town houses like the ones near the square. They were detached single families, a mishmash of architectural styles that reminded me vaguely of New England.

The broader streets meant more room for trees and the tall cedars shaded us from the sun. Their green boughs were strangely still in the dirty-tasting air. The lack of wind, and the faint red tint, and the sluggish heat made the place feel like it was waiting for something to happen.

The clinic was located in a converted two-story saltbox with gray clapboard siding and a cherry tree behind a white picket fence. Only a few hard, unripe cherries still clung to the dark branches, and the lack of rotting fruit meant someone had been picking it.

"So you're not selling the Inn & Pub to Anwir?" I asked Luna.

She shook her head. "I spent the past two years of my life restoring the place. Why would I want to give it up?"

"I hear the money's good. Tilly said once-in-a-lifetime good."

"I moved back home looking for a community, not a payday." She opened the door to the clinic and we walked in.

The clinic was air-conditioned, thankfully, and of the old school. The brown wooden chairs were polished from use. The counter was clad in chipped Formica. Shelves upon shelves held real paper files, labeled with handwritten names and faded color stickers. The only concession to the past thirty years was a glossy new computer monitor next to a black box with blinking green lights.

A bored woman looked up and brightened when she saw Luna. They fell into a tumble of gossip full of names I didn't recognize, and you-know-what-I-mean looks. I didn't feel left out, though. It was like rolling in with a VIP. Sure enough a few minutes later (barely enough time to flip through the two-year-old copy of *Glamour* magazine on the side table) we were led through a door marked PRIVATE, past an old beige scale with balance beam and weights, past a digital scale that looked like it was for babies, to an office door.

Dr. Green gave the impression of vigor softening at the edges with age. He was a black man, probably in his fifties. His dark curly hair was cropped close to his head, and his neatly trimmed beard flecked with gray. He wore aviator-style prescription glasses, a pink polo shirt with an emerald-green cardigan. Under the cold stream of air whooshing in from the AC vent overhead, it made perfect sense.

"Glad to see our computer bugs didn't scare you away for too long," he said, clapping Luna on the shoulder. "And who do we have here?" He looked at me like he knew me but couldn't quite remember my name.

"Holly Nightingale," I said. We shook hands and his felt warm and dry.

"Nightingale, eh? I thought I recognized you, but I was

having trouble placing you at first. Has anyone ever told you you look like Stella?"

"I've heard that."

"My condolences. Forgive my saying so, but your grandmother was one stubborn woman. I never thought she'd pass. To tell you the truth, I expected her to outlast all of us. But what am I thinking? Come on in. Sit down."

He led us into the small office. Hazel and I sat in two low-backed visitor chairs in front of a desk piled high with more of those manila case files, and another shiny computer. Dr. Green walked around to the other side of the desk and sat in a broken-in leather-backed chair. Behind him, a honey-oak bookshelf held dozens of medical books, framed photos (including one, of the doctor next to a young woman in robes and a mortarboard), and a collection of about a dozen antique cameras.

"You're in luck," he said. "I'm usually booked out a few days, but we had a last-minute cancelation. Now what can I do for you? Are you looking to establish care, Holly?"

"Nothing like that," I said.

Luna leaned forward. "We heard that they called you in about the murd—um, the, uh, dead person, the person who died at the police station."

"Gossip travels fast."

"That's what everyone tells me," I said. *Word gets around too quick in this town for people to have many secrets.*

"And we were wondering," Luna said, "if maybe, possibly you might be able to give us a little information *about* the dead person?"

"You know that's confidential,"

"But is it?" Luna said, "He wasn't a patient of yours, so it's not a HIPAA violation or anything like that to tell us. You know I had to read those rules pretty closely when I set up your computers, and they only apply to living

TANGLED CHARMS | 121

people, er, people who were alive when you examined them."

"Be that as it may, there's a certain understanding when the authorities ask me in on a case. They pay upfront, and I don't go blabbing about what I see."

"There's a reason we're asking you," I said. "My sister saw the man shortly before he died. She didn't go through the proper channels. We're afraid Deputy Sprout is going to assume she killed him, and come after her."

Dr. Green shook his head. "That does sound like something he would do. The good deputy hasn't been quite right since the sheriff went missing, what was it now, six years ago? I tried to tell him, Barney, you keep looking for trouble and your blood pressure's never coming down, but he didn't feel like listening. Most people don't."

The doctor looked at Luna, then me, and I got the feeling he was sizing us up, making a decision.

"It really tore your grandmother up when your mom and dad left. She didn't talk about it much, but older folks see a lot of their doctors and she let a word slip every now and then. If she was here I know she'd tell me to do anything I can to help you and your sister. And, well, after last night I think we all owe you. I wasn't there, but words travel fast and I know what you did for the town."

"Thank you."

"Don't thank me yet, because you might not like what I have to say." He paused. "Do you know Reina Flores? She takes care of the day-to-day over at the police station. She called me just after I got back from lunch. Told me about the prisoner. Said she was bringing him his food, but he was passed out on the floor. Didn't seem to be moving. Seemed to be dead. He certainly was when I arrived."

"How did he die?"

"Well, we found what the test kit told me was a cyanide

capsule in his cell. However it hadn't been taken, obviously. Cyanide poisoning is a messy way to die. No, I'd say it was the knife wound below the ribs, angled up."

"Could he have done it himself?"

"It's a hell of a way to kill yourself, but I guess it's possible, if you believe all those stories about the samurais committing seppuku. Still, I'm inclined to believe someone else inflicted the wound. The angle of it would be awkward to self-inflict."

"Are you able to tell the angle just from looking at the cut?"

"Doesn't take a genius, when the knife's still in the wound."

"Ouch. Was there anything else?"

"Minor burns on the arms, pretty strange-looking but hardly lethal. Likely vitamin D deficiency. That's it."

Dr. Green took off his glasses, wiped them with a small brown microfiber cloth he kept on his desk, eyed them for specks then put them on and pushed them up onto the bridge of his nose.

"In my professional opinion, it's likely murder. Of course Barney wants it to be suicide."

"But this is a police station, they have cameras everywhere. Why can't Deputy Sprout just review the security footage? It would be pretty obvious if someone had visited him."

"That was the first thing the good deputy checked after they found the body. But obviously didn't have Luna here set up their system, because the thing was fried. Some sort of power surge. Totally out of commission."

I didn't know whether to be happy or sad. On the one hand, the lack of security footage meant there was no easy way to place Hazel at the scene, not unless they found her fingerprints or something. But on the other hand, it made the incident even more confusing, and I was getting tired of being confused.

"Whatever the answer is," the doctor said, "it doesn't look good for the deputy. It's an elected position, due in November. By the end of the day, everyone on the island will know he either let a prisoner get murdered, or let him commit suicide, and the tapes that might have cleared it up never got recorded."

"He might get voted out?"

"Change is in the air. Folks were restless, even before what happened with the Inquisition. There was even talk of replacing certain people on the city council. Now, especially after this murder, I wouldn't be surprised if a lot of the old guard get handed their walking papers this fall."

23

*L*una and I walked through the still neighborhood, the clinic and its cherry tree far behind us. We didn't have a destination, not exactly, but we were heading in the general direction of the square.

The air still had its smoke-red tinge. My eyes stung and I blinked them watery as the last breath of cool air from the clinic's AC leeched out of my jeans and cotton top, replaced first by not-unpleasant warmth, then mugginess, then pinpricks of sweat that wicked into the fabric and darkened it.

"Our next step is to interview Reina," I said. "We need to know the exact timeline. If she saw the inquisitor alive after Hazel stumbled across him…"

"She won't talk to us," Luna said, tucking a strand of pink hair behind her ear. "She's with the police, and she won't tell us what happened just because we ask nicely."

"It worked for the doctor."

"Only because I know him and he owed me."

"You don't know Reina?"

"It's a small town. I've seen her walking to city hall and

stuff, but we've never talked. She's been to the pub maybe once, when it looked like her friends dragged her in, and she drank half a beer and left. Some people just don't like being around alcohol, and people with kids don't get to go out much."

"Too bad you didn't install the police station's computers," I said.

"That was a favor to Dr. Green. It's not something I really do anymore."

"But it used to be?" And now that I mentioned it, what was Luna up to before she moved back to Charm Haven? The Inn & Pub had been vacant and boarded when we grew up. It must have cost a small fortune to restore it.

"I just helped Dr. Green because he's helped me out a lot getting some of my medications delivered. There's no real pharmacies out here, you know?"

I didn't know, but it made sense. I had a vague memory of a pharmacy, Johnson's, or Jorgenson's or something like that. It was an anachronism even back then, with a real chrome soda fountain and an old man in a paper hat who would make you root beer floats with ice cream that smelled like a freezer. The place had probably been jumping back in sock-hop days, but it was gone by the time I hit middle-school. By then, all the cool kids hung out at The Sandman, a coffeehouse just down the street. Now both of them were shuttered, victims to time and changing fashions.

"We could wait until Reina's off work," I said. "It's three thirty now, and most people get off at five or six."

Luna raised her index finger and opened her mouth but didn't get a chance to answer, because my phone started to buzz in my pocket. I took it out and saw Hazel on the caller ID, then slid my thumb over to the big green *answer* button and wondered if one day it would be like the rotary phone on Vincent's desk, like the soda fountain and Sandman Coffee. Of course it would. That's how it goes.

"Holly." My sister sounded nervous. "You won't believe what I found."

We'd left the house less than an hour ago. What could they find in so little time? And what was the cause of the anxious note in Hazel's voice? I glanced around. The street was empty, except for me, Luna, a fire hydrant with chipped yellow paint, and a small tabby cat, its tail swaying as it walked away from us.

I motioned to Luna to lean close, and when she did I angled the phone out so we could both hear it.

"Did Dana find some dirt on Anwir Holdings?" I asked. "Luna's listening in too, by the way."

"Not yet. She ran into some problems but is still digging. I found something though, in Gran's library. You were right, that place is amazing. It's like a museum."

My mind went back to yesterday, when I'd found the missing library. The room had been lined with shelves filled with books, their spines a kaleidoscope of colors and titles. In the center had stood a large table with maps, scrolls. Two well-worn leather armchairs had sat in front of a dark fireplace. And the fireplace had come alive on its own. Flames had leaped up, casting a warm, flickering light that had danced across the floor and nipped at my toes.

"Holly? Are you there?"

"Sorry," I said. "I'm listening."

"At first I thought there was no way I'd be able to find anything useful. There are so many books. Then I noticed one sticking out a little from the shelf. I didn't know where else to start so I pulled it out and started skimming. Turns out, it was an old history of Charm Haven, and you'll never guess what it said."

TANGLED CHARMS | 127

"Something about a thirteenth daughter?" Seemed as good of a guess as any.

"Close, but not everything's about you. It talked about the magic the original settlers brought with them. They had a ton of it, but there weren't very many people. When the Inquisitors came, they couldn't fight them off. Instead, they stole a ship, and sailed it here. They used the magic to keep their ship safe, to find food, and when they got here, to clear the trees, dig wells, and set up the village. Like, imagine all of those stores about Paul Bunyan and his ox named Babe… but with witches and magic."

"I remember it from school." But I wasn't surprised my sister hadn't. Hazel had been in—what, second grade?—when our parents moved to the mainland.

"Did they teach you what happened next?"

Now that she mentioned it, all the stories I remembered hit fast-forward after the initial landing and breaking ground. They picked up about a hundred years later during a food shortage.

"Everything went fine for a few years after they landed," Hazel said. "But then their magic started acting up. At first it was little things. Spells misfiring, then quitting altogether. Lifelong friends getting in screaming matches, then fistfights, then magical duels."

I glanced at Luna. "Do you remember any of that from history class?"

She shook her head no.

"It only got worse," Hazel said. "One night, the magic they used to protect the settlement failed. Huge, monstrous beasts emerged from the wood. They tore the settlement apart and destroyed their stores."

"They didn't teach us any of that," I said.

"Then the trees came alive and marched on the town."

"Excuse me?"

"Yeah. The trees."

"That… I would say that sounded crazy, but it's pretty close to what happened at Tilly's. How did they get it under control?"

"It only says that a bargain was struck, that no more land was to be cleared, and that the remaining forest was to be left untouched."

The remaining forest? I looked back, down the street leading toward the clinic. Far past it, the land rose up, and the light green of summer grass became darker cedar green. I'd been there last night. I could still feel the weight of those heavy trees. I could still smell the musty moss and pine, and something ancient and damp that had drawn the heat from my shoulders and pricked my skin into goose bumps.

"The remaining forest must have been the Crone's Wood," I said. "That would explain the taboo against entering it." The trees there had been enormous because it was a primeval forest, never touched by steel. "You said the founders struck a bargain. With who?"

"It doesn't say. It's weird. The book is super detailed everywhere else. Want to know what plants the settlers ate? How they searched the land methodically for native settlements to ask permission to build? How they broke down the ships into lumber to build their first houses? It's not a short book. But when it gets to the part about magic going haywire, and especially about the deal, it tightens up like someone pleading the Fifth."

"What else?"

"I've told you everything I know. I'm going to see if I can find any other books that might fill in the details."

"Ask the house."

"Huh?"

"Just try it. Talk to the house. Explain what you want. Say please and thank you."

TANGLED CHARMS | 129

"And what exactly will that do?"

"I have no idea, but if you feel a breeze where there shouldn't be one, be sure to look around. By the way, we made some progress on the inquisitor. The doctor thinks it was murder."

"Wow, okay, keep me informed."

"Will do. You let me know if you find any more about the bargain."

"It's a deal." I tapped the red End Call button.

Luna let out a low whistle. "I've never heard that story about the trees, or the bargain or any of that, and you'd think they would have covered that in civics. Mr. Bunnel would have made that a whole semester. He was the worst, wasn't he? Did you have him?"

"In my class we called him Mr. Grumble."

"But never to his face, right, because he would have flipped. So why didn't he tell us about it? I mean, I know people try to protect kids from things in the world, but this was like a million years ago and it would have been way more interesting then memorizing the names of every single person in the founding families."

"Mr. Grumble probably didn't know. We're talking about something that happened five hundred years ago. And it must have been pretty traumatic for everyone involved. Think about it. You're fleeing the Inquisition, and finally find somewhere safe. Then your magic, the one ace up your sleeve, stops working and your safe haven comes alive to try to kill you."

"Sounds like a very bad day."

"When it was over, they probably didn't feel like talking about it. After a few generations of not talking, people must have forgotten it had ever happened, just like they forgot about the legend of the locket and the thirteenth daughter."

"So," Luna said, "magic is going haywire now, just like it

130 | TABATHA GRAY

did back then. They made a deal to fix it. We could do the same thing."

"Why not?"

"Simple." Luna's cockeyed smile said it would be anything but simple, and I agreed. Where would you even start? We could go back to Gran's library and help Hazel flesh out the story. We could focus on Reina Flores, and nailing down that timeline. Or…

The idea came to me slowly, like the morning sun breaking through lazy clouds, its golden light watering the night-black world like rain. When the idea had formed fully and perfectly in my mind, I turned it over, looked at it fully from all angles.

"I might know where to start," I said. "We know that the Crone's Wood is mixed up in this. And who knows the most about the Crone's Wood?"

"Who?"

"The crones! Think about it. All of this forgotten history was preserved in Gran's library. Maybe they have their own library, with their own books that don't skimp on the details."

Luna's eyes were saucers. "I know it's silly and I'm not a kid anymore, but I spent my whole childhood hearing how if I didn't clean my plate, mind my parents, walk and talk and act the way they wanted me to, the crones would come out of the wood and drag me away and nobody would ever see me again."

"Those were all just stories."

"I know, but tell that to my nervous system! It's not every day you find out your bogeyman is real, and 'oh, why don't we go ask them about the finer points of local history?' That forest is creepy, and huge, and where would you even find them?"

I was wondering that too. I thought of Silas, with his

cabin at the edge of the wood. But despite living so close, he was terrified of the place. He'd only entered it last night because of his misplaced faith in me, along with a little liquid courage.

Then I remembered what Lucas had said last before he'd shifted into a jaguar and carved an escape route through the inquisitors.

Silas lives near the wood, he'd said, *but he doesn't have the freedom of it. My family does. We are allowed to hunt under certain conditions. I can't protect you from everything, but I can at least make sure you don't walk into a trap.*

24

Lucas's store was shuttered when we arrived. The wooden tables where he normally displayed boxes of fresh produce on the sidewalk were folded up and stacked behind the steel grate.

I walked over to it and stood near a dark splatter spot on the pavement that smelled like overripe cantaloupe, a strange accompaniment to the air's dirty taste. I wrapped my fingers around one of the metal grate bars, warm where it was raked by a shaft of sunlight. I pulled, but the grate caught and rattled. It was locked.

Not that there was any chance of Lucas having simply forgotten to unlock his storefront. I couldn't imagine him sitting in the dark, wondering why business was so slow. I cupped my hands around one eye and peered through the grate, looking for any movement, any sign of someone inside. The only light inside came around the edges of the double doors leading to the store's back room.

"Let's try the back entrance," I said. "Lucas used it when I needed cream to give to the whittlers."

"Is that what they're calling it these days?"

TANGLED CHARMS | 133

I laughed. "Shut up. It wasn't like that, okay?"

"What, you have to admit he's cute."

We passed through an unlocked chain-link gate to the alley, where a gray steel door and a small loading dock cut into the building's redbrick exterior. I grabbed the door handle, and gave it a tug. It swung open.

Okay, didn't expect that to work.

The light was already on inside the room with the big, rumbling walk-in cooler taking up most of it, and cardboard produce boxes filling the rest. It was chilly inside and smelled like bananas.

"Lucas?" I'm not sure why I called out. It's not like there was any place back there to hide. I walked to the big swinging doors and poked my head through them. The public part of his store was dark and nobody seemed to be—

Clank.

I whirled around just in time to see the walk-in cooler's heavy door swing open and a woman walk out. She was older than me, with hair in a short bob, so neat I wondered if it was real. She wore a drapey hot-weather top with linen pants and hard eyeliner (probably not because any influencers wore it, but because she had never stopped).

She saw us and stood there with her mouth hanging open a little, holding a glass milk bottle in each hand, her nude-manicured nails wrapping around their necks like talons. She looked familiar, but I couldn't place her.

"Mom? What are you doing here?" Luna said.

"And I suppose I should ask you the same question. What are you some kind of hooligan come to rob the place? Outrageous! I should think that my own child, a Sinclair no less, should take advantage of a hardworking businessman, should rob a store so vital to the community, and for what?" She seemed to notice me for the first time. "And who is this? A bad influence? A Jezebel? What would your father (rest his soul) think if he saw you being led around like this?"

Silence hung in the air, thick as a Wild West standoff, until Luna let out a sort of hissing sound and broke into a laugh.

"I'm forty years old, Mom."

"All the reason for you to get your life—"

"My life is together! I literally own a hotel."

"And a bar." She said it like it canceled out the hotel.

"...which you still haven't visited."

"You know your father wouldn't approve—"

"How long does he have to be dead for you to stop being afraid of him?"

She didn't reply to that. Just clinked her milk bottles down on a table and sucked in a breath through her closed teeth. It made a wheezing kind of sound.

"And anyway," Luna said, "it's pretty wild you accusing us of stealing, when you're the one carrying two jugs of milk."

Luna's mom closed her eyes and shook her head slightly, like she was saying a prayer for the strength to deal with the idiocy of the world. "I am not stealing."

"Let me guess, you're borrowing."

"I ran into Mr. Lucas this morning. I inquired as to why his store was still closed, and he informed me he was taking the day off, as he wasn't feeling too well. Not sure why he was running toward the park instead of staying home."

Lucas was sick? He had been fine last night. Could he have been injured during the fight with the inquisitors? Could he have gotten zapped by a bolt of unruly magic? It was even more reason to find him, even if he couldn't lead us to the crones.

"...so he just gave you the keys?" Luna asked.

She held up a scuffed aluminum carabiner with about a

dozen keys on it and jingled them as proof. Those were Lucas's, the ones he used last night.

"I impressed on him the importance of getting my two quarts of milk, because Ronald drank it all last night and I'm making my ooey gooey butter cake for Tilly's fete, she told me Rachel, it simply would not be a fete without your ooey gooey butter cake. And speaking of, I expect that you'll be going this year. Hattie asked about you."

Hattie. Henrietta Thorn. I'd almost forgotten about the battleship of a woman with her oversized jewelry, and her snobby way of talking, and her fete. (Who uses that kind of word, anyway?) Luna had said Hattie and her mom were peas in a pod, and I could see why.

Luna and her mom were also an interesting pair. They both talked like pots overboiling, but somewhere in the conversation, Luna had transformed from her batty, chatty, anxious self into a sullen teenager. The same thing happened to me when Mom was alive.

What other depths did Luna have? What must it have taken for her to restore the Inn & Pub? Even with a little money, a big restoration project like that would require a ton of work, a boatload of tenacity, and more than a little knowledge about greasing wheels.

"...lly Nightingale." I heard my name and snapped out of my thoughts. They were both looking at me now, and it hit me just how much they resembled each other, twenty years apart. Luna looked bored and embarrassed. Her mom was grinning ear to ear.

"Such a pleasure to meet you! Why I was so excited when Hattie told me you'd be attending the fete. Your grandmother, Stella, was a great friend of mine, a revered member of the community, and I really must know everything, absolutely everything, about you and your parents and your sister. Why the last I saw her she was in pigtails!"

136 | TABATHA GRAY

I guess I wasn't a Jezebel anymore. "Unfortunately the invitation was kind of last minute, and I already have a lot planned for this evening."

"Nonsense! All of the founding families will be there, and a few others, like the Trembols, and Lancasters, and it wouldn't be the same without a member of the Nightingale family in attendance." When she started talking about families, she didn't just sound like peas in a pod with Henrietta Thorn, she sounded exactly like the old battleship, and I shuddered at the idea of being in the room with them both, outflanked.

But she had said the Trembol family would be there. Lucas's family. If he was attending, we could ask him about the crones. And if he wasn't, we could ask his family where he was, if he was sick, or had gotten better.

"Okay," I said. "Seven o'clock, right?"

"Yes, though you could stand to be a little early."

"I'll be there."

It earned me a sharp look from Luna, but an even wider smile from her mother. I'm sure it was my imagination, but in that moment it seemed like I could see each and every one of her teeth.

"Wonderful!" She said. "I look forward to seeing you. You too." She glanced at Luna, grabbed the milk bottles and walked out. For a second you could see the red-tinged light of the alley, then the gray steel door thudded shut.

"*I look forward to seeing you too*," Luna said, imitating her mother. She bit back whatever she was about to say next.

"What's the matter? I thought you would be happy that I agreed to go to that silly dinner party—sorry—fete."

"It's nothing. You wouldn't understand."

"You sure about that? I had parents too. Nobody in the world knew how to push my buttons like my mom, or, I mean, she wasn't trying to do it. Just her existing in the same room as me was enough to drive me up the wall sometimes."

"It's not that," Luna said. She looked at me and sighed. "Do you really want to know?"

"Of course I do." Luna had been one of the first people we'd met when we came to Charm Haven. And today, she'd dropped everything to help Hazel and me out. Besides, I liked her. If we were going to be friends, that meant lending a shoulder sometimes.

"It's probably going to seem like nothing to you, but did you notice how when she left, she said, 'I look forward to seeing you, too.'" She wasn't crying, but the corners of her eyes were wet.

"Yeah?"

"She didn't say my name. She never does."

"A little strange."

"And did you notice how she referred to me as her *child*?"

"What's wrong with that?"

"She didn't call me her daughter."

"Oh."

"I told you, you wouldn't get it. I mean, it probably seems like I'm just looking for some reason to be upset, and if it was only this once maybe you'd be right."

"It's not?"

Luna ran her hand through her pink hair. "It's been like this for years. I'm her *child*, her *offspring*, a *citizen*, a *Sinclair*. I'm *you*. I'm *they*. I'm never Luna. I'm never her daughter. Do you understand how weird that feels?"

"Have you tried discussing it with her?"

"I've brought it up, sure, but she pretends like she doesn't know what I'm talking about. It's like she thinks she's found a clever little loophole where she can make it clear to me she doesn't approve of who I am, without coming right out and looking like a bigot."

"Yikes."

"Tell me about it."

"So I guess you won't be coming to the fete with me?"

Luna laughed and rolled her eyes. "She only asks because she knows I won't come. She does it to needle me. I'd bet you anything, she made up that little story about Henrietta asking after me. But you know"—a mischievous grin spread across her face—"maybe it's time to call her bluff."

I was right. Luna did have depths. Maybe I'd never experienced anything like what she described, but she was wrong to think I wouldn't believe her. I was starting to get the feeling we'd be good friends.

25

*L*una and I said goodbye in front of the Inn & Pub. She had to get back to work, to make sure Judie was still alive, and to get ready for the fete. It turned out that dinner party didn't just have a fancy name. It had a dress code, not exactly tux and tails, but miles above the jeans and wrinkled cotton tops I'd stuffed in my pack.

Thankfully, we were about the same height, so she was able to lend me a couple of dresses to try on. They were in the slick, heavy-plastic shopping bag I held a little away from my body, so it didn't cut off the airflow and make me sweat even more. My throat felt like the desert. I'd have killed for a cup of iced tea, though I resisted the urge to park myself in the cool, dark pub, and stay there until a fiery sundown cooled the stagnant air.

My number one goal had been to find Lucas, but he was missing. My first instinct had been to track him. Luna's mom had said he was walking toward the park, which, it turns out is what they called that the grassy buffer between the town's paved roads and the Crone's Wood canopy. They didn't use to call it that, but it hardly mattered, because I didn't believe for a second that Lucas was going there.

He was headed for the wood itself, where his family hunted, in their shifted animal forms. If he was in the wood he was far out of my grasp. I couldn't hope to track him. My best bet was to go to the fete, see if he was there, and if not, ask around.

I considered stopping by the police station to trying to talk to Reina, but that place made me nervous. Not only had a man died there this morning, but it was also the domain of Deputy Sprout, who always seemed to be watching me, waiting for me to slip up. And Luna had been right. She wouldn't talk to me unless she had a reason. Perhaps a good word form Henrietta could loosen her lips.

So the only thing to do, was to walk back to the house, kill time for an hour or two then get ready. I'd been on my feet for a long time, and was starting to wish I had a car, or a moped, or a Segway, anything to avoid having to walk up that hill one more time, breathing the forest fire air.

Or a broom...

But that was a joke. No matter how much I tried to find it, the magic just wasn't there. I was emptied out, hollow, and who knows if I'd ever be refilled. I could reach out my open hand all I wanted, but the broomstick would never come. So I had to make the climb by foot.

By the time I reached Gran's wrought iron gate, the sun was dipping west, and I began to regret being cocky about my newfound leg power. They felt like Jell-O and I steadied myself on the gatepost, eyeing the orchard up ahead, wondering if the gnarled old trees would come to life one day and try to evict us.

Hazel was there, a burst of yellow, picking dark, sweet-looking plums from a sagging tree. A wicker basket bounced

TANGLED CHARMS | 141

against her dress, its long loop of a handle resting in the crook of her elbow.

She noticed me and waved. I couldn't tell if she was smiling, because she wore a red bandanna around the bottom part of her face. I knew it was for the smoke, but it made her look like a desperado. *Hands up, pardner, now move real slow and give me all them plums.*

"What are you grinning at," Hazel said, her voice muffled.

"It's nothing. Just happy to see you. By the way, you'll be happy to know there's not any security footage of you at the police station."

Hazel turned toward me. "There's not?"

"Yeah, they had some sort of malfunction this morning. Any progress on the research front?"

"I've found a lot of information, but no smoking guns so far. You were right about asking the house, by the way." The tree leaves rattled as she plucked a plum. She held it up and inspected it, then laid it gently in her basket. "I felt like a dim bulb talking to the empty room, but I asked it to help me find books about magic going haywire, about how they fixed it, about the deal."

She picked another plum, held it up and inspected it. It was so dark and juicy with the faintest frosting of white that fresh plums have. She held it instead of basketing it, and a memory of sour sweetness made my mouth water.

"And the house helped you?" I asked.

"It wasn't like the teapot and chairs grew eyes and started talking," she said, "but I felt the breeze you mentioned, then I saw that several other books had been pulled just a little bit out. They might have been like that before, but when I checked them, they all were histories that covered that time period. Dense reading material, but it feels like it might have answers."

"Then what are you doing picking plums?"

She tugged her bandanna-mask down around her neck, brought the dark purple fruit to her mouth and bit into it. A little stream of clear juice ran down her chin. She wiped it away with the back of her hand.

"I needed a break," she said, "and from the looks of it, you do too. Come on in, I'm making us a galette, and you're just in time to help."

I didn't know what a galette was, but anything my sister baked was sure to be the best thing I'd eaten all day, so I followed her along the flagstone path, and up the front stairs, and I thought about asking how it had been spending all that time with Dana, if there had been a deeper connection, or even a spark of something romantic, but I didn't know where the reporter was and didn't want her overhearing.

When the door closed behind us I breathed deep. It must have been the house's magic keeping the smoke from seeping in. Back in Seattle, even when I'd lived in an apartment on the eighth floor of a new building, the smoke had only needed minutes to creep in through cracks and crevices. But the air inside Gran's house was utterly clean, and after an hour in the prickly haze, it almost tasted sweet.

I followed Hazel to the kitchen, and set the bag with Luna's dresses on the breakfast table next to Uncle Max's lawsuit letter. It was still there, so I guess the house only tidied things that needed tidying.

My nose still prickled from the smoke, but I still caught the high spicy note of cinnamon. Three large ceramic canisters and several smaller jars sat on the center island's butcher-block counter. And there, next to them, sat a single, fresh lemon.

A lemon? Where had it come from? The kitchen hadn't been restocked since Gran passed away, Lucas's grocery was closed. The garden had no lemon trees, and we were too far north for them to thrive anyway. It didn't make sense.

TANGLED CHARMS | 143

"Yeah, it surprised me too," Hazel said. It was annoying being so easily read. "But there's a whole pantry back there full of fresh fruit, lemons, onions, carrots, flour, nuts, pretty much any ingredient you might need."

My mind flashed back to Lucas's store. "A walk-in refrigerator?"

"No." she put the basket of plums on the counter by the sink and pulled a brass colander from where it hung on the wall. "It's just a pantry."

"Another win for the magic house," I said.

She finished transferring the plums to the colander, then ran them under water from the sink, shook off the extra droplets, and brought them over to the center island and set them on a white dish towel that was printed with a repeating pattern of crooked witches' hats and arched-back black cats.

There it was again, that glow I'd seen the other day, that only really came out when Hazel was creating something delicious, working with the tools and ingredients she knew like the back of her hand.

She had had always been a whiz in the kitchen. I still remember the oohs and aahs from Mom and Dad, and a few of their friends from work, when Hazel and I brought out trays of strawberry mousse she'd made from berries from the garden. The friends had been impressed enough when they thought I'd made it at seventeen. They almost couldn't believe it had been my eight-year-old sister.

"Here," she said, setting a cutting board and knife in front of me. "You cut up the plums. I'll make the crust. Just cut them in wedges. They don't have to be perfect."

So, I thought to myself, *a galette has a crust.* Good to know. My stomach growled, and I realized I hadn't eaten anything since fish and chips at the pub.

I picked up one of the plums. It was still warm from being outside, and its skin felt smooth and taut. A seam ran from

144 | TABATHA GRAY

the stem to the bottom of the fruit. I slipped the small paring knife in and ran it around the hard middle stone, then I set the knife down and twisted the fruit apart and it smelled like sweetness and the promise of summer.

I flicked the stone out with my knife, cut the flesh into pieces, and before I put them in the bowl, I took a slice and popped it into my mouth. It was sweet and sour and sharp and mellow and watery and warm, and all at once the dirty taste from the smoky air was gone. I ate another.

"Save some for the galette," Hazel said. Her voice was chiding, but she wore a smile. She had been cutting butter into small cubes and now scraped them into a bowl full of flour. She plunged her hands into the mix, pinching the flour and butter together like Mom had taught us when life was simpler.

I fell to work cutting, and Hazel added ice-cold water to the dough, rolled it out and spread it flat on a cookie sheet.

When I was done, she added sugar, cinnamon, zest from the lemon, and a few other things to the fruit and tossed it until it glistened. She spread a thin layer of crushed almonds (the pantry really did have everything), then dumped the fruit on top, and folded the dough edges up to make them thicker.

So that's what a galette is. The kind of pie Picasso might have made, flat and oddly shaped but gorgeous.

Hazel slipped it into the oven and dialed thirty minutes into a timer shaped like an owl. She turned to me and smiled the way only she can and said, "Let's see how Dana's—"

There was an earsplitting electronic warble that sounded like a car alarm trying to sing opera. It took me a second to figure out it was coming from the landline phone attached to the wall.

Who would be calling? Maybe one of Gran's friends, who didn't know she passed away? Maybe it was Deputy Sprout,

TANGLED CHARMS | 145

calling to accuse me of a crime. I didn't want to pick it up, but what if it was important? And on a landline there was no way to mute the ringer.

Hazel pointed at the door and said something about checking on Dana, but I could barely hear her over the ringer. I nodded and she left. I sighed and braced myself and lifted the hard plastic receiver to my ear.

"Hello?" I said.

"Post office here. I have a package for Holly Nightingale." It was a raspy woman's voice, strangely familiar, but I couldn't place it.

A package? That didn't track. The hairs on my arms stood up. "This is Holly speaking."

"Are you alone?" The raspy voice asked. I was sure I'd heard it before, but where?

Was I alone? It seemed like a dangerous question, the sort of thing, an axe murderer might want to know before they made their move. But even if that was the mystery caller's play, they couldn't exactly charge through the small window above the sink. Besides, the house wouldn't let them. It would go into lockdown mode like it had with the inquisitors. So the question might have seemed dangerous, but I was safe... and I was curious.

"Nobody's in the room with me, if that's what you mean."

26

IN CLEARING BY THE CRONE'S WOOD

The beehive was glad to be back on soft ground, surrounded by grass, with the elder trees ahead, and the people and their strange ways far behind it.

Well, most of the people.

The beehive wasn't certain if the person it was following was the one who had used iron to separate it from its roots. But this person wore the red and black shapes that the others with iron had worn. He was larger than the other people, as the bad ones had been. The pelt on the front of its top box looked the same as theirs had too, like a tangle of fine brown roots.

The beehive watched the person walk across the field and enter the forest. As it followed it felt a strange sort of buzzing in its bottom box. It wondered if the bees were growing restless. But as it followed the human into the wood, the beehive realized it had just learned what happiness felt like. It was happy because it had found the person who could unmake its disgusting shape. Happy because its long journey would soon be over.

27

I pressed the hard plastic telephone receiver against my ear. My arm was already getting tired from holding it. I had been pacing and was now on the other side of the kitchen. The long coiled phone cord stretched to the wall, draping like a springy jump rope.

I felt the heat from the enormous cream-colored oven where Hazel's galette was cooking. It had been seconds since she left, but I already imagined I could smell the sweet plums and buttery pastry.

Had it been a mistake to admit I was alone? The mystery caller (definitely not from the post office) hadn't said a word after hearing it. There had only been a series of scraping sounds, claps like doors slamming, and now I was pacing, jamming the receiver into my temple, heart drumming, straining to hear anything that might tell me who the hell this was, and why they were playing games.

"Sorry," the raspy voice on the other end of the line said so loud I almost dropped the phone.

"Who is this?" I asked.

"I had to let the dog out."

TANGLED CHARMS | 149

"What?"

"If I don't let her out she pees all over the carpet."

"You said something about a package?"

"She has bladder issues."

"You're not from the post office, are you?"

"Who ever heard of the post office calling on the phone?"

"Then why—"

"I didn't want your sister getting suspicious. You and me, we're on the same side right?" Now I knew where I'd heard that voice. It had been only hours ago, in front of Vincent's office, when a bony finger had jabbed into my sternum.

"Lin," I said.

"Who else?"

The owner of the bakery had said she'd find me, and she had. I glanced at the kitchen door and felt as dirty as the smoke-tinged air. What right did I have to go behind my sister's back? To conspire with a stranger to keep Hazel in Charm Haven? To steer her toward a business, a bakery, a decision she might regret?

…but what if it wasn't so simple?

I'd just seen my sister come alive when making that galette. I was sure I could smell it now. That sweet, buttery, floral aroma wasn't my imagination. Ever since Hazel was a kid, she dreamed of owning her own bakery, and here it was, the opportunity you got once, maybe twice in a lifetime. If she passed on it now, the chance might not come again, and the only thing holding her back was a misplaced fear of spending Mom and Dad's life insurance. And if she stayed, well, it would be a lot easier to protect her from Caleb and the too-alive plants and everything else that was sure to come after her.

"You there?" Lin said.

"Okay, you said you had a plan. I'll listen to it. Keep in mind I'm not agreeing. But I'll listen."

"Can't tell it over the phone. Have to show you. Come to the bakery tonight after sunset and you'll see."

"I'm not sure if I can."

"You want your sister to stay in town? Then come."

"I have to go to the fete," I said.

"That stupid thing? Nobody cares about the founding families."

"Henrietta Thorn sure does."

"She only wants to feel special because her husband cheats with the secretary."

"Really?"

"He left last year on a business trip. Never came back. What do you think is going to happen when the pretty young actress gets old? She pretends it's nothing. Says he got promoted. But she's not fooling anybody."

"An actress, huh?" I couldn't see it.

"I tell you what, you go to the party. Then you come to the bakery after. Should be over by ten. I'll wait."

Her voice was as unrelenting as the finger she jabbed into my chest back in front of Vincent's office. *Hold on.* There was something there, something about that encounter that snagged my attention, that wouldn't quite let it go. It didn't have to with the unease I felt about Lin's mysterious plan. It was something else, but what?

"Well? Do you agree?"

No, it wasn't Lin's plan at all. Then I saw it in a flash. Lin had taken the elevator down to the first floor of city hall at precisely the time the inquisitor was being stabbed.

"I'll come on one condition."

"What?" It was a voice used to making deals.

"Tell me what happened after we met."

"What are you talking about?" Maybe she didn't know about the inquisitor.

"Do you want me to come or not? Just answer the question."

"I went down in the elevator."

"To the first floor?"

"No, to the second, planning. I had to talk to someone there about a permit. They were still at lunch."

"What did you do then?"

"*Then*, I went to the first floor."

"Did you notice anything unusual?"

"Your sister, walking out the front door."

"Did you talk to her?"

"You think I'm crazy? I went out the back. Why are you asking dumb questions?"

I didn't want to have to tell her. She'd find out soon enough. "I only have one more. When before you left the building, did you notice anything weird at all? Anyone running? Any shouting? Any people you didn't recognize?"

"No," she said as if it was the final, reverberating thud of a tomb door closing.

I let out a sigh and tried not to let my disappointment get out of control. I had been smart to make the connection, to realize she had been on the scene. I could be proud of that, even if it hadn't turned out like I hoped. And it wasn't as if I'd lost anything. I would have gone to hear her proposal anyway. It helped to tell me these things, but it didn't completely stop the heaviness that had touched down on my chest and settled in.

"Except…"

Maybe the door wasn't closed after all. "Except what?"

"You said a scream. It wasn't a scream. I didn't hear it in city hall."

"What was it then?"

"I left through the back door. There's a path. It goes by

the side of the building. When I walked on it I heard a shout. I looked but saw nobody."

"Did it sound like a man or a woman?"

"It was a deep voice."

"What did it say?"

"Couldn't make it out. I thought it said *hell*, but that doesn't make sense. Who's yelling that in the middle of the day?"

"And you didn't see where it could have come from?"

"Nobody else was on the street. It had to come from the building. It seemed to come from underneath the building."

"What happened then?"

"I went home? What kind of stupid question is that? You think I have all day to hang around and listen to crazy voices? Is that what you wanted? You'll meet me at the bakery at ten?"

"Yeah. I'll be there."

The line went dead and I wondered what sort of deal I had just made. I wandered back across the kitchen and hung up the phone. The cord, having been stretched to its limit, clenched into a tangled mess that wouldn't ever come undone.

Lin had heard a man's voice at the time of the murder. It had come from city hall, below, where the holding cells were. Could it have been the inquisitor crying out? Or was it the shout of a killer?

What a strange person Lin had turned out to be. Not exactly what I imagined when I thought of cookies and cakes, but I'd watched enough reality TV to know chefs are eccentric. Maybe the same was true for bakers, and Hazel was the exception proving the rule.

I didn't like going behind my sister's back, but it was for her own good, wasn't it? Besides, there was no harm in listening to Lin's plan. I could always walk away.

28

I found Dana and Hazel conspiring in the library, sitting in the two leather armchairs Gran's ghost and I had used the other night. They didn't look up as I entered and I felt like a ghost myself.

The work table was filled with books, the histories Hazel had told me about. They were organized into two piles: a large one on the left, and a small one on the right. In the middle, in front of a chair, sat a single leather-bound volume, splayed open, next to a battered, blue-ruled composition book I recognized as belonging to my sister. She had her work cut out for her.

Beyond the table, at the far wall, the darkened fireplace was flanked by two stained glass windows that glowed red and amber from the westering sun. A long full-length mirror stood in the corner. Next to it, leaned against the white plaster wall, was a wooden staff, made from a smooth brown tree branch, gnarled around a clear crystal orb.

It was Gran's staff. She had used it last night to unlock the memories that had been sealed away to protect me. (And without my consent I might add.) I still felt salty, but I could feel my anger softening. I reached out and wrapped my hand around the staff's smooth wood. It felt oddly warm, and the crystal orb flickered blue before fading to nothing.

"Who was it?" Hazel asked.

I blinked, not understanding.

"Who was on the phone?"

"Oh... Nobody." It wasn't the most convincing lie, and I felt like a jerk about telling it, but it was for Hazel's own good.

"Okaaaay." She looked at me funny. "Dana was just telling me about what she's found on Uncle Max."

"Really?" I asked, leaning Gran's staff back against the wall. I walked around to the front of the fireplace and knelt to get on the same level as the other two. Hazel was still giving me the stink-eye, so I focused on Dana, who had her tweed blazer spread across her legs like a blanket.

"I came to an impasse while researching Anwir," Dana said in her broadcast voice. "I needed to use certain databases that aren't available to the public, but I lost access to them when I was fired."

"Damn." I had been looking forward to knowing more about the company that was trying to gobble up Charm Haven. "Is your investigation dead in the water then?"

"Definitely not," Dana said. "I still have friends with access to those databases. I'll get the information, though it will take time. While waiting, I've been looking into your famous uncle, Maxwell Amp. I saw his letter on the kitchen table and read it. I hope it wasn't an intrusion."

"I don't mind," I said.

"It screams *frivolous lawsuit*," Dana said.

"Some lawsuits aren't meant to be won." I echoed Hector's words. "They're meant to apply pressure, to make us give up. Uncle Max has enough money to keep a team of lawyers working round the clock until the sun goes supernova."

"But why?"

I glanced around the library. "He wants the magic house?"

"On an island he hasn't visited in over thirty years?"

"I didn't say it was a good explanation."

"Hector told me about the ambiguous comment in your grandmother's will. 'If love were enough to pay your debts, I would have paid them ten times over.' Do you have any idea what these debts might be?"

"I didn't know until a few days ago that he was one of the richest people on the planet. He was just this weird guy that showed up in old family photos from before I was born." My mind went back to the picture of Mom in the drawing room, with the man who had been cropped out.

"Would you like me to fill in the blanks?" Dana reached under her blazer and pulled out a small, spiral notebook, the kind reporters always used in old movies. She opened it and flipped to a page filled with writing so small, the paper was more black than white.

"Absolutely. Fill them in."

"The first mention I could find of your uncle, was in a 1983 court document. He petitioned San Francisco County to change his name from Maximilian Nightingale to Maxwell Amp. As part of that procedure he was required to publish notice of the name change in a newspaper, which he did in the *San Francisco Chronicle*."

"Eighty-three?" I asked. "I thought it would be later, for the car company."

"Your uncle's name change occurred roughly thirty years before the Amp Electric Vehicle Company was founded, though he was involved in a number of failed ventures before that."

"What kind of ventures?"

"His first company, Harmonic Stride, sold jogging shoes with quartz embedded in the soles. It was a play to capitalize on the jogging craze of the eighties along with the New Age ethos that San Francisco is known for."

"Sounds like a scam," I said.

"An unsuccessful one. Its business registration lapsed after the first year. But six months later, your uncle created a new S corp based in Reseda. It specialized in pay-per-minute telephone psychic lines."

"You mean those 1-900 numbers? I always wanted to call one but Mom never let me."

"A lot of people drained their savings to learn they were about to meet a tall, handsome stranger. Most of that money went into Maxwell Amp's pocket."

"Another scam."

"It was his first taste of success, and it brought more media attention, including one item I found interesting."

She held up her phone and showed me a scan of a blotchy old newspaper photo. It was a red-carpet event, with a dozen or so high rollers, permed and shoulder-padded, standing in front of a theater marquee. Right there in the middle, talking to a blonde with an enormous bouffant, stood the phantom who haunted our old family snapshots: Uncle Max.

"It was a fundraiser," Dana said, "for a group known as the Resonant Household."

"Never heard of them," Hazel said.

"Maybe you've heard of the mystery of the lead masks?"

"Sounds like a Nancy Drew novel," I said.

"Oh no, it was very real. In Brazil, 1966, two men, both electronic repair technicians, left their small town to travel to Rio de Janeiro on business. They were found dead the next day on a local kite hill."

"I'm guessing they didn't get mugged."

"The bodies were lying face up, like they had been stargazing. However, their eyes were covered by crudely fashioned lead masks. They showed no signs of trauma. Toxicology came back negative. And, to answer your question, their wallets *had not* been taken. Both were filled with cash."

"That's weirder than Nancy Drew, for sure."

"Because there was no obvious motive, authorities looked into the victims lives and found that they both were acolytes in a new movement: electrical spiritualism."

"Hold up," I said. "Spiritualism is like séances, right? What does it have to do with electricity?"

"That's where things get muddy. The movement was in its early stages, and its practitioners had an empirical streak. Remember, the two victims were electronics technicians. They sought to understand spiritualism in the same way they would understand an electrical circuit. By analysis, and by performing their own experiments."

"Did they get killed during one of their experiments?" Hazel asked.

"Some members of their local group claimed they hadn't been killed at all, but had contacted a higher-order being, and had ascended to a higher plane of reality."

"So they're nuts," I said.

"Maybe so. But one of them, Manoel Castelhano, went on to found a group named Lar Ressonante, which became quite popular in Brazil. He immigrated to San Francisco in the 1970s. The organization took on the English version of their name."

"Resonant Household?"

"Bingo."

"I've heard about cults targeting rich people," Hazel said.

"I believe it's why he changed his name to Maxwell Amp in 1983. Maxwell was taken from James Maxwell, who discovered the laws of electromagnetism. And Amp is the unit of electrical current."

158 | TABATHA GRAY

Far away, from outside the library, came the muted sound of clapping bells. The kitchen timer was ringing.

Hazel stood. "I'll get it."

I took her chair, slumping back and wondering what it all meant. Dana was silent, too. I guess she ran out of pages in her reporter's notebook. It wasn't that I didn't believe her. It was just all so strange. But strange or not, I was starting to feel a sharp reminder in my stomach that I hadn't eaten since lunch.

"Should we go check out this galette situation?" I asked.

Dana said yes, so we stood and followed the tantalizing aroma to the kitchen, where the big, cream-colored oven radiated heat.

Hazel put an apron over her yellow dress and cut the galette into wedges. The plums had melted purple together, and the crust had turned golden brown and sparkly with sugar crystals. I took the slice she handed me and went over to the gallon tub of vanilla ice cream we'd found in the freezer. I took a scoop and plopped it on top of the warm galette, then used my spoon to create the perfect bite, one with crust, filling, and ice cream all together.

It smelled like summer flowers and it tasted like heaven, the bright sweet hot plums against the cold cream, the rich almond base that had been saturated with juice and the crisp buttery crust. I swallowed and shivered and took another bite.

I was still trying to figure out what I thought about Uncle Max and his culty name change. If you believed Dana's theory, he'd moved to San Francisco in the eighties and fallen in with the Resonant Household, a cult with some funny views about electricity. Its leader had known the masked men in Rio. He might have even been involved in their experiment to contact higher-order beings.

In the past week I'd had my world blown open. I'd

learned that magic was real. I'd flown on a broom and inherited a magical house. I couldn't help but wonder: Did these higher-order beings exist?

And what was the hold that Manoel Castelhano had on Uncle Max? I'd seen enough cult documentaries to know that charismatic gurus have a way of wrapping their tentacles around you, until even the most successful, charming, beautiful people could be brought to heel like dogs. Was this the debt Gran had mentioned? The one even love couldn't pay?

I might have felt sorry for Uncle Max, if it weren't for the lawsuit. But our lawyer, Hector, had talked about leverage, and here was some leverage of our own. *The Silicon Valley Billionaire and the Cult.* The story writes itself. Not only would it be Dana's ticket back into the journalistic limelight, but it would wreak havoc on the Amp Company's stock.

I was just spooning up the last soupy bite of my galette à la mode, when my eyes landed on the plastic bag on the table. I had told Luna I would meet her at six thirty in front of the inn. I needed to shower, shave my legs for the dress, and wash and dry my hair. I needed to hurry.

29

The sun was arcing west when I reached the Inn & Pub, and the tart sweetness of my third slice of plum galette still lingered on my tongue. The square was empty except for a handful of people treading the cobblestone home after work. Lucas's store remained dark, and in the distance the statue of Augustus was a shadow against city hall.

The jade dress Luna had lent me fit perfectly and felt light in the breeze blowing in from the ocean. Pants, I decided, and especially jeans, were the stupidest things ever invented. Maybe that was Hazel's secret to happiness. She never wore jeans.

I had left my sister and Dana in the kitchen, had found my pack and lugged it upstairs and claimed the first bedroom I came upon. It was larger than I expected for such an old house and featured a private bathroom where I had taken a glorious shower. My hair had, thankfully, dried in time. Instead of tying it back in my usual pony, I let it fall in a feathery curtain around my ears and neck.

Now, the pub door opened and Luna walked out and I

TANGLED CHARMS | 161

gasped because she looked so pretty. She was wearing a simple black dress with dangly diamond earrings and her pink hair tied back in a bun. Her lipstick was a subtle shade of pink as well, and she'd done her eyeliner with a hint of a wing that was more perfect than anything I could manage.

"You look amazing!" I said. "You're making me feel like a barbarian over here." After all, I was wearing sneakers under my dress, and my only makeup was some CC cream and a coat of tinted Chap Stick. The magic house hadn't come with a mystical shoe store, *or* an enchanted makeup counter. What was the world coming to?

"I just went a little overboard tonight to show up my mother. You look great too, and didn't I tell you that dress would fit you perfectly? I just hope our ride gets here before I chew off all this lipstick."

"Our ride?" We hadn't discussed how we'd actually get to the fete. I'd assumed we'd walk, like I'd been walking up and down the hill to Gran's house all day. But now that she mentioned it, I didn't actually know where the Thorns lived. I hadn't gone to school with any of them, so I'd had no reason to.

A sharp crack sent me jumping and an antique, cherry-red pickup truck rumbled in from a side street and came to a stop in front of the Inn & Pub. It was the sort of truck you'd see on a Christmas card, carrying a fresh-cut spruce home to trim with lights and tinsel. I'd seen it before, when a fatherly man with a golf cap had been unloading wood to make the Litha bonfire.

Silas left the truck running, hopped out, and came around to meet us. He was wearing a gray flannel three-piece, and had traded his normal golf hat for a spiffier one made of the same flannel. Even in the breeze, I'd have been sweltering, but he didn't seem to mind.

"Ladies," he said, touching his hat in a strange, old-fash-

162 | TABATHA GRAY

ioned gesture. "You both are beautiful as the Goddess herself. Shall we be going?"

I glanced at the truck's cab and felt a prickle of doubt. The passenger's side of the bench seat was filled with stacks of papers that tumbled onto the floorboard. They seemed to be photocopies of old handwritten documents.

"I know she's not a limousine," Silas said, walking around to the back of his truck and opening the tailgate. "But I'm afraid she's all I have. Still, I did my best to make her comfortable for you." He gestured to a couple of square bales of golden-colored straw.

Luna grabbed the polished wooden stake rail, stepped on the low rear bumper and hauled herself into the truck bed like she'd done it a thousand times.

Could this really be safe? I eyed the bed warily and wondered how long the walk would be. But it would be rude to refuse. I climbed into the truck bed and plopped down on the prickly straw.

Silas went around to the driver's side, hopped in, shut the door and leaned out the window with a thumbs-up and rosy smile that made me wonder if he'd kept drinking after lunch. I wasn't feeling thumbs-up confident, but I gave one in return. He popped the clutch. The truck lurched forward in a cloud of blue exhaust.

I felt every cobble in my clenched teeth as we rolled a block or so across Charm Haven Square. The next street was smoother, thank goodness. I was worried that the wind would mess up my hair, but the air was relatively still in the lee of the cab.

As the truck picked up speed, I felt an unexpected, bubbly kind of happiness. I'd been bracing for a fancy dinner party full of snooty people, but I hadn't expected to arrive there in such... style. It was so ridiculous, I couldn't be upset.

TANGLED CHARMS | 163

I turned to Luna. "Why do I feel like I'm seventeen, taking a hayride to the fall festival?"

"I was just going to say that but prom."

"They don't have hayrides at prom, though, do they?"

"I wouldn't know." She laughed. "I skipped it."

"Didn't know you could do that."

"Some friends and I camped on the beach over by Crystal Cove instead. You remember Jane Finch, and, uh, Mike Hunt?"

The names sounded kind of familiar. I knew they belonged to that distant homeland, where music came from stores and we were all so worried about being cool. *Jane... Jane... First period math?* I couldn't remember her face.

"They both live on the mainland now," Luna said. "Jane's an accountant and Mike, I think he wound up on a fishing boat in Alaska, but it's been years since I heard from either of them."

"Where's Crystal Cove," I asked. "Is it on-island?"

"Yeah, but it's cut off by some cliffs and you pretty much have to take a boat. The school was remodeling and getting rid of a bunch of old wooden chairs—remember those?—so we stole them from the dump and hauled them out and made a big bonfire and played bad Flaming Lips covers on acoustic guitar and went diving off the hanging arch."

That rang a bell. "I've definitely heard of the hanging arch. Didn't one of the seniors break their neck diving off it?"

"I heard that rumor too, but I'd bet my life it never happened."

"Really?" An image flashed up, a memory of a school assembly, but it was vague.

"It was always just *a senior.* They never told us his name."

"Sounds suspicious now that I think about it."

"Yeah, if a kid died in a town this small, everyone would know about it. I'd bet you anything the adults invented that story to scare us away from diving. I can't blame them, I guess, because the place looks scary and there's probably a million ways you could break your neck, but we were okay."

I looked out from the back of the truck and saw Charm Haven city center, getting smaller in the distance, pushing lower as the land rose under us. Past it, far in the distance, the sun was sinking into a dazzle of pink-and-yellow water. Smoky days always made the best sunsets.

"And what about you?" Luna asked. "Did you go to prom on the mainland?"

"Oh… yeah."

"So it wasn't the best time."

"Are you kidding? A new school where I hardly knew anyone? An acne breakout? No money for clothes? It was a total blast. I went with a guy named Ryan Humbert, or Herbert, or something like that. Barely knew him, but he was nice enough until he got drunk and tried to feel me up."

"Gross."

"I punched him."

Luna laughed. "Good for you."

"God, I haven't thought about that in years," I said, and bit my bottom lip and felt the world wash over me. "But that Flaming Lips album was pretty good."

"Right? I played the CD so much I wore it out."

"Didn't know that was possible."

"Neither did I. I don't even have a CD player anymore. It's weird how long ago it was."

I looked at the lights in the distance and wondered which of them belonged to the Inn & Pub, which to Tilly's, and which to Gran's. From out here you couldn't tell. They swirled into a single nebula, barely visible in the long summer twilight.

"Sometimes it feels like another lifetime," I said. "But sometimes it might have been yesterday."

It was cooler out here away from the city center, and the breeze was livelier too. It gusted cross-ways across the truck. I swept my hair back and held it to keep it from flying and wondered if I should have borrowed one of Hazel's cardigans.

"Hold on to your hats!" Silas called from the front, then we made a sharp turn to the left and started up a hill. I braced my feet against the sheet metal bed and tensed my legs against gravity. The rumbling engine revved to a throaty roar and we started up the long driveway. As we did, the first words of a nursery rhyme came back to me in my mother's voice: *Seven houses on seven hills. Seven families were magic dwells...*

30

I held on to the stake rail as the Silas's antique pickup roared uphill toward the Thorn house. The drive was lined with those tall skinny evergreens that rich people planted to make their house seem more like Versailles. Only now, with the wind rising they whipped back and forth with a bushy sound, cracked as the branches bent too far.

The wind had blown away the smoke, thankfully, and the air had a brisk briny taste, and piney scents from tall finger trees, and flowers from the rose bushes, and a green smell from the dark surrounding forest that even now seemed to press in, encircling the Thorn house like a hand closing around a beetle.

Thorn house was a white-and-green mansion in a gaudy old style obsessed with windows. The glazing blazed with orange and pink. Not from a fire, but from the sunset behind us, which was no longer a dazzle, but had been transformed into a vast, burning leviathan sinking into the abyss, whipping flaming tendrils toward us, red and orange and yellow, to drag us with it.

TANGLED CHARMS | 167

In front of the house, the drive dead-ended in a round-about with a fountain where a nymph in tarnished bronze poured water endlessly from her jug, into a basin lined with bronze turtles and frogs, with bronze dragonflies and cattails.

An electric light in the bottom of the basin shone upward through the splashing water, bathing the nymph and the pillars and the house front, and the swaying trees in undulating liquid shadows. And the world seem to slip its mooring and drift away from shore.

A sharp pain cramped my stomach. Motion sickness. The back of my tongue tasted bitter. I clenched and closed my eyes to keep it from getting worse. The truck squealed to a stop, and I felt Luna touch my shoulder.

"You okay?" She said, the water-light catching her dangly diamond earrings.

"Yeah." Though with the wheezing way I said it, I wouldn't blame her for keeping her distance.

Luna offered me her hand. I took it. I let her lead me to the edge of the truck bed, and down, crunching onto the smooth round pebbles.

"Thanks," I said, as the spinning world slowed, then stopped. I took a tentative step and didn't fall over.

The wind picked up and howled and blew my hair around my face. I gathered it and looked up at the Thorn house, looming, a great white beast with too many eyes.

Ivy snaked up its brickwork, and I had an impression—the strangest feeling—that I was watching a slow-motion struggle, a battle waged over centuries by the hairy brown vines, to swallow the house and reclaim its bricks for the earth.

The ivy's dark green leaves flapped like pennants, pounding against the brick, rattling windows, and I

168 | TABATHA GRAY

wondered just for a second if those waxy leaves didn't move a little too much. If they weren't a little too alive.

"You ladies go ahead," Silas said, clanking the tailgate shut. "I'll park and see you inside."

"Got it," Luna said. She turned to me. "Ready to go in?"

I shook my head to clear it, and saw that we were alone on the circle drive, unless you counted the bronze nymph. Now that we were closer to the windows, I saw past the gaudy sunset reflection. The house was full of people, men mostly in suits, women mostly in dresses. On a normal night the sounds of their conversation might have carried through the antique single-pane glass. But outside there was only the wind.

Luna led me up the stairs to a front entrance larger than the one at Gran's house. It was a double-door setup, with one of those half-circle windows on top. The glass on the doors and windows was stained glass, a decorative motive of rose-bushes and vines. She didn't knock. She just opened it into a world of electric light and a murmur of voices, and the sound of a string quartet, and the closing door swallowed the howling wind, though the ivy still tapped against the windows.

"Do I look like the bride of Frankenstein?" I asked, trying to pat my hair down.

Luna took a break from brushing hay off her black dress and looked over and flashed me a thumbs-up.

We were in a large foyer that up ahead, broadened out into an enormous room with a grand crystal chandelier hanging above twin staircases leading up to what I figured must be the more private quarters. Many, many tables had been set up in this room in a long line, and they were filled with enough food for a Vegas buffet. A steady stream of partygoers lined up, got their helping, then went away.

"Luna! Holly!" A voice called out. I turned and saw

TANGLED CHARMS | 169

Vincent walking toward us. He was wearing a black suit and a bow tie, and with his hair slicked back, his pale skin and his high cheekbones, it was easy to imagine that he was a long-lost heir to an extinct royal family.

"You both look as lovely as a moonlit night in summer." He clapped his hands then gave me a conspiratorial wink. "So, ah, you've come to rescue me?"

"Sorry," I said. "I came because I was told in no uncertain terms that if I wanted to have a life in Charm Haven I'd better suck it up and kiss the ring."

"Whoever told you that was smart." He smiled at Luna. "Though with any luck, the days of kissing rings might soon be past us this fall. Still, the city council meets tomorrow and if I want my ordinance to pass, the wheels must be greased."

"I heard that Lucas's family would be here. We're looking for him, but he didn't open his store today."

"I noticed. And you think he'll be here?"

"Not exactly, but Luna's mom saw him going toward the Crone's Wood. I figured if any of his family members are here, maybe they could give us a lead on where to find him."

"Ah yes, I believe his family has a small temple in the wood. I imagine he would go there if he was distressed."

"Did you see him distressed?" I asked.

"Many people are distressed today. Simply look around you." He made a gesture with his arms that indicated the whole room. And sure enough, now that he pointed it out, I saw the tension. Cords standing out on necks. Thin, globular wineglasses gripped dangerously hard. People going through the usual dance, the social act, peacocking and strutting and fawning, but doing it with gritted teeth, as if each of them was barely holding together their own private world, and subject to snap at any moment.

"Deputy Sprout said the equilibrium's been thrown off. Old rivalries are flaring up."

170 | TABATHA GRAY

"Deputy Sprout is a silly man, but in this case he is correct."

"But there's no magic here."

"You can't feel it?"

"I just mean that nobody's casting fireballs. The drapes haven't come alive and tried to murder the couch." And even though I didn't trust the ivy, it had yet to try to bury me in the garden.

"The room is filled with magical energy. It's the reason for the distress. But I forget, you were never trained in these things, so there is no reason you would know them." He paused and looked at me as if he were making up his mind to take a step he could never take back. "Would you... like me to show you?"

"What?" My heart started hammering.

"Would you like me to show you how to feel it? I'm not an expert, but I do know this."

"Ummm, okay?"

"Open your hands and hold them palm up."

I did what he asked, and he spread his hands out palm down and held them an inch or so above mine.

"Now close your eyes and feel the distance between our hands."

Feel the distance between our hands? Was this some kind of weird vampire pickup line? After all, what was there to feel? What could I possibly—and I felt it. A rustling, cracking energy swirling in that tiny space, a miniature atom bomb waiting to detonate. My heart was in my throat and every nerve was a needle and I felt the urge, wild, almost uncontrollable, to throw myself into Vincent's arms, then to run out of the room screaming because I couldn't trust myself, but somehow I held it together. I opened my eyes and found his and, for a moment that seemed to stretch to eternity, we looked at each other. My heart settled down and I had the strangest feeling. My lips parted slightly and I looked up at Vincent and… and…

"So, um, you two, I'm gonna go get something to eat," Luna said, in her best nonchalant voice. "Give you two some privacy for your, um, little experiment."

"I like experiments," I said, and then I died inside, because God what a stupid thing to say.

31

I walked with Vincent out of the main hall, and into a less populous part of the house, where roses in big vases perfumed the air. We stopped in front of a bank of three large windows. One of the ivy vines had come loose on the outside and flailed wildly in the wind, slapping against the glass again and again like it wanted in, although any sound it might have made was lost among the sweet violin and cello rills drifting in from the next room over. The party, this house, the music and light felt like it was bracing against a storm.

Vincent seemed totally at ease in his black formal wear as he put his hand behind his back and looked out onto a world being swallowed by night. My turquoise dress felt impossibly thin as it brushed against my smooth legs. Though our experiment with the hands was over, I still imagined I felt some fragment of that cracking energy racing between us, like a magnet drawn to iron but held away.

"I'm not an expert in magic," he said, "but I have known those who were. The demonstration we just finished was common in the past, when knowledge of magic was passed down more formally." He spoke of the past like he has been there, and I thought of that moment in his office, that dramatic call when I'd seen through his charming exterior and glimpsed something ancient.

"Vincent," I asked, "how old are you?"

"Do you need to know?" His eyes held a sadness I couldn't understand.

"I guess not. It's just—"

"Most people," he said in a lecture-hall voice, "in this new, mechanized world of ours imagine magic to be a thing, a power, an energy that can be controlled, like water behind a dam, or electricity in a battery, or money in one of your stock markets. They view its practitioners like the ancient Romans might have viewed someone with a television, or an automobile, or a gun."

Had he cut me off because he was angry with me? Or had I touched too close to a wound?

"They are mistaken," he continued. "Magic is not a thing. It is a relationship. A spark. A tension. A wise person once told me that magic holds the world together, that it stretches between everything and everyone like the strings of a harp."

"I felt a spark when we did the hand thing."

"That was a teaching exercise, one of the first ones given to children."

Was I a child to him? Was he so ancient that all of us here were children? I had that urge again, stronger, for him to hold me, because if anyone could handle the dark wind, the leviathan sun, the robed assassins, the whiplash magic, the blackmail, everything, it had to be Vincent.

"Were you one of those children they taught it to?" I finally asked.

He shook his head slowly. "My kind have no use for magic."

It was a voice that had suffered and passed beyond

suffering and grief, to a fixed understanding, an absolute certainty that no one was coming to save you. That no one ever had been.

My breath caught and I stepped back and looked at him like a fawn must look at a wolf, except the wolf just smiled sadly and shook its head as if to say, *See? See the tragedy of the world? That no matter how long we frolic and pretend it might be otherwise, no matter how many times I prove my better nature, you will never trust me fully, nor would it be wise for you to do so.*

Something came to me then. Maybe it was that spark, that string pulled taut between us, but I knew the sadness in his voice.

"Who was she?" I said. "The one who taught you all of this."

He seemed surprised by my question. His brow went up and he pursed his lips and he stared out at the night like looking off the edge of a cliff. He mumbled something too low to hear. He shook his head.

Heat rose up my neck at my presumption. "I'm sorry."

"Think no more of it."

Thank God for that string quartet, because I wouldn't have been able to stand the silence. I felt like a grave robber. I felt like an idiot. *How do you recover from that? Is it even possible to change the subject?*

"So, um, how is the city council thing going?"(*Oh God, could I be any more obvious?*) "I mean, have you been out here wheeling and dealing? Are you going to get the ordinance passed to fend off Anwir Holdings?"

He sighed. "It is still uncertain. Henrietta is pressuring several council members. The others, let's just say that the strings connecting them have been thrown out of tune, and the discord amplified by the wild magic."

(*So it's my fault.*) "Well, you, uh, might be happy to know

TANGLED CHARMS | 175

that we're doing a little digging on Anwir. Trying to find out who's controlling it."

He glanced at me and raised an eyebrow. "Who?"

"I don't know—not yet. It's a bunch of shell companies and Dana's got some of her journalist friends on it, and have you met Dana? She's great."

"I'm sure."

"So, um, I'll bring that information by your office whenever I get it. I mean when she gets it, I mean. Have you heard anything else about the inquisitor, Albinus?"

Vincent went absolutely still. He didn't blink. He didn't shift his feet. He didn't even seem to be breathing. My heart sped up, and my skin pricked to gooseflesh. I had the strangest notion that Vincent was gone, that he'd been abducted between heartbeats and replace by a statue, a wax one from Madame Tussauds, like the Princess Diana I'd seen after I celebrated the end of college with a two-week whirlwind European trip. It had been London where Laurie and I had found a charming pub, with low ceilings and darkened beams and smooth, uneven plaster, and a shiny pitted plank of a bar where (according to a plaque on the wall) Henry of Monmouth (before he was King) had swilled a dozen flagons of mead and challenged the local cobbler to a duel. Laurie and I didn't beat his record, but we had enough to give us wild, screaming headaches the next day. We'd slept in until noon, then stumbled into a small shop that served mystery meat pies with a bland green sauce, then stumbled into Tussauds and saw Diana, who probably looked more alive than we did.

"Yes." Vincent's voice snapped me back.

"You've learned something else?"

"The death is deeply troubling."

"Why?" (*Wouldn't he be used to death?*)

"It reminds me of something I've seen before." There was

more of that silence, then he touched my arm, and the distance between us flew to zero. The spark discharged and left me breathless. But something in him contracted.

"Please excuse me," he said. "I'm afraid I must go."

As if I didn't know he was already gone, as gone as that distant time ago when laughter was measured in flagons, and wonder was a colored clump of wax.

"Of course," I said. (*Don't.*)

As I watched him walk away, I felt hollow. I'd failed a test I didn't know I was taking. Or perhaps I'd misread the situation entirely, and the spark had only been in my imagination. After all, Caleb had never loved me. What made me think this could be any different?

I turned back toward the window and looked out, alone now. The string quartet brought its song to a close. Silence fell on the room and I didn't have any choice but to take it. Silence, except for the ivy tendril beating against the windowpane: *crack, crack, crack.*

32

The world outside the window was dark and the cloying scent of roses gagged me. Roses for love. Roses to show you care. Roses at the Thorn family's house. A bit on the nose, don't you think? Then again, Gran's house was swimming in pictures of nightingales. Was this really so different?

Maybe people were more earnest in the past. Maybe they didn't grow up in a world obsessed with being cool, unfazed, unbothered by the stones the life throws at you, the little heartbreaks like thinking you might feel something for a man, and thinking he might too, only to have it poof away with a single question.

Who was she?

It wasn't that I was wrong. No, it was obvious that this vague, faceless, magical practitioner he spoke of had been someone dear to him. She must have been very close for her to talk about magic. The Inquisition we barely escaped last night was only a shadow of its former self, back in the days when it had brought kings to heel.

They might have been in love for all I knew. And the odds

178 | TABATHA GRAY

weren't in her favor. I still had no idea how old Vincent was, but it was pretty clear he wasn't a millennial. He spoke of the distant past like he had been there, and I could only assume she had been there too. Most likely, she had never left.

Vincent hadn't glossed over the mystery woman because she was unimportant. No. She was a treasure too valuable to share. And me with my questions. *Who was she?* How dumb could I have been?

The string quartet in the other room launched a new number and it didn't sound like Brahms, or Beethoven, or whatever. High notes from the violins soared like gulls above the cello's choppy ocean. They dove and skimmed the water, then flew back up into a melody.

I knew that melody.

It was a song from that Flaming Lips album that Luna had mentioned on the ride up. I remembered listening to it when it came out, and thinking how strange it was, but exciting, young, and fresh. But this string quartet version had been caught and chloroformed and placed under a bell jar in the National Museum of History.

"Can you believe this song?" Luna said behind me. I turned and saw her approaching, her diamond earrings bobbing under her pink pulled-back hair as she walked. She carried a plate of food in each hand. "I saw Vincent leave through the front and thought you might be hungry so I went to the buffet and got you some food, and then I got seconds for myself because it wasn't so bad, and I guess I'm just trying to say I hope you like chicken."

I chuckled and took the plate, real porcelain, heavy, no paper plates at the fete. It had a skewer with what looked like grilled chicken, peppers, and onion. A green-beans dish that looked so fancy I suspected they called it *haricots verts*, a roll, a sprig of salad, and a lump of something suspiciously brown.

TANGLED CHARMS | 179

Luna caught me looking. "It's not a fete without my mom's ooey gooey butter cake."

"Heaven forbid." I caught myself laughing again. I was glad Luna had come when she did.

As enticing as the brown blob looked, the thought of anything sweet and rich made my stomach squelch. I'd eaten half of Hazel's damned galette instead of dinner, and was starting to feel grumpy and strung out from the sugar. I picked up the skewer and ate one of the piece of chicken. *Not bad. A little dry.*

"So did you guys make out, or what?" she asked.

I choked, then coughed, then swallowed and wheezed back to normal. "It wasn't anything like that."

(Who was she?)

"Really? That's kind of a surprise because that hand thing? I mean, that was intense, right? You closed your eyes but I didn't. And the way he looked at you? I've never seen Vincent look like that at *anybody*."

"I must just look funny."

"A sort of smoldering—"

"It was just a normal conversation, okay! He told me some stuff about magic being like harp strings, and the reason everybody's acting so strange is because the locket knocked them out of tune."

"So would you say your conversation was... *magical?*"

"He said something about the dead inquisitor too. He'd seen somebody die like that before. I'm not sure if he meant being stabbed, or in a jail cell, or by suicide or what."

"So that's all you talked about?"

"Yes."

"Really?"

"Yes!"

"Magic going haywire, a dead guy, murder, suicide, cyanide?"

"That's it."

She rolled her eyes at me and sighed. "No wonder you never made out."

I punched her lightly in the arm, because if she was going to pretend to make fun of me, I could pretend to beat her up. And I smiled, too, because Luna was becoming a real friend. Not just someone to pass at work or wave to at the grocery store.

"Have you seen your mom yet?" I asked. I remembered her leaving Lucas's walk-in, holding two bottles of milk by the neck. It was the first time anyone ever called me a Jezebel.

"I haven't run into her yet," Luna said. "We'll probably find her wherever Henrietta is."

"They're peas in a pod."

"How'd you know?"

33

*L*una and I left the dark window and the smell of roses and walked back to the large open room with the buffet. After downing the chicken, the *haricots verts*, the bread, and salad, I'd been left only with the brown lump of cake and had tried it. If you can imagine burned (not caramelized) sugar formed into a sort of sponge, then soaked in butter until it wept, you wouldn't be far off from the taste that still coated the roof of my mouth.

Murmuring conversation surrounded us from the fifty or so guests in suits and ties and dresses. Food was laid out on a dozen tables arranged in an enormous *U* shape. Racks of skewers had chicken and lamb and veggies sizzled under heat lamps. Dozens of chrome chafing dishes were labeled with small printed cards (pilaf, stuffed peppers, pakora…) There was a whole table full of bread (slices, rolls and miniature baguettes). Past it a trio of three-tiered fountains circulated sparkling punches in ruby, orange and violet.

It was a professional production, catered, except for one dish, pushed to the end of a table where you could hardly reach it. A brown lump on a chipped cake stand. A handwritten card beside it read: Ooey gooey butter cake. Only one slice had been taken, by Luna out of filial loyalty.

"Hey," she said, smoothing her black dress, "weren't you looking for Lucas? Well, there's his brother." She pointed to a guy at the punch table. He seemed to be trying to figure out how to fill his glass from the burbling fountain without spilling punch everywhere.

I remembered him, Arnie, a dirty kid with messy hair and freckles. He'd always tag along when Lucas and I wanted privacy. I felt bad about ditching him as often as we did.

He was all grown up now and squeaky clean. I saw the resemblance around the eyes, and the way he stood. Subtle, but it was there. I wondered if he preferred Arnold now.

Arnie spotted the clear-plastic ladle on the other side of the wide punch bowl. He grabbed it and transferred a glug of the ruby liquid into his wide-rimmed champagne glass. He took a sip and nodded, then headed away, toward back of the house.

I turned to Luna. "Should we tail him?"

"Obviously."

We walked past the buffet, waving at Silas who was piling his plate way higher than Emily Post would approve of. He waved back but didn't say anything because of the roll stuffed in his mouth.

The big door led to a parlor, and the sound of a piano. The room was larger than Gran's drawing room, and obviously made for the public. Enormous windows stared at the night from powder blue walls. Satin curtains lined them, their fabric picking up the reddish-brown of the gilt picture frames and aging oil portraits. Three empty couches in powder blue sat in the center of the room around a low glass table. A large gold urn on the table held roses on the vine, spilling out and down the sides of their container. I supposed the arrangement was meant to give a lush, garden feel to the

TANGLED CHARMS | 183

room, but it made me uneasy. It looked too much like a many-armed, thorny monster giving birth to itself.

Music pulled my attention away, to the back of the room where twenty or so people gathered around a semicircular bump-out lined with darkened windows. A tilted grand piano lid jutted above the crowd. It shone, black and slick under the crystal chandelier.

I couldn't see the pianist, but I knew the tune. I'd heard it not too long ago on an oldies station as I was driving back from the Northwest Booksellers convention in Spokane. It was a story song, one of those weepy ballads from the fifties. The lead singer had killed his best girl when he lost control of his souped-up Oldsmobile during a game of chicken against a greaser and an oncoming train.

I spotted Arnie, with his glass of punch. He was probably the youngest person there and I could tell from his smirk what he thought of it. Farther in, Henrietta Thorn was wearing a beautiful emerald dress, a string of what might have been real emeralds around her neck. She looked less like a battleship now that she wasn't hopping mad, and more like a retired opera singer. Lin had said she'd been an actress. I could see it. Luna's mom was on the outside of the crowd, trying to push in closer.

The song was winding toward its final stanza, where it slowed and sounded like a funeral. Nobody was singing, but I remembered the story from the radio. The boy hoped to reunite with his best girl up in heaven. I couldn't help but wonder how happy she'd be to see him. If it was me, I'd meet him at the pearly gates with a slap to the face and kick to the groin for getting me killed. But I guess in the fifties, they hadn't heard of women's lib. He probably expected a martini and a shoulder rub.

The pianist played the final note and held it long, until it faded and left the room in silence, except for those window-

184 | TABATHA GRAY

tapping vines. Just before the crowd applauded, the piano exploded into a quick bright tune, like music from an old Bugs Bunny show. The notes went quicker and higher and higher and quicker until the piano ran out of keys, and the pianist played that old chestnut: shave and a haircut, two bits. The fall board clapped shut, and everybody laughed, even Arnie. The show was over. The crowd dispersed, and I saw the pianist for the first time.

He was in his mid-sixties, tall with light blond hair and a tan. Unlike everyone else, he wasn't dressed formally. He wore a teal polo shirt, with chinos and well-worn leather flip-flops.

It was Maximilian Nightingale, aka Maxwell Amp, aka Uncle Max, aka the richest guy in the world, secret cult member, and the guy with the lawsuit that wasn't made to win. He saw me and his eyes sparkled in recognition. He smiled and gave a little wave.

34

Uncle Max stood in front of the oil-black grand piano. He was the only person in the room not dressed to impress, and I supposed that had its own way of impressing. *Look, I hate to say it but I'm so far above you folks that to wear a suit and tie would only bring me down to your level. Call me when you have your own chopper. Call me when you have the president on speed dial and he picks up. Call me when you don't have to check the market in the Wall Street Journal, because you are the market, kid.*

He was smiling at me in a way that might seem friendly. A normal uncle seeing his normal niece unexpectedly, ready to catch up about the family. But I'd only met him the other day and I didn't trust that smile.

"Oh, Maxy, Maxy, that was simply wonderful, breathtaking, tell me where did you learn to play like that?" The woman looked like a girl at a Beatles show.

"You're embarrassing yourself, Hannah," Henrietta Thorn said, as she sashayed up to them and hip-checked—yes, hip-checked— the other woman, sending her flying off like a

186 | TABATHA GRAY

bumper car. "Your husband is in the other room. He'll be waiting."

Hannah might have had someone waiting, but Henrietta's husband was long gone, on that never-ending business trip of his. Henrietta didn't seem to miss him too much. She put two hands on Uncle Max's shoulder, and dipped forward in a way that screamed *look at little old me, I'm throwing myself at you. Won't you catch me before I fall?*

When I'd first seen Henrietta at the tea shop, she'd struck me as a battleship of a woman. Later, she'd been an aging diva. And now? A coquette, and she was pulling it off. Her way of moving, her voice, her facial expressions all made her seem twenty years younger. I suspected she hadn't only been an actress, but a good one.

"Thanks again, Hattie, for inviting me to your little shindig," Uncle Max said. "A lot of memories in this place."

"Why, I thought you forgot, Max."

"How could I forget?"

"You're not leaving are you? I'd be positively bereft if you didn't play us another song."

"Maybe later."

From the way the red came to her cheeks I got the idea that later meant later, in private to her. I wondered what it meant to Uncle Max.

I felt a tug on my dress sleeve, and turned to see Luna, her diamond earrings sparkling in the light from the chandelier. She was pointing toward Arnie, who seemed to be casually walking toward the door. The surprise appearance of Uncle Max had distracted me, but it was Arnie we were after. He could tell us where to find Lucas, and Lucas knew the way to the crones and information about the haywire magic.

"Arnie!" I heard myself call. By the way everybody looked at me, I could only guess that I'd used my outside voice.

Arnie paused, then turned and looked at me, confused.

His lips crept into a hint of a smile as he walked over. He held his glass of ruby-red punch delicately between his thumb and forefinger.

"Me?" He glanced between me and Luna in a help-me-out-here sort of way.

"You are Arnie Trembol, aren't you?" I said.

"Of course he is!" Luna said.

The man laughed. "I haven't been called that since I was a kid."

So he did prefer Arnold. I couldn't blame him. He didn't look much like an Arnie anymore. The word *refinement* came to mind. Somewhere over the past twenty years he'd acquired a mess of it. I wished I could ask him where he found it.

"Do I know you?" he asked.

"You did, when you were a kid." I stuck out my hand. "Holly Nightingale."

"Well I'll be…" He seemed mystified. "I heard you might be coming back because—I'm so sorry about your grandmother."

"It's okay. My sister and I arrived a couple of days ago for the will reading."

"Hazel's here?" He looked around.

"At the house. Do you know her?"

"We were in kindergarten together, or was it second grade?" He took the last sip of his ruby punch. "And you, I remember you and Lucas were joined at the hip. I guess I didn't make it easy on you, did I?"

"I'm looking for Lucas. Have you seen him?"

"He's not here. I heard he wasn't feeling well."

"I heard that too. He never opened his store today. Luna's mom saw him heading toward the Crone's Wood."

Arnold lifted his empty glass toward his lips but stopped halfway and frowned at it. "That makes sense. Our family has

188 | TABATHA GRAY

a place in the wood. Not a house, exactly, but it's a sort of consecrated space where we..."

The silence got to me. "Where you hunt?"

"You know about us?" He seemed surprised.

"I didn't until last night when Lucas shifted to save me from the inquisitors."

"In front of you? That's surprising. Our family likes to keep that side of things discreet. I'll bet you didn't know he had that ability even when you were dating."

"I didn't. Why do you keep it discreet? Isn't Charm Haven the sort of place where people wouldn't bat an eye?"

"People are people. They can be closed-minded wherever they live. Our family powers aren't exactly a secret, but we don't advertise them. It helps keep the peace."

"You sound like Deputy Sprout," I said. "I'm not looking for Lucas to catch up. Magic is going haywire. I thought he could lead me to the crones, and that they would be able to help. I don't suppose you could take me."

He shook his head. "Even I don't venture that deep into the wood. It's easy to lose your way. Once you go deep enough, paths shift, almost as if the trees themselves are moving. Still, Lucas might know the way. One of my earliest memories is of him and our parents walking into the wood to renew our family pact with the crones."

"Then tell me where to find him."

Arnold hesitated. He twirled the empty glass, its stem between his thumb and forefinger. "If Lucas shifted in front of you, he trusts you. That's good enough for me. If he's ill, he likely went to our family temple in the wood. It's a holy place for us, a place where we commune with nature and our ancestors. Healing energies are strong there. But it's a private place. If I tell you how to find it, do you promise to keep it a secret?"

"Absolutely."

"You too?" He looked at Luna, who nodded. "Okay, then."

"How do we reach it?" I asked.

"I've never traveled there in my human form. When I'm shifted it's more about the smell of the ground cover, the spongy feeling of the forest floor, and something else that's hard to describe, a feeling like the one that calls birds south for the winter. Give me a moment." He closed his eyes and I saw them moving under his eyelids like he was dreaming.

If you go far enough into the wood, the trees start moving, huh? I didn't like the sound of that. When Hazel told me the story of the trees coming alive and marching on the town, I sort of assumed at the end of it, they marched back to the wood, and started acting like upstanding citizens again. For a plant, that meant staying planted. But what if they were still out there?

"I think I have it," Arnold said. "At any rate, it'll get you close enough for him to scent you. Do you know where Silas's house is?"

"The one by the edge of the wood?"

"Go to his house. Don't enter the woods yet. Just walk north along the perimeter until you see a tree that's been split in two by lightning. That's where you'll enter. You'll be moving west. Keep going in that direction for a while, I'm not sure how long it will take you on two legs. Eventually you'll hit a stream. Follow it uphill until you hit a clearing with a big stone ledge jutting out above the water. Stand on top of the stone and you should see the temple."

"Okay, lightning tree. Follow the stream uphill. Find the clearing. Got it."

"Be careful," he said. "It's easy to lose your way in the wood, especially now. Things have started changing there. My father went on a hunt this morning and came back swearing he had sensed a presence. Something foul. He attempted to track it, but couldn't..." I got the impression that he wanted to say something else, but he held up his empty glass and wiggled it. "I think I'm due for a refill."

"Thanks again," I said, turning to Luna. "What do you think? Should we go there?"

"Go there?" She chewed her bottom lip. "Like, now? At night? With a foul presence running around?"

I remembered tripping through the undergrowth, looking for my sister last night. It had been dark, almost impossible even with the hagstone's magical assistance. It would be hard, almost impossible to find the landmarks Arnold had told us about.

"I guess you're right," I said. "We have to wait until morning. I've had a long couple of days, anyway, I could use some sleep." Just saying the word *sleep* was like a floodgate opening. I stifled a yawn and felt a weight press down on me. "Do you want to see if Silas can give us a ride home?"

Luna opened her mouth to reply, but didn't get a chance.

"Holly!" It was Uncle Max, walking toward me, his arms spread wide.

35

Uncle Max walked toward me, a dumb grin on his face. His leather flip-flops made a stupid thwacking sound with each step. But why were his arms spread out like that? Was he pretending to be an airplane? Did he want me to crucify him?

No.

Oh no. I realized with a sudden twist of nausea: Uncle Max wanted a hug.

A hug!

My heart sped up and my neck felt hot and I clenched my teeth so tight I felt the muscle in my jaw quiver.

A hug!

As if he didn't show up out of nowhere to demand Gran's house and sue me into oblivion!

My mind flashed back to Women's Self Defense, a class I took at the Y just after college. When an attacker came in to grapple, you had a couple of options. The best thing in most cases was to run. To splash a drink or throw dirt in the attacker's face and take off. If you couldn't run, couldn't get away, couldn't avoid being grabbed, there was a move. You

192 | TABATHA GRAY

stepped in, hooked your leg behind the attacker, and pushed. It would send them down and buy you time to escape.

But if I threw him, he'd fall into Henrietta. She could ruin my life in Charm Haven if I offended her, and I was pretty sure turning her fete into WrestleMania would do the job. (Some people just don't know how to have a good time.)

If judo was out, so was running. (I wasn't about to walk back to town.) My only option was head-on, but I wasn't about to hug the bastard. I stuck out my hand. He took it with an eagerness that seemed almost grateful.

"Holly! I'm so glad I caught you. I was just telling Hattie here that I couldn't let my niece get away without catching up."

I noticed a strange webwork of scars running up his right hand. It was like he'd caught a lightning bolt, and it had left its mark in fine white scars that you could only really see when the light was just so.

"Maxy, Maxy!" Henrietta said. She trailed behind him like a woman whose dog just broke leash. I wondered if she had any other characters to hit him with. The coquette routine didn't seem to be working.

"Hattie, dear," Maxy said, "won't you give me a moment with my niece? We're all still reeling after my mom kicked the bucket, and I know you think family is really important."

"Family? Why there's nothing in the world more important than family. Without it who would we be?"

"So, uh, can we talk," he said.

"Why certainly." She didn't move.

"I had an idea we'd do it in private, Hattie."

"Oh. Oh, yes, of course." She looked almost bereaved.

"Hey, Henrietta," Luna said. "Why don't you and I talk? I don't think I've seen you down at the pub much, and I know that it's not everyone's thing, but you should totally come down sometime and bring my mom too, and, oh, where is she? Right over there! Why don't the two of us go say hi?"

Luna slipped her arm around Henrietta's and led her away. She probably thought she was doing me a favor, but I wasn't so sure. Uncle Max had come into my life like a wrecking ball, and he was probably lining up for a second pass.

"Mint?" he said, pointing something cylindrical toward me. It was a half-eaten stick of Mentos. When I shook my head no, he popped one in his mouth and slipped them into the pocket of his chinos.

"Will you come out with me and have a chat?" he asked. "I seem to remember a balcony around that corner there."

"I'm not sure what we have to chat about."

"Why not? I'm not such a bad guy am I?"

"You tell me."

"Are you mad about the lawsuit?"

"Of course I'm mad about the lawsuit!" There was that outside voice again. Everybody looked at me like a two-time loser. "Fine," I said. "Let's find the balcony."

It really was just around the corner. A French door led out onto a stone landing that overlooked darkness. Wind whipped around the sides of the building, and the little pocket where we stood felt like the eye of a hurricane, perfectly still. It smelled of pine.

"What do you really want?" I said.

"Maybe you and I got off on the wrong foot."

"Do people usually send you flowers when you sue them?"

He paused for a second, then let out a sigh. "The other day at the will reading I thought I was doing you kids a favor. It was my mom's house, you know, and sure, it rankled a little that she didn't leave it to me, but I've never borne the two of you any ill will."

He had a funny way of showing it.

"She and I never saw eye to eye. But that's not your problem, is it? I thought, hey, why's she dragging the kids into it? They lived their whole lives in the city. Why would they want that old house?"

"It's a magical house."

"This is Charm Haven. Half the houses here are magical. But what does that really mean? They clean up after you when you're not looking? They restock the pantries? Nothing that a maid or a cook couldn't handle."

"But you tried to buy it from us before we knew."

He seemed confused. "Wait, you didn't know it was magical? I thought you grew up here."

"Yeah, but..." My anger collapsed. Uncle Max couldn't have known Gran wiped my memory to protect me. "... I forgot. Why do you care about the place anyway?"

"I grew up there. It was my home. A long time ago, sure, but I missed it. I wasn't trying to take advantage of you. I honestly thought I made you and your sister a generous offer. I never expected for you to turn me down."

"So you sued us?"

He shook his head slowly. "I've spent the past thirty years waging never-ending corporate war. Heck, before the will reading, I had to go quash an uprising of some activist investors who were trying to force me to use a cheaper source of lithium that was mined by slave labor."

"Do you want a humanitarian award?"

"No. I want you to understand. This is the world I inhabit. I've adapted to it, but it's a messed-up world, one where people don't act like people, and the easiest way to get your wife to come to dinner with you is a subpoena. When you turned down my offer to buy the house, I called my lawyer and asked them to send you that letter. It was a reflex. Part of a dance I've done a thousand times. If you were

TANGLED CHARMS | 195

General Electric, you would have been expecting the lawsuit. You'd reply with your own, along with a counteroffer."

"You expected us to sue you back?"

"Sounds stupid when you say it out loud." He laughed. "I forgot I was dealing with actual people. I wasn't acting like much of a person myself. I'm sorry."

I looked out at the night sky and the forest which was darker. In the rushing wind, it sounded like the ocean. Lucas was down there, somewhere, healing from his mystery illness in his family temple. The crones were down there too. Maybe they would know what to do.

"I'm not sure I accept your apology," I said.

"Fair enough."

"Are you going to drop the suit?"

"There's no way you'd want to sell me the house? Even if I, doubled my offer?"

"It's not my decision to make. The house belongs to Hazel too. But if it were up to me, I wouldn't sell. I like it here."

Uncle Max sighed and leaned on the rail. "I don't blame you. I haven't thought about this place in a long time, but coming here tonight, and seeing all the old faces makes me wonder if I ever should have left."

He straightened up. "If you girls want to keep the house, that's your right. Mom gave it to you, along with everything in it. But there's one thing that she didn't have the right to give, because it was never hers. When I moved away, I only took what I could fit in a single backpack. So I had to leave something behind, a book that was given to me on my eighteenth birthday. It's not worth much, but it would mean the world to me to have it back."

Could it be so simple?

"I'd need to talk it over with Hazel."

36

SOMEWHERE IN THE NORTH PACIFIC

*C*aleb Robinson throttled the sleek gunmetal trawler away from the rendezvous coordinates. Behind it, already lost in the night, a tanker would be steaming in the opposite direction.

The docking at sea and the cargo transfer had been difficult, yet Caleb Robinson had not doubted. For he was the Lord's right hand. He could not fail, and he had not.

He looked out onto his ship's front deck. The halogen flood lamps cast hard shadows. Dark-robed brothers moved within them, lashing the steel oil drums together, making their final preparations.

Caleb Robinson whispered a prayer for the souls of the witches. They had been condemned by God to die, and therefore were already dead.

37

$\mathcal{I}$ sat on alone in the back of the red pickup as it chugged up the hill to Gran's house. The wind wasn't as strong here as at had been earlier, but it brought a briny smell and cool dampness that sucked the warmth from my bare shoulders and left me shivering. The truck crunched to a halt behind the big purple Victorian. I grabbed the stake rail and pulled myself up, then smoothed my dress and brushed the prickly tag-along straw from my dress.

Silas came around and fiddled with a latch, and the tailgate clanked open. He held out his hand to help me down. I took it. It felt nice, rough and dry, and when I hopped down to the gravel he touched his felt golf cap in that old-fashioned way of his.

"Thanks again," I said. "You didn't have to bring me all the way home. I could have walked from Luna's. But it's nice that I didn't have to."

"It was nothing, miss. Did you enjoy the party?"

"Was there a party?" I laughed. "It just seemed like one dramatic thing after another, first with Vincent, and then my Uncle Max. I'm exhausted."

"Did I ever tell you I knew your Uncle Maximilian? He and I were just a few years apart coming up."

"It doesn't surprise me," I said. "The fete was like a high school reunion for him. Henrietta and this other lady were basically throwing themselves at him, too. I guess being rich has that effect on people."

"It might be so, but Maximilian was always a bit of a ladies' man. I shouldn't be saying it, and you didn't hear it from me, but your uncle used to go with all the girls. Most of all he went with Henrietta Tilby, before she became a Thorn, you understand."

"So that's why she was crushing so hard on him."

"After they started going steady, some folks noticed that Henrietta Tilby was eating a second helping of ice cream at night and then disgorging it in the morning, if you know what I mean."

"She… got pregnant?"

"Can't say for sure, but some thought so. Many did. Then her parents took her to the mainland and she came back right as rain. The word was that she'd been to a private clinic. Soon after, Maximilian left town."

"Wow."

"Didn't think ya'd be coming home to land right in the middle of an episode of *The Young and the Restless*, did you?" He laughed and clanked the tailgate shut. "Those were my dear old mother's favorite stories."

"Did Max tell anyone why he left?"

"Didn't breathe a word to any of us, and he never came back until now. But plenty of water has flowed under the bridge since then. The tale of young lovers, wilted to gossip in the mouths of old men."

"Hey, thanks again for the ride," I said, watching him climb back into his truck.

"The pleasure was mine." He clanked the door shut, touched his hat, and chugged off down the gravel drive.

I turned and looked at the back of the house. It felt strange and unfamiliar. When Gran had lived here, we'd only used the normal walking path with the big wrought iron gate and the trees heavy with sweet fruit. I looked and found a small path leading around the side of the house. I took it.

Gossip in the mouths of old men, huh? I couldn't help but wonder if the story was really over. The way Henrietta had thrown herself at Uncle Max certainly suggested the past wasn't entirely dead.

Mom had told me once that in the days before the pill, it wasn't uncommon for girls to slip away and have something done that was prudent, if not entirely legal. And it wasn't too strange for the guy to get lost after. Either scared off by the thought of a baby, or by the girl's older brothers.

Could this be the debt that Gran talked about?

I wanted a connection, a rope to pull to make the curtain drop. To make the past make sense. But there was another possibility, and it went like this: *Life is messy. People aren't arrows shooting toward a target, even if they might look that way in hindsight.*

I climbed the steps and opened the door and kicked off my shoes and left them. I felt heavy. I'd been on my feet all day.

I glanced around the empty foyer and shouted: "Honey, I'm home!"

"We're in the drawing room!" my sister called back.

I found the two of them sitting in the half dark, watching some sort of movie on Hazel's phone. Hazel had added a cardigan to her yellow dress. Dana's tweed jacket was folded over the back of a chair. I couldn't see what they were watching, but the soundtrack pegged it as an action movie.

They were sitting close. (They had to be if they were both

going to see the tiny screen that Hazel had to balance on her leg.) But the tops of their arms were touching and it seemed to me that neither of them minded it too much.

"How was Fancytown?" Hazel asked.

Fancytown was a bad joke from when we were kids. *Why were Mom and Dad dressed up?* It wasn't because they were going on a date. No, they were headed to Fancytown. It was a place we never visited ourselves, but we imagined it was full of people like Thurston Howell III from Gilligan's Island. It was the type of place where people wore sparkly clothes, and used cigarette holders, and drew out their vowels, *daaaahling.*

"Simply maaaaavelous," I said. "We ran into Vincent."

"Oooooh!" Hazel said it in that high-pitched way that was usually followed by *girl, you're in trouble.* But this time she let it hang.

"It wasn't like that," I said, tamping down my disappointment. *(Who was she?)* "And you will never guess the person I ran into next."

"The queen of England?"

"Our crazy, cult-member, rich-as-sin uncle."

"Oh my God." Hazel paused the movie. "Are you okay?"

"Yeah, strangely. He was… nice?"

Hazel frowned. "Are we talking about the same guy here? Tall. Cargo Shorts. Gross sandals?"

"He wore chinos tonight, but yeah, same guy. He apologized for suing us. Apparently that's pretty normal in the circles he travels in? When we turned down his offer to buy the house, he thought we were hardball negotiating. He says it's fine with him if we keep it, but he would like to come get a book of his. Something he left when he moved out years ago."

"Seems reasonable," Hazel said.

"Do you believe he's trustworthy?" Dana asked.

I shook my head. "I just don't know. He seemed earnest.

Just like a normal person. I mean, a little weird, but anyone with money like that is bound to be. Did you find any more dirt on him?"

"No," Dana said. "After that fundraising event for Resonant Household, there's nothing unusual. He has a paper trail, of course, including a few peccadilloes in the society pages, but it's all what you would expect for a rich white male CEO."

"When does he want to come look for his book?" Hazel asked.

"I said I needed to talk to you first, but he's going to drop by tomorrow sometime before noon."

"We did find some additional information about Resonant Household, itself," Dana said.

My curiosity stalled before takeoff. The engine sputtered and died. I was beat. "If it's not an emergency, can you tell me tomorrow? I just want to make myself a cup of chamomile and go to bed."

"Sure."

I left them, arms still touching, and wandered toward the kitchen. My shoes had been lined up neatly on a shoe rack by the front door. It hadn't been there a moment ago.

Max had said the magical house was just like having a cook and a maid, but something seemed off about that. A butler is explainable. But a magic house is… magic, right? But maybe if you grew up around magic that's all it became, a sort of invisible servant.

In the kitchen, I put water on to boil, then spooned some loose-leaf chamomile into a steeper in a cup.

Then again, hadn't Vincent had told me magic wasn't a thing? It was a relationship, or a string or something. God I was tired. I felt my brain slowing to a molasses crawl. Maybe all of this would make sense in the morning.

When the kettle whistled, I poured boiling water and

considered just leaving it there, crawling up to my bedroom and collapsing. But the open-air truck ride had left me with a chill, and I can never fall asleep if I'm cold.

"Howdy," Hazel said, walking into the kitchen. "I… just wanted to ask if you mind if Dana stays over."

I thought about giving her the old *Oooooh!* as she'd given me, but I didn't have the energy.

I smiled. "Yeah, of course."

"It just, uh, seems kinda rude to have her walk down to the inn so late, and when we have this gigantic house."

Was she blushing?

"And one other thing… I've been thinking about what you said about the life insurance… I think you're right. Our parents got the policy for a reason. They wanted us to have the money."

That was a big deal. I turned to face her. "Hey, sis, are you okay?"

"Yeah." She flashed me the most beautiful smile. It looked just like Mom's. "I am. It feels like a weight's been lifted, you know? All this time I thought I was keeping hope alive by leaving that money in the bank, but it was more like an anchor."

I saw the change in her. She stood taller. Her smile came easier. Not only was she out of her funk, but she was even more herself than she had been. I went in for a hug and she returned it so tight I felt tears welling in the corners of my eyes. I wiped them.

"I think…" She hesitated. "I think I might talk to Lin tomorrow about the bakery."

38

I walked to the counter by the big cream-covered oven and lifted the steeper from my cup of tea. Steam sent up a sweet floral aroma. I lifted the cup and let it rise around my tired eyes, then sipped and felt the delicious warmth in the back of my throat. I shivered as the last of my chill left me.

"Do you mind if I make a cup of this for myself?" Hazel asked, walking over. She was pulling the two sides of her cardigan closed. I guess she had been warmer back with Dana.

"You don't need to ask me. This is your place as much as mine." And now that she was staying it might be really true.

I leaned against the counter and enjoyed the quiet crunch of her spoon digging into the loose chamomile tea. She loaded it into a clean steeper, a little tin star full of holes. It clanked as she put it in the big ceramic mug. She brought it over and held the mug out with both hands around the handle like a kid. I filled it and she put her face into the steam and closed her eyes, just like I'd done. I wondered how many more little mannerisms we shared.

204 | TABATHA GRAY

"I always think chamomile smells like apples," she said.

I took another sip of mine and wasn't sure I picked that up. If it was there it was barely noticeable.

"Then again," she said, "I'm never sure if it really does, or if I just think so because I always used to order the *té de manzanilla* from this little café by my host family's house in Guadalajara."

"I don't follow."

"Manzanilla is Spanish for chamomile. And apple is—"

"Manzana," I said. "Even I know that one."

She laughed. "And Manzanillo is a city on the beach, about four hours from Guadalajara."

"And Manzanita is a beach town in Oregon not far from where they filmed *The Goonies*."

"Touché."

"Are you sure you won't miss traveling?" I asked. It was funny how I'd been trying to get her to stay in Charm Haven. But now that she was going to, I worried she'd regret it.

"Just because you have a home base doesn't mean you have to stop traveling."

"But a bakery—"

"Can close for a month once a year. Or maybe I won't need to because I'll have help." She gave me a big wink.

I had no doubt who her help would be. Any other time, I would have objected. I wasn't about to win any blue ribbons for my personal baking specialties: lumpy rubber bread, salt-instead-of-sugar cookies, or my favorite, burned-to-cinders box-mix brownies. But the thought of working alongside my sister was too pretty of a balloon to pop.

It was a fine feeling. Happy enough to cover up the tendril of shame that snaked around my guts whenever I forgot something important. I was supposed to meet Lin an hour ago. She was probably getting ready for bed now, and cursing me as a flake. But she wouldn't be upset for long. She was getting what she wanted, after all.

And it was better for Hazel to come to the decision on her own. I could see now that whatever Lin's plan had been, I would have turned it down. Hazel deserved to chart her own course without anyone leaning on the tiller.

"You *will* help, won't you?" she asked.

"Of course, daaaaling!" It came out in my Fancytown voice. I was either hilarious or past exhaustion to punch-drunk mania.

"Why not indeed?" She raised an eyebrow at me like a challenge. *Okay. Game on.*

"We're sistaaahs, ducky, the same blood flows through our veins. It'll be easy for me to take over when you step out."

"Why, we're practically identical!"

"Indubitably! I'll just pop on your chef hat, and your name tag and the fools won't know a thing has changed."

"Maavelous," she said, "although there is one hitch, ducks."

"What ever could it be?"

"You and I are different heights."

"I'll tape shoe boxes to my feet."

That got her laughing, a big snorting laugh. It was the sweetest sound in the world, so I had to keep it going. "And if people ask why the croissants are especially wooden this month, I'll tell them it's the latest fashion in gay Paree, oh yes, they eat 'em like hockey pucks over there."

"A good plan," she said. "But unfair."

"How so?"

"If you get to impersonate me, daaahling, then I should get to return the favor."

She reached up and pulled her hair back tight like I usually wore it, then scrunched her face up in a way that looked just like me and sent me whooping. But before I could ask her how long she practiced that in the mirror, the phone on the wall rang.

Hazel was closest, so she picked it up and pressed it to her ear. "Hello? ... Why, yes, this is *Holly*." She gave me a big stage grin and a wink, and I wanted—I wanted to die.

"Lin?" she asked.

I wanted to dig a hole and jump in and die, because I knew what was coming. She was nodding along and saying uh-huh and it was like watching a freight train scream down the tracks toward a minivan full of puppies.

A burning heat rose up in my chest, just like it had when I was ten and found a hundred-dollar bill in the dryer. I'd been at the mall with Stacy the night before and she'd bought that cute polka-dot top on her dad's card, because her dad felt guilty for being out of town. They had the top in purple, too, and I wanted it worse than anything, but it was eighty bucks. Might as well have been a million, until when I found that hundred-dollar bill in the drier and then it was like the loaves and the fishes. Of course Mom noticed the money missing. She asked me about it and I shook my head no even though I knew very well the bill was stashed in my back pocket. As the worry blossomed on Mom's face, something happened. I started to feel a burning sensation creep up my throat. It made me want to puke, because there was Mom who touched my forehead with her cool hand when I was sick, who sang me to sleep sometimes even though I was getting old for it. And here was me, a liar. It burned until I couldn't take it, so I went to the bathroom, where the dryer was, and slipped the bill back in. I flushed the toilet and said, *Hey, Mom, didn't you run a load of laundry earlier? Maybe it's in there.* And then I was the hero, to her at least, but now I wouldn't have even that.

I heard the clunk of the phone. I looked up at my sister. Every hope I'd ever had turned black and bitter in my mouth.

"Were you... talking to Lin behind my back?" she asked, as if she couldn't believe it.

"I ran into her outside Vincent's office."

"And you came up with a plan to... manipulate me into buying that bakery?"

"*She* had a plan. I don't even know what it was."

"She called earlier too, didn't she? When we were making the galette."

"Y-yes."

"You told me it was nobody."

"Look, Hazel, she doesn't take no for an answer. She wanted me to tell me her plan after Henrietta's fete. I felt queasy about the situation. I'd basically decided to tell her no."

"Basically?" She said the word like she was holding up a dirty sock. "It didn't stop you from hiding it from me."

"But I didn't go, did I? That's the reason she called, wasn't it?"

Hazel seemed uncertain. "Did you miss your little appointment on purpose?"

It was like that hundred-dollar bill, burning in my pocket. I shook my head from side to side. "No. I forgot about it."

"This is messed up, Holly. I thought..."

She thought I was better. She thought I was strong. She thought she could trust me. Yeah. So did I.

"I was scared for you," I said, tears swelling in my eyes. "I was so damned scared for you last night! You almost died! Caleb almost killed you and he's still out there. Now, to make things worse, magic's going haywire. Then you tell me you're leaving, and going somewhere I can't protect you."

"It's messed up," she said again, turning away. The distance between us might have been measured in miles.

From another part of the house, I heard a bang. Then another, and another. Someone was knocking—no, pounding on the front door.

"Police," a voice shouted. "Open up!"

39

*D*eputy Sprout looked like a boy standing on the porch in his oversized uniform. In the half darkness I might have imagined the pistol on his belt was nothing more than a hollow plastic toy. But he had changed from earlier. Maybe it was the inquisitor's death, or his election worries, or maybe he was just dog tired. In any case, the dark circles under his eyes and the dead slant of his mouth told me he wasn't enjoying the game as much as he usually did.

"Is your sister home?" As soon as he'd said it he looked past me, at Hazel who I heard approaching.

He pushed past me—"Hey!" I shouted—and a quick flash of steel clapped around Hazel's right wrist, then her left.

"Hazel Nightingale, you are under arrest for the murder of Mr. Albinus, first name unknown."

"But I didn't murder anyone?" *Why did it sound like a question?*

"She didn't murder anyone!" I gave it the oomph it deserved.

"Then why did an eyewitness see her enter the station at the time of the killing?"

"I think the question is why weren't *you* at the station taking care of your prisoner?"

"We've confirmed it too," he said. "We matched the prints from the holding cell area to ones from your sister's passport. We might be a small town, but we're not completely cut off from civilization."

"Oh, so now your computers work? But your surveillance cameras mysteriously shut off right before the guy died?"

"Look," he said, anger flashing, "Do you think I want to arrest your sister?"

"Yes. Probably makes you feel like a big man or something."

"I'd have killed him myself if I could have!" Sprout didn't look like a little boy playing dress-up anymore. For a moment the only sound was the wind moaning through distant trees.

"That freak," he said. "That group of freaks, came to *my* island, and tried to burn your sister at the stake. Hell, they tried to kill the rest of the town too, didn't they? You ask me, Albinus got what he had coming to him. If your sister did the killing I'd say it was a fine piece of work. I'd throw her a parade myself if I wasn't in such hot water."

"But I didn't," Hazel said weakly.

"Look, miss, you had motive, means and opportunity. And I'd shake your hand instead of cuffing it if my own hand wasn't being forced."

"Do you seriously think my sister could break into a locked cell and make a grown man take a pill he didn't want to?"

"Didn't half the town see the both of you flying around on a broomstick? I heard that in the woods you yourself brought her down from the burning stake just by thinking it. How hard would it be to spring a lock, or force a man to take a pill?"

TANGLED CHARMS | 211

"Harder than you think. Good luck telling that to a jury on the mainland. They'd lock you in a padded cell."

"I wish they would. It'd be more peaceful. And I hope she beats the charge, I really do. But we all play our roles." He turned to Hazel. "You have the right to remain silent—you need me to loosen those cuffs?"

She shook her head no.

"I wouldn't have you in those darned things if I could afford to take any chances." He led her down the front porch steps. "Anything you say can and will be used against you in a court of law."

"We'll fix this, Hazel! I'll get Hector!"

Deputy Sprout lead her around the same side path I'd used, his voice fading into the distant moaning wind. "You have the right to talk to a lawyer…"

40

I had a hell of a time getting to sleep, and when I did it was only halfway. I never quite lost the sense of lying in the bed, my cheek on the coarse linen pillowcase.

I dreamed I was ten years old, wearing a purple top that cost eighty bucks and Deputy Sprout cuffed me and tossed me in a cell, but it was the Crone's Wood and I ran toward Hazel as the flames shot up like a wall, and I jumped and felt a shock of cold and tasted brine and the water stung my eyes when I looked down into the abyss and swam up toward sun, and breached, and heaved, and cleared my eyes, and saw the Charm Haven ferry steaming into the fog, and…

… and it went on and on like that, horror after half-awake horror until part of me wondered if the inquisitors didn't kill me after all, if this wasn't hell and the devil himself wasn't knocking on the inside of my skull.

Knock.

Knock.

Knock.

"Holly?" a distant voice said.

TANGLED CHARMS | 213

I shot up and opened my eyes. I squinted at the light. I was in a bed. In a room with an old-fashioned armoire and two large lace-curtained windows. My pink-and-yellow pack leaned up against the wall. I was in Gran's house.

"Holly?" The voice belonged to Dana. The weight of last night sank onto me and I wished I was back in that hellish dream. It was better than a world where I'd betrayed my sister, and she was in jail for murder.

"I'm awake," I said, blinking away the echoes of the dream. I could still feel the saltwater sting my eyes and the devil knocking in my head.

"Your, uh, uncle is downstairs at the front door."

Anxiety jolted me fully awake. Uncle Max was here already? How long had I slept? I looked to the side table, where a small alarm clock told me it was just past ten. Holly was rotting in jail and I'd slept in. Real Sister of the Year material.

"Tell him I'll be down in a few minutes," I said, forcing my legs to kick the covers off and swing around. I winced. My head was throbbing, probably from all the sugar I ate yesterday. Had to be, unless that really had been the devil knocking.

I stood and winced, but the deep pile rug felt squishy and nice under my toes. I walked around to the big armoire and opened it. Sure enough, my clothes were laid out neatly inside. Luna's dress was hung up, too, although I'd left it in a crumpled heap on the floor last night. Thank goodness for magical houses.

Last night I'd made a plan while trying to get to sleep. First, I'd track down our lawyer, Hector. Then he and I would march to the police station and free Hazel. I wasn't sure how we'd spring her, but Hector had a good track record. Two for two. A hundred percent success rate. I was sure he'd think of something.

214 | TABATHA GRAY

But what if... What if it wasn't so simple? Deputy Sprout had said a few puzzling things last night.

I'd throw her a parade myself if I wasn't in such hot water.

I'd shake her hand if mine wasn't being forced.

Could he be worried about the upcoming election? Dr. Green had told us the inquisitor's death might hurt his chances. Or was someone powerful pressuring him? Had he received his own birthday card? *Your secret is not safe with me.*

If Deputy Sprout really was in hot water, he might not release Hazel without proof of her innocence.

An eyewitness had seen Hazel at the police station. This could only be Reina Flores, the fading bombshell in horn-rimmed glasses who had carried a stack of papers into the station, then disappeared.

How could she have seen my sister if she, herself, was nowhere to be seen? I felt a hard certainty in my chest and nodded to myself. I had to confront her. I had to ask her point-blank, then look her in the eye and see if she was lying.

I hoped Uncle Max could find his book and get out of here quickly.

I put on my clean pair of high-waisted jeans and a tight white cotton top that was as wrinkled as wadded-up paper. I looked around for my shoes before remembering I'd left them by the front door on that miraculous shoe rack. A glance in the bathroom mirror told me my hair looked like crap, so I pulled it back tight in a messy bun. Not great, but as good as it was going to be, so I pasted on a smile and went downstairs to see Uncle Max.

He was in the foyer, inspecting the portrait of Augustus Nightingale on the far wall. He glanced over his shoulder at me. "Funny how this old thing's been here all this time. It was in this exact spot when I was a boy."

I noticed he had changed back out of slacks into those

awful cargo shorts. His polo shirt was the same make, but forest green, and he wore the same ugly leather sandals.

"Did you enjoy the shindig last night?" He asked.

"It was… something."

"Hattie really knows how to lay a spread."

"You two were getting along."

"Did that surprise you? Well, me too. She and I share a lot of history and not all of it's good. I half expected her to chase me down the front lawn with a rolling pin. Although there's always time for that." He laughed. "In fact, I could have sworn I saw her following me after I left the party and walked down to the pier where my yacht is parked."

"Weird." My headache was pounding, and I had more important things to worry about. "So, does this make us even? You get your book and you drop your lawsuit over the house?"

"Even Steven. It's funny. I used to ride my tricycle through this front hall. Used a clothespin to clip an ace of spades so it hit the spokes and made a sound like a machine gun once I got going. I saw the older kids doing that on their bikes and thought, why not on a tricycle? Most innovations are like that, you know. The trick is to take something that's already out there and give it a little twist. Put it somewhere unexpected."

"Should we start in the library?" I asked. "I don't know how much has changed since you lived here, but we haven't moved anything. A lot of the books don't look like they've been touched in a long time."

"I would be very surprised if the book wasn't where I left it."

"Where's that?"

"Somewhere unexpected." He grinned and lifted the portrait of Augustus off the wall. Behind it there was a small

216 | TABATHA GRAY

door made out of a dark pitted metal that might have been cast iron.

"After the tricycle, I graduated to roller skates," he said. "Now there's an innovation for you. Take eight boring wheels and put them on a pair of boots and *zooom*! Mom hated the skates, of course, and she never let me use them inside. But one afternoon she was gone, and whee! I knocked this painting right off the wall. That's how I found this little box. It took a few years to figure out how to open it, but…"

The door had six different buttons, each of them engraved with a vaguely astrological shape. Uncle Max pressed them in a quick sequence. There was a little click. The door loosened.

"This is where I stored all of my treasures. My butterfly collection. My favorite comics. and…" He opened the door took out a small book. Scratch that. Book is too fancy of a term. It was more like a pamphlet made from translucent parchment and bound with coarse red string. Its cover had a single word, written in old-fashioned script: *focus*.

"This was written by our ancestor, Augustus himself. It was given to me by my grandfather on my tenth birthday. He was a wonderful man. I could tell you stories. It will be nice to have something to remind me of him, of family."

Family? It was strange to think that this rich, famous man could be related to me and Hazel. But if that was the case…

"Hazel's just been arrested," I said.

"Really? Why?"

"She was in the wrong place at the wrong time, and the deputy thinks she was involved in a murder. I wouldn't normally ask—"

"You don't have to." He pulled out his phone and started tapping. "I'll have my lawyers get on it immediately. They're good at applying pressure."

I was just glad they weren't doing it to me anymore.

41

The front door clunked shut behind Uncle Max, and my stomach growled. I walked down the hall to the kitchen, through the door that was always propped open, into the big room with its massive, cream-colored stove. The morning had made it cooler and quieter than I remembered. It would have been nice to linger there, to make eggs with pancakes and eat them outside, at one of the tables on the wraparound porch. But I only had time for a quick bite to dull my hunger. Hazel needed me.

I went to the pantry and found a box of Pop Tarts. I brought it out to the island counter. Last night's jar of chamomile tea, the steepers, and mugs had been put away. I took out a pastry. It smelled like sugar and probably wasn't the best thing for my pounding head. But the buttery crust, the hard icing, the red gash of strawberry filling called to me. I took a bite and it tasted like childhood. My headache eased a little, too. *Hair of the dog, I suppose.*

I took another bite and walked over to the wall-mounted phone, and found the slip of paper full of telephone numbers. Hector had been Gran's lawyer long before he was ours. His name was near the top of the list. I took the receiver off the hook and dialed, each number playing a screechy note in an unmelodic song. The phone rang five times then went to voicemail. I left a message and hung up.

"Calling Hector?" Dana stood in the kitchen doorway. She was wearing the same white blouse and tweed blazer, though everything was a little more rumpled.

"I tried to call him but nobody picked up," I said. "I guess I'll need to walk down there."

"How was the meeting with your uncle?"

"Fine, I think. Uncle Max got what he wanted and he's dropping the lawsuit. Toaster pastry?" I tipped the box toward her.

"Don't mind if I do." She took one of the shiny sleeves out of the box. It crinkled as she tore it open. "I haven't had these things in years."

"I'm sorry I can't offer a real breakfast, but I need to round up Hector and check on my sister."

"And I'm going with you. It's the least I could do after you and Hazel helped me yesterday."

"Really?"

"Yeah."

We left the wrappers on the counter and munched as we prepared to leave. The front door stuck a little in the frame, but it wasn't hard to open. Outside, the wind had completely stilled. My nose prickled.

"Looks like the smoke is coming back," I said.

Dana sniffed. "You're right. I hoped the wind had cleared it."

I looked at Dana, chewing her pastry, with a rumpled shirt and slept-in makeup and I felt a swelling, almost pathetic gratitude that she'd stayed. My dreams last night were bad. They would have been worse if I woke up to face them alone.

"I'm… sorry," I said, "for calling you a vulture the other day when you showed up."

"Did you call me that?"

"If I didn't, then I meant to."

She laughed.

"I was pretty mad," I said. "Hazel almost died the night before. And it was only a week since I lost my job, my home, my fiancé. After the explosion, reporters stuck cameras in my face. They asked questions, but they didn't really care—I saw in their eyes they didn't. I was just grist for the mill. A human-interest story for the viewers back home."

"I *was* a bit of a vulture," she said. "The industry makes us into that. I'm sure you know the old chestnut: *If it bleeds it leads*. But… I'm trying to do better. I really do want to help."

"I know."

Being up and moving was doing wonders for my headache. By the time we reached the end of the garden path, it was reduced to a shadow of itself. The wrought iron gate didn't click open on its own, but it wasn't locked so I pushed it open. I looked forward to the walk downhill into town.

"I'm still waiting on my contact to get back to me about Anwir Holdings," Dana said. "But I did find some additional information about the Resonant Household. It's a strange organization. Very secretive."

I popped the last of my toaster pastry in my mouth and chewed it. "Aren't all cults secretive?"

"Most of them will have a spokesperson. Some even pretend to be self-help groups or professional development trainers."

"Like a Tony Robbins–type of thing? Release your inner lion?"

"Yeah, but the Resonant Household is different. They don't have a website or any social media accounts. Members don't announce their membership to the world. And strangest of all, their founder, Manoel Castelhano, hasn't appeared in public for fifteen years."

I swallowed the sugary buttery pastry and wished I had some water. "Maybe they went out of business."

"I was beginning to wonder, until I found this message board. It's an online support group for parents whose children have disappeared into a cult and cut ties. But it's more than that, too. Parents share information about the cults, so they can understand what they're up against."

"Sounds bleak."

"Someone shared a video from a Resonant Household meeting held in September of last year. There must have been a thousand people there. The members call themselves Householders. Half a dozen speakers laid out the organization's vision for the future. They're continuing the work that was started in Brazil, by the men with the lead masks."

"They're trying to make first contact?"

"Not exactly. It's hard to explain. The Householders believe that the universe was created by higher-order beings. They call them HOBs."

"Sometimes I think the world was created by an SOB."

She laughed. "It's a shared-language thing. A way to separate the in-group from the out-group. The Householders don't say *created*. They say the HOBs *innovated* the universe, but as far as I can tell, it means the same thing."

We reached the base of the hill and turned down the cobblestone street leading to Hector's law offices.

"So, the SOBs are gods?" I asked.

"More like cosmically powerful engineers. They were on track to create a perfect world where they could live with their creations (us) in peace and harmony, yada yada yada. But something happened."

"Something always does."

"The HOBs were forced to stop the act of creation, and

flee, leaving humanity to fend for itself in an imperfect, incomplete world."

"Story checks out."

"But here's where things get interesting. Householders believe the HOBs left so quickly, they didn't have time to pack up their tools. You know, the ones they used to create the universe? The tools are still here, lying around, waiting to be picked up and used by anyone who knows how."

"Use for what?"

"To finish the original act of creation. To make the world perfect like it was meant to be. And they think they know how. They just need a source of energy."

"So these Householder people are nuts," I said.

"Yesterday I thought you were nuts when you told me about flying a broom."

"Did you see Uncle Max in the video?"

"No. I looked and couldn't find him, though it doesn't mean much. The video was highly compressed, it was hard to make out the faces in the audience."

"It would surprise me if he was," I said. "The more I hear about these Householders, the more I think that Uncle Max can't have anything to do with them."

"Really?"

"I mean, sure, he kept the electrical name, and he's weird but... business-book-at-the-airport weird, not SOBs-constructing-the-universe weird. I guess it doesn't really matter, though. He's dropping the lawsuit so we don't need dirt on him."

"You're right," Dana said, though her tone said she wasn't so sure. She was a journalist, and this was a hot story, lawsuit or no lawsuit.

We turned a corner and up ahead I saw the streetlamp where a lifetime ago I'd kissed Lucas. I wondered if he was in the Crone's Wood. Hector's office was dead ahead. I walked up to the door and twisted the handle. It didn't turn.

"It's locked," I said.

Dana stood back so she could look up through the windows. "It's dark inside. The lights are off. Maybe the office is closed today."

"What kind of law firm is closed at 11 a.m. on a Wednesday?"

"This kind, apparently. What now?"

Good question.

My plan had been to grab Hector and march over to the police station. While he was sparring with Deputy Sprout, I could corner Reina Flores, the blond woman with the horn-rimmed glasses. I knew she wouldn't admit to anything, but I hoped I could rattle her, to shake loose some nugget of truth that could free my sister.

The first part of my plan had fallen through, at least for now. But I could still go see my sister, to let her know help was on the way. And I could still find Reina Flores.

"Let's split up," I said. "I'll go to the police station. You try to track down Hector. My sister was able to reach him at home. I don't know the number, but Luna at the Inn & Pub will be able to help you track it down."

"Sounds good. I saw the Inn & Pub when I arrived in town yesterday."

"Luna's the woman with pink hair. She's a friend. You can tell her anything."

42

ucas's store was still dark as I passed it and walked toward the statue of Augustus. The smoky air was filled with birds, streaks of gray and black, hovering with chuffing wings around the statue's outstretched hand. They dove and sparred, fighting over the pile of birdseed, knocking bits to the ground where a dozen more birds (either lazier or smarter) waited for the manna to fall from heaven.

Just yesterday I'd found my sister leaning against this statue, feeding these birds bits of bread. Now she was jailed in the basement of the four-story city hall building ahead. I wondered how many tons of brick were pressing down on her tiny cell.

The police station door was heavy but it swung open easily. I entered the room where I'd once been accused of murdering my great-aunt. It felt like walking into a barely remembered dream. There were the filing cabinets, the cork-board, the desks (built with enough steel to storm the beaches of Normandy), and the uncomfortable chair that had dug into my back. I remembered them all. They all were here, but none of them seemed entirely real.

The woman was real, though. She sat behind the nearest desk, hunched over some papers. She wore her dark hair up and her red lipstick was perfectly applied. I had never seen her before.

"Can I help you?" she asked. Her voice told me exactly the level of crap she was willing to put up with: zero, nada, zilch.

I cleared my throat. "My sister is being held here. I hoped I could visit her."

"Visitation is at three p.m. Come back then." She pointed at a big chrome clock on the wall. The little hand was at eleven. The big hand pointed to the space between thirteen and fourteen. She looked back down at her work, something involving tables of numbers and lots of highlighters.

So that was it? Come back at three? I'd have to leave my sister down there, wondering if I'd forgotten her, wondering if the cavalry would ever come?

"Forget about visitation," I said. "My sister has a right to meet with her attorney, doesn't she? Do attorneys have to wait?"

She looked at me, seemed to be judging my jeans and wrinkled white top. She raised an eyebrow so sharp it might have cut me. "You're her sister *and* her lawyer?"

"Well, no. Hector Morales is her lawyer. I'm sure he'll be here any minute. If you could just—"

"When Hector gets here, I'll talk with him." She looked down and dragged the pink highlighter over the paper. It made a high-pitched sound like nails on a chalkboard. It left me with a strange, tingly feeling at the back of my neck.

I could tell I wouldn't get anywhere with this woman. Like it or not, I'd have to wait until visiting hour at three. But I wasn't entirely helpless. I still had my other lead: the blond woman with the horn-rimmed glasses.

TANGLED CHARMS | 225

"There's one other thing." I swallowed and my throat felt dry. "I'd like to talk with Reina Flores. Would you happen to know where I can find her?"

The woman set her highlighter down and squinted up at me like I'd grown horns and a tail.

"What did you want to talk to her about?" She seemed cagey and I remembered an article I read about how cops never testify against other cops, even the corrupt ones. The article was titled "The Blue Wall of Silence." I wasn't sure if the wall included everyone who worked in police stations, even if they weren't cops.

"It's a personal matter," I said.

"Oh really? Are the two of you old friends?"

"Not exactly."

"Are you her doctor or something?"

"I'm nobody's doctor."

"Then what kind of personal message could you have for Reina?"

"Look, I just need to talk to her, okay? I know she works here at the police station. Could you at least tell me if she'll be in today?"

"Oh, she's working today. Trying to, at least." The woman stuck her hand toward as if to shake "Reina Flores. Pleased to meet you."

I shrank back. This woman, this *petite* dark-haired woman *not* the tall, horn-rimmed blonde from yesterday. Even if she dyed her hair blond and put on glasses and platform shoes, her body type was too different. Could she be lying? Playing a prank? I didn't think so. People didn't usually pull pranks at their place of work.

I realized suddenly that I'd only assumed Reina Flores was the mystery woman we'd seen enter the police station. Dr. Green had given us the name, but not a description.

"What's the matter? Cat got your tongue?" she asked, drawing her hand back.

"No, well, yes. I thought you were someone else, or, I guess I thought someone else was you. She was taller, and blond and wore horn-rimmed glasses. I thought she was the witness who had seen my sister. I'd heard someone named Reina Flores worked at the police station, so I assumed that was her name. I wanted to find her and talk to her."

She let out a hard laugh. "You thought I was the person who placed your sister at the scene of a crime. So what? You wanted to threaten me? To shut me up? You know that's illegal."

"No! I just wanted to ask you, uh, her some questions."

"So would Deputy Sprout," she said. "That tip came from an anonymous informant. He's out looking for her now, so he can find out what else she saw."

"Oh." I felt suddenly heavy. My lead didn't amount to a hill of beans. I didn't know what to do.

"Look. I get that you're upset about your sister. But you're not Nancy Drew. Leave the detective work to the professionals. Now, if you'll excuse me, I've got a lot of work to get through. Come back at three."

"Okay, thanks," I said, as though the building's hundred tons hadn't dropped on me all at once. I turned and walked toward the honey-colored door, the door that was heavy but easy on its hinges.

"One more thing," Reina called from behind me.

"What?"

"If you find your mystery woman, you send her straight to Deputy Sprout, do you understand? Do not pass go. Do not collect two hundred dollars. Do not ask her questions, or say anything that could influence her testimony. If you do you won't need to wait until visiting hours to see your sister, because you'll be in the cell next to hers."

43

I walked out of the police station into the hall and heard the heavy door shut behind me. So that was it, huh? Come back at three?

I leaned against the wall, next to a bank of brass mailboxes. It felt cold, but I didn't care. My one lead was up in smoke, and I'd better not go looking, better not say, better not ask any questions that might influence her testimony. And that was it. The game was over. My sister was in jail and I couldn't help her.

Something dark and even colder than the wall turned over inside me. It kicked up a bitter taste in my mouth. I tried to swallow, but my throat felt sandy and dry with the memory of yesterday's words: *How can I protect her if she leaves?*

What an idiot I had been.

I should have known Charm Haven was crazy, unsafe. I should have known there were forces at work I didn't understand. For all my talk of coming home, all my memories, all my hope I'd finally found a place to belong, I'd been away for too many years. I was an outsider. So was Hazel. And Deputy

228 | TABATHA GRAY

Sprout was just another small-minded, small-town cop who saw a target on the back of every stranger.

(If your sister did the killing I'd say it was a fine piece of work. I'd throw her a parade myself if I wasn't in such hot water.)

And if Sprout didn't have it in for us, that made it even worse. It meant some vague, unseen force was working against us, for reasons I couldn't fathom. Maybe it was the horn-rimmed woman herself (the hunted become the hunter). Could she reach my sister even in jail? Murder her like the inquisitor was murdered?

Charm Haven wasn't home. It wasn't an island. It wasn't a town. It was a puzzle box, smooth and lacquered. I could pick it up, turn it over, and probe with my thumbnail for seams. But even if by some miracle I found a hidden button, pressed it and released the lid, I would only find another box inside, smooth and lacquered, and in it, another. I would never make it to the heart of this place. I would always be an outsider.

(How can I protect her if she leaves?)

Hell, I should have packed her bag for her, taken her to the airport and bought her ticket to Bali myself, as if I had the money. But I was broke, and I'd lost everything, and magic hadn't chosen me.

(Wasn't I the woman who charged into a nightmare forest to rescue my sister? Didn't I prevent a mass murder at the festival? Hadn't I just defeated that little shop of horrors on Tilly's roof? It wasn't magic. But it wasn't nothing.)

Of course it was nothing!

I was on an island where beehives were sprouting legs and plants were coming to life. I was part of a magical family. I had my own prophecy for crying out loud. People looked at me with their mouths a little open because they'd seen me fly on a broom. But what did that get me?

Nothing! Not even my sister.

TANGLED CHARMS | 229

Tears welled in my eyes. I wiped them on my sleeve. More came and carved hot gashes in my cheeks. They fell to the floor like raindrops.

"Holly?" a familiar voice said. "Are you well?"

It was Vincent, looking at me with his deep, kind eyes. He held a half-collapsed black parasol in one hand and a worn leather briefcase in the other. He seemed like he was coming back from a meeting, and he'd stumbled upon me and didn't know what to do so he asked me if I was well.

"No." I sniffed. "I'm really not."

He paused, probably thinking back to last night, when I'd pried too far and offended him. He held out his hand.

"Here, come with me."

I didn't understand. Why would he care? And where did he want to take me? I looked around at the dingy hallway, with its off-white walls, its doors the color of honey, its hard terrazzo floor now slick with tears. Anywhere would be better. I took his hand. It was cool. We rode the elevator up and walked down the hall as I told him what happened with Hazel. I finished the story as he opened the door to his office and gestured me inside.

The velvet drapes were closed, and the room was dark and quiet. A click behind me illuminated the sconces with soft, warm light that reminded me of candles. Vincent walked to the ancient-looking wooden desk in the center of the room and deposited his briefcase next to the Rolodex.

"If I could order the deputy to release her I would," he said, leading me to the small sofa in the room's corner.

I sat, wiping the leftover tears from my face. I was suddenly nervous about my wrinkled shirt, my jeans, my face, probably swollen like it always was after I cried. I wiped my cheeks with my palms and patted down my hair and tried to blink away the stinging feeling in my eyes. But the thought of last night only made it worse. I needed a distraction, so I watched Vincent as he went to a small table and fussed with something. He came back a moment later holding two glasses curved like tulips. He handed me one. It contained a small amount of a brown liquid.

"Brandy," he said. "Just a splash. It's an old custom to help with shock."

I was about to argue that I wasn't shocked. I was… I don't know, crushed? Frustrated? Humiliated? (*Trying not to think of last night?*) Maybe it didn't matter. It was only a bit of brandy, not enough to make me drunk. What did I have to lose?

I tipped it back and it hit my tongue with a heady explosion, a fruity burning that slid down my throat like honeyed fire. It warmed me from the inside, then pushed out, making every nerve tingle with energy. I shivered, and felt… still sad, still frustrated. But it wasn't all I felt.

"I'm not sure who might be pressuring the deputy," Vincent said, drinking his glass. He took mine and placed it on a tray by his desk, then rejoined me. "And I can't imagine why anyone would want to have your sister imprisoned."

"Maybe it's nothing then. I could have been over—"

"No," he said, "I'm certain some larger scheme is playing out. I simply don't know who could be behind it."

It was a cold comfort to learn that I wasn't the only one who couldn't unlock the puzzle box. But even a cold comfort is still a comfort, I guess.

"I received another birthday card this morning," he said. "This time, there was no doubt that I was the intended recipient."

"Really?" I leaned in. I remembered Vincent showing me the first card. It had been vague, saying *your secret is not safe with us*. But it hadn't been addressed, and Vincent wasn't sure if it was meant for him. The case had basically vanished, as far as I could tell, and he hadn't mentioned it last night. (*Don't think about last night!*)

"The new card was much more... explicit. It instructed me to withdraw my proposed ordinance before the city council meeting this afternoon."

"The one that would keep Anwir from buying up all the land in Charm Haven?" I asked.

"If I don't withdraw it, they say they will release compromising information to the public. I'm not sure what that might be, but there is an election this November. They must imagine they can replace me with a more friendly candidate."

"Do you have any idea what the... compromising information is?" I asked.

He shook his head. "I've lived in Charm Haven for twenty years, without a hint of scandal. The residents know me, and trust me. I can't believe they would turn against me because of an anonymous accusation."

"It's not anonymous though, is it? Anwir has to be behind all this. They're the only ones who stand to gain from you withdrawing your ordinance."

"The property owners stand to gain as well."

"People like Tilly? None of them would blackmail you."

"I don't think so either, but one never knows for certain. People have a way of... surprising you. And even if Anwir is the culprit, we don't know who controls it."

"Believe it or not, *I* actually have someone working on that. The owners of Anwir are hiding their ownership behind a series of shell companies. Dana is digging through the paperwork to find them."

"That's excellent news."

"It's the least I could do after last night." *Shit.* My breath caught in my throat. Last night I'd failed the test. I'd overreached. And now I was *reminding* him of that? Smooth. Real smooth.

Vincent's expression was distant, like he was thinking

about something far in the past, then his eyes focused and he looked at me with barely contained emotion.

"Are *you* well?" I asked, laughing, and immediately wanted to die.

"I felt like a fool leaving you last night. It was rude of me."

My heart started pounding. He was rude to... me? I turned to face him on the couch, moving my whole body around, cocking one leg onto the springy cushion.

"It was my fault," I said. "I never should have asked that stupid question. Your past is your business. You had every right to be upset."

"I wasn't upset, and your question wasn't the reason I fled."

It had seemed so clear to me there was someone in his past, someone who he had cared about and was gone. And when I had asked my stupid question (Who was she?) it had brought up all those old memories. The pain had been too much to bear in public, so he had gone. But now he said that wasn't it at all.

I felt heat creep up my neck. "Then why did you leave?"

He looked at me with those kind gray eyes that hinted at depths I could only imagine. I saw uncertainty and it looked strange on him, like ill-fitting clothes. He reached out and gently touched the back of my hand. An electric shock went through me and I was a live wire with a swimming head and a heart about to jump out of my chest.

"I left because I was afraid," Vincent said, his voice barely above a whisper.

The admission hung in the air between us. His hand, which had been barely touching mine, pressed down overtop it, and I felt giddy then terrified. What about Hazel? And hadn't Caleb held my hand like this? Hadn't I thought that was something real? Could I trust myself? But I'd done all I could do for my sister at the moment, and Vincent seemed so sincere.

I leaned closer, hardly daring to breathe. "What were you afraid of?"

"Afraid of how strongly I'm drawn to you, Holly. It's unexpected. And perhaps unwise."

"I… I don't think caring for someone is ever unwise."

A ghost of a smile touched his lips. "Perhaps not. But it can be… dangerous."

"Life is dangerous."

Vincent's eyes searched mine, and I thought he might pull away. Instead, he raised his hand and gently touched my cheek. I bit my bottom lip and looked into his gray eyes.

"Ever since I left last night," he said, "I haven't been able to stop thinking of you. Your warmth, your vitality, they're intoxicating."

I leaned into his touch, my eyes closing for a moment. When I opened them, Vincent's face was closer.

"Holly," he said, "may I—"

A sharp knock at the door made us both jump. Vincent pulled back, clearing his throat as he stood. I tried to compose myself, smoothing my shirt and running a hand through my hair.

"Come in," Vincent called, his voice steady despite the tension I saw in his shoulders.

The door opened, and a harried-looking woman poked her head in. "Sorry to interrupt, Mr. Mayor, but I've got a call for you on line two. It's Mr. Orimund from the council. It's about the meeting."

44

*V*incent walked to his desk and picked up the black rotary phone. He spoke in quiet tones I couldn't hear, but I could see traces in his posture of what I'd glimpsed before, that powerful being who was used to command. I caught myself holding my breath because I'd... We'd almost—

"Well whaddaya know? If It isn't the girl with the broomstick." It took me a second to recognize the bright, slightly nasal voice. It was the voice from the telephone when I'd tried to call Vincent yesterday.

The woman walking toward me was dressed like a secretary from an eighties movie. Her red hair was a halo of tight curls. She stopped in front of the sofa and looked me over with something a little fonder than suspicion.

"Maybe I was wrong, hon."

"What do you mean?" I asked.

"Maybe the mayor *is* buying what you're selling."

My cheeks went hot. What were you supposed to—

"And good for you, I say. The poor guy needs a little relaxation in his life. He works all hours, day and night, night and day. Linda, get me that report. Linda type this letter. Linda, Linda, Linda, It's enough to drive a girl batty, pardon the expression, especially if her name is Linda."

She collapsed on the sofa next to me and looked at me slyly. "So tell me, hon—what was your name again?"

"Holly."

"So tell me Holly," she looked me dead in the eye, "Is the mayor a good kisser?"

I stared at her.

"And where do the fangs go? Sometimes he has them. Sometimes he doesn't. Do they retract? Do they flip out like little switchblades or what?"

My mouth hung a little open as I tried to figure out a response.

"Does he like to use them to, you know, get a little kinky?"

"Excuse me?"

She grinned and put her hands up in mock surrender. "Never mind. Never mind. Just teasing. But for real, did you ever find out more about the, ah"—she glanced toward Vincent—"murder? Monique in planning said it was a stabbing. She said she heard one of other psychos, ya know the ones with the robes, must have stolen the master key and sneaked in there and *hwacht*"—she pounded on her chest— "right through the heart. And there's no getting up after that one, let me tell you."

"That's what I hear too," I said, although the version I heard didn't come with sound effects. I wasn't in a hurry to tell her that my sister had been arrested for the crime. I was sure that if I did, she'd run out of the room to call Monique in planning, and within twenty minutes half the town would know. But something she said stuck in my mind.

"There's a master key?" I asked.

"Don't get any ideas, hon, even the mayor himself doesn't have a copy."

236 | TABATHA GRAY

Vincent hung up the phone with a clunk, then turned to us. "Linda, Orimund needs the latest version of my proposed ordinance. Take it yourself if you don't mind."

Linda winked at me. "Anything you say, Mr. Mayor. I'll take it right now, and did you know that Alice and John went over to see about that road issue? You're going to be up here by yourself, well, maybe not *all* by yourself."

"I think I can handle it."

Linda slapped her hands onto her knees and stood. She took a document from Vincent then walked through the door to the hall, about as subtle as a wrecking ball, but I couldn't help but like her.

"I apologize for the interruption," Vincent said, sitting next to me.

He was in the same spot he'd sat just before. I was too, but the moment had passed. Vincent seemed preoccupied.

"What's going on?" I asked.

"The city council is meeting this afternoon." He sighed.

"To keep Anwir from buying up Charm Haven?"

"To vote on my proposed ordinance, yes. But hostilities between members is boiling over. Today, Mrs. Blackwell, the bursar, ran into the council's secretary, Mr. Fletcher. He and Mrs. Blackwell have a long-standing disagreement about a budget issue. He believes that money for fixing potholes should come from the road construction fund, while she believes that it should come from the infrastructure mainte-nance fund."

"Sounds like not that big of a deal."

"Normally, it's not, but the man I just spoke with, Orimund, witnessed them screaming at each other earlier this morning. She apparently cast a spell that turned his beard into a nest of green snakes."

My stomach felt hollow. I remembered fighting off the too-alive whipping vines at Tilly's. I remembered their sick-

TANGLED CHARMS | 237

ening green smell and the sight of that red tendril of corrupted magic reaching toward my sister.

"You have to understand that Mr. Fletcher has a quite impressive beard," Vincent added. "And he became so angry that the parcel Mrs. Blackwell was holding spontaneously burst into flames. That parcel apparently contained architectural plans destined for Henrietta Thorn, the council chair. I can only wonder what she will do in revenge. For all I know, the council may not reach a quorum. If they don't, they'll be unable to vote on my ordinance."

"And Anwir will be able to keep buying up Charm Haven…"

"If the council fails to pass the ordinance, it could be too late. Anwir will have already completed its purchases."

I sank into the couch and let out a sigh. So, the haywire magic was striking again. Charm Haven might be bought up by a faceless corporation. It would be bad enough if Anwir was an ordinary developer wanting to build cookie-cutter condos. But this wasn't just any real estate venture. Its owners were so scared of the limelight that they had spent a fortune in legal fees on dozens of shell companies. Why?

What if—*oh God, what if it was the Inquisition?*

What if the bomb at the festival had only been their plan A? Could they have made a backup plan in case it failed? *If you can't burn 'em out, buy 'em out.*

And the name, Anwir. (An old Welsh word meaning liar. Well, the devil's a liar, miss, and I'll be damned if this ain't from him.) The Inquisition was the closest I'd ever come to the devil. And Caleb—hadn't every word he ever said to me, every kiss he ever gave me been a lie? I glanced at Vincent and wondered if I was lying to myself. I stood and began to pace the room.

I had led the Inquisition home to Charm Haven. I had released the wild magic that was causing so much chaos. I'd had good intentions, sure, but I'd done it. If it meant that Vincent's ordinance didn't pass, that Anwir bought out Tilly, and the bookshop and the flower shop and Silas's family property, and countless other properties, well, that was something I couldn't live with. Especially not if Anwir was a front for the Inquisition.

My sister would always come first, but I was dead in the water until visiting hour at three. I had no doubt that Dana would find Hector. And Hector could work his legal magic without me in the room.

"Vincent," I said, turning to face him. "I know what I need to do."

"What do you mean, Holly?"

I took a deep breath, inhaling the scent of old books and polished wood. It was a comforting smell, but my decision was no comfort at all, not even a cold one.

"There's a temple in the Crone's Wood. It's sacred to the Trembol family. Lucas's family."

"I've heard whispers of such a place, but…"

"Lucas has been sick, so he went there to recover. He's the only one who knows how to find the crones, and they're our best chance to fix the haywire magic."

The magnitude of what I was proposing hit me all at once. My heart leaped into my throat and my breath felt shallow. I was going to venture into that nightmare forest where last night I'd stumbled blindly, as sounds not quite like voices called to me from the trees and lights not quite like eyes stared down. The place where Hazel had almost died.

Vincent placed a hand on my arm. Even through my shirt, I felt the coolness of his touch. It sent a shiver down my spine, but a warmer feeling rose to meet it.

"Are you certain?" he asked. "The Crone's Wood is a dangerous place. Most humans who have ventured into it have never returned. The few who have speak of trails shifting, compasses spinning. I know that you entered the wood last night, but you had your grandmother's hagstone and Augustus's familiar to guide you, did you not?"

Part of me wanted to melt into his arms, to stare into his centuries-deep eyes, to surrender to that voice of command and let him protect me from whatever was coming. But I couldn't. This was my mess to clean up.

"I have to try. And I don't think I'll get lost. Arnie—I mean Arnold gave me directions to the temple. Once I find it, Lucas can guide me the rest of the way."

Vincent gently squeezed my arm, and for a moment I thought he might try to stop me, but he let go. A small, sad smile played at the corners of his mouth.

"I understand," he said softly. "I would come with you if… if I thought my presence wouldn't be a hindrance."

A hindrance? Why? I opened my mouth to ask him, but suddenly I understood. Lucas had told me that he was suspicious of Vincent's kind. He might not look too kindly on Vincent showing up at his family's most sacred place.

Vincent walked over to his desk, pulled out a drawer, withdrew something shiny from it. He came back and offered it to me on his two upturned palms. It was an ornate dagger.

"If you're going into the woods, you should be prepared. This has been in my family for generations."

"I don't think I'll need—"

"You don't know what you'll need. Neither do I. That's why you must be prepared. Take it."

I took it. Our hands touched. I looked into his eyes and saw hunger, longing, sadness, and… Maybe it was a trick of the warm, guttering light glinting off the dagger's watery blade, but for an instant I saw—could have sworn I saw—something else in his eyes, too.

I saw flames.

45

$\mathcal{I}$ stood in the hallway on the fourth floor, watching the yellow elevator light count its way up. What had happened back there in Vincent's office? Had we really almost kissed? Hazel had teased me about it the first time I'd come up here, but it didn't seem possible that anything could happen. Now, it almost had, and it was so much, so soon, so overwhelming I could barely think about that moment on the sofa without my memory overheating and cutting to staticky white.

Vincent's gift, the dagger, was in my right hand. I held it in front of me, away from my body, like it was one of the snakes in Mr. Fletcher's beard. It was a heavy, awful, beautiful object, with a walnut handle and a silver blade shaped like an elongated heart. The blade and the pommel were both inlaid with gold-and-lapis-blue scrollwork so fine I couldn't imagine how it was made without machinery, but it must have been, because the dagger was in Vincent's family for generations, and you could tell just by looking it was old, maybe ancient.

It belonged in a museum. It would make sense there. You

could stroll by after a heavy brunch and wonder sleepily: What kind of person would ever own a knife like that? How much did it cost? Did it ever kill anybody? If it had killed someone, it would be more intriguing than disturbing, because that curtain had closed centuries ago, and everyone involved had long since passed.

The dagger would have made sense in a museum, but it was all wrong here, in this dingy municipal hallway that smelled like floor wax and burned coffee. I felt wrong holding it, too, like a thief.

The elevator dinged and its steel doors shuddered open. I stepped into the humming fluorescent-lit box with its washed-out wood paneling and the pink safety certificate. The doors closed behind me. I moved the dagger to my left hand then pushed the button for the first floor. Something above me whirred and I felt lighter as the car descended.

Above the elevator door, the number four went dark, and the number three lit up. I felt a pang of worry needle me just above my stomach. If the elevator stopped and someone else saw me, what would they think of me with my dagger?

The number three blinked off and the number two lit up.

I needed to stash the knife, but it hadn't come with a scabbard or sheath, and I didn't have a purse or any sort of bag with me. If this were an action movie, I might have stuck it in my waistband, but that seemed like a great way to get a surprise appendectomy.

The number two blinked off, and the number one lit up with a ding. The elevator came to a jerking halt, and the door machinery clanked into action. My heart sped up and in a rush of panic I thrust the knife behind my back, hiding it behind my body.

The doors slid open, but there was nobody waiting on the other side. All my tension melted, and I found myself grinning, because the knife-behind-the back move was so over-

242 | TABATHA GRAY

the-top, so comically arch, so Colonel-Mustard-in-the-library-with-the-revolver that I couldn't help but smile, then laugh because the only thing worse than a psycho with a dagger is one who is also grinning.

I stepped out of the elevator into an empty hall. The floor by the brass mailboxes was dry, though I imagined I could see the faintest rim of white on top of the red and white terrazzo pebbles.

Past the mailboxes, a blue wire rack held a stack of large white priority envelopes. I took one and slipped the dagger in and nodded to myself in a satisfied sort of way. If you walked down the street holding a dagger by the handle, you were a threat. But if you put the dagger in an envelope, you were, what? An antiques dealer?

I kept walking toward the rear of the building, past the tiny post office, past the meeting room with the city council schedule taped to it, to the back door Lin had told me about. I opened it and stepped out into a hot, red haze of wildfire smoke. It had gotten worse, but it didn't matter. I had my instructions: *Go to Silas's house. Find the lightning tree. Follow the stream uphill to the clearing.*

I followed the same path I'd taken the night of the fire, past Lucas's store (still closed), through a residential neighborhood, out to the outskirts of town where small industrial buildings gave way to a rocky ledge overlooking the clearing where I'd once attended an Ostara egg hunt as a toddler. Tilly had told me the story recently, to embarrass me in that way older relations always try to do. But since recovering my memory, I had my own impression of it, hazy like a dream.

It had been cool that morning, and cooler still, because I had been running. The bigger kids were ahead, a wall of pastel blue and pink. They made an incredible noise, yelling and shrieking as they plucked bright colored eggs from the grass and put them in their baskets. It was a

TANGLED CHARMS | 243

feeding frenzy, and I was the runt, and I worried all the eggs might be gone. Then my eyes landed on it, a smooth object, nestled in a tuft of grass. It wasn't dyed like the others, but the egg fascinated me because of its strange translucent yellow white. I remember the pride I felt as I picked it up and turned around to show my parents. And confusion, when the thin shell crumpled in my hand, and revulsion as the watery, rotten egg spilled down onto my arm and face and into my nostrils. Even now I could still smell that sulfur stink. My stomach turned, and I wondered if I might have to throw up on the side of the narrow gravel road.

The heat wasn't helping. The sun, red-tinged by smoke, was overhead, slightly in front of me. My forehead was sweaty and my jeans felt like a sauna. The back of my throat had that familiar dirty taste and raw feeling.

I stopped, shaded my eyes with my nondagger hand, and scanned the field ahead. Silas's house was up ahead, a small red shack, like a drop of blood against the tall black trees of the Crone's Wood. His truck was gone.

It was a small house, only a shack, really. I doubted it had more than one bedroom, and wouldn't have been surprised if that bedroom doubled as the kitchen.

This wasn't the McIntosh family house, of course. The McIntoshes were one of Charm Haven's seven founding families. (Seven houses on seven hills, seven families where magic dwells.) Their house and, I supposed, their hill was farther away from town than even the Thorns' had been.

No, this shack was something else. Perhaps it had once been used by hunters, or loggers, or maybe Silas had built it to get away from an overbearing family, though it seemed odd that he would choose to live next to a forest that obviously terrified him. That was a mystery for another day. I had my instructions:

Walk north along the perimeter until you see a tree that's been split in two by lightning.

My right arm was tired from carrying the dagger envelope, so I shifted it to my left and wished I'd brought a compass instead. I was supposed to walk north, but which way was that?

A couple of years ago, when I still had my bookstore, there had been a hot new series, a sort of *Little House on the Prairie*, but with werewolves. The plot was all over the place, and the characters were a little thin, but there had been a scene where little Moxie Anne (That was really her name.) got lost after bandits attacked the family's covered wagon. She was able to find her way home because she knew it was to the north, and moss grows on the north side of trees.

Well, I had a lot of trees, and they had the glorious, bright green lichen-studded moss that I've only seen in the Pacific Northwest. The moss was on the right side of the trees. So to go north, I just needed to turn right. As if to confirm it, I heard a gull cry from my left, and felt the gentle slope of the land down to where it would eventually meet the ocean at the ferry dock on the island's south side.

I headed right, through the low grass. Far above me, the trees caught the wind coming off the ocean. Their upper boughs swayed with a distant rustling. I became suddenly aware of how small I was. It was flash-fire panic that left me feeling like a gnat buzzing around the legs of giants. If the trees had eyes I would have seemed a frantic thing, a blur of speed and worry that was born and blinked out in half a heartbeat. And lonely too. So alone.

The trees were packed into the forest so tightly that they had never been alone. Their canopies merged to create a permanent twilight, made darker still by my sun-constricted eyes. To me the forest seemed like a great dark mass, a smooth black wall, blank and inscrutable except up ahead where part of an enormous tree leaned heavily over the clearing.

Once, it must have stood taller than city hall. Now it was split down the center. Its two halves leaned to opposite sides, making a splintery *V* shape. The exposed heartwood had turned a silver gray. At the top, around the edges, the wood had been burned to black cinders.

I reached out and touched the rough bark of the lightning tree and thought I felt some trace of the power of the storm in it, like lightning always lingers in your vision a second after it strikes. When I looked through its cleft, the dark forest seemed... clearer somehow. Less murky. I saw faint outlines of the forms within, of the enormous tree trunks, fallen branches, ferns, mushrooms, and...

A shadow passed across the already-dark image. Something with no outline, as if the night itself had wandered across my path. My stomach turned, but not from the heat, and I remembered Silas's story. The story his grandmother had told him when he'd played at her feet. The story that wasn't a story at all, but a warning:

If you go into the woods, keep your eyes down, don't look up at the trees. If you look up in the trees, and see what's in the branches, you'd better hope that it doesn't see you. And if you see, and it sees, you better act as if you didn't. Let your eyes drift slowly away. Walk away slowly, too.

And never, *never run.*

46

My eyes were playing tricks on me. They had to be. If I didn't enter the wood at the lighting tree, I might never find the stream, or the temple, or Lucas. Magic would stay broken, and Anwir would win, and I would have returned to Charm Haven after twenty years, to have it slip through my fingers like sand.

The shadow I'd seen through the lightning tree cleft had only been a side effect of my sun-dazzled eyes adjusting to the forest gloom. And there was nothing in the trees. That scary story was just something Silas's grandma had told a child to keep them from wandering too far into the woods. Wasn't it the same story we'd all heard growing up? If you don't clean your plate, the crones will get you.

But I'd met the crones. They might not be normal, but they were decent people, or witches, or whatever. And hadn't they told us themselves that a lot of the scary noises and spooky things people associated with the wood were just tricks played to keep people away?

I'd been scared when I ran into the wood to find Hazel.

But I would have been scared in any forest at night. And now that I thought about it, when I looked through the hagstone, searching for my sister, I had looked up into the trees and lived to tell the tale. The only monsters I'd found in the Crone's Wood were people who didn't belong there.

My eyes were definitely playing tricks on me, and my mind was in cahoots. This was an ordinary forest, with ordinary trees and people I knew in it. People I needed.

I shifted the envelope with the dagger back to my right hand, then walked past the lightning tree, into the Crone's Wood.

It was cool in the canopy shade, and my sweaty forehead and upper arms felt clammy. The forest floor felt spongy under my shoes, and I wondered how many feet of fallen spruce needles and dead-fall branches I would have to dig through to reach the dark loamy topsoil. All around me, the massive cedars creaked slowly, as the upper wind caught their canopies like sails. But below, where I was, the air was still and damp with musty moss and mushroom smells, and a strange absence of prickly wildfire smoke. As my eyes adjusted to the dim, I saw that it wasn't uniformly dark. Sunlight peeked through the rustling canopy, moving with the wind, lighting the forest floor with dancing rays of sunlight.

It was... beautiful.

And in here, somewhere, were the crones. They lived in the wood. They would know the wood better than anyone. Hopefully they would know about the deal the founders had made to keep the trees from attacking. But to find them I needed Lucas.

Walk west until you hit a stream. Easy enough. I was already walking west, and I could tell I was from the moss growing on the tree to my left.

Who were the crones, exactly? From their witchy clothes to their camper van bubbling with green smoke, I'd was certain they knew a spell or two. They'd gone around the world in that van, and come back with the souvenirs to prove it, and yet they'd only been gone for a couple of days.

Maybe they knew more than a spell or two. Much more. Maybe they could fix the haywire magic themselves, or look into a crystal ball and see who killed the inquisitor. That is, if they wanted to help. On that score, I was hopeful, because the scary stories weren't the only stories people told about the crones. While most of the few people who went into the wood never returned, the ones who did had curious stories.

Hadn't Dotty Lundgren told me about her crazy uncle with the bad leg who had wandered into the Crone's Wood on a dare? He'd come back a week later walking straighter than he had in years, but he was crazier, too. Kept babbling about giant chickens. Dotty told me in a can-you-believe-this sort of way and I'd relayed it to my parents and they'd told me that Dotty Lundgren's uncle had a problem controlling himself with certain mind-altering substances, and that if he walked into the room that I was to leave. Maybe they were right, but someone had fixed his leg.

A cracking sound overhead snapped me back to the present. I tensed. My hand tightened around the dagger inside the envelope, but it was probably just the trees, swaying, creaking in their normal way. Either that or the echo of a cracking branch I'd stepped on without realizing it. I let out a sigh and tried to relax.

I was heading west, past trees with trunks so big you could carve a tunnel and drive a car through them. Enormous roots snaked underfoot, studded with bushy ferns that rustled as I scrambled past them. The roots were smoother than the trunks, and redder too. The rough bark on the

TANGLED CHARMS | 249

trunks was dark, except for the trees on my right, which were covered in bright green moss.

I stopped.

My right side? Hadn't the moss been on my left just a moment ago?

I retraced my steps in my mind. I'd been walking north in the clearing, and turned left at the lighting tree. I was supposed to keep west until I hit the stream. Moving west, the mossy sides of the trees would be on my left, like they had been when I was started. Now they were on my right, which could only mean I'd gotten turned around.

"Okay," I said to myself in a thin, tight voice. "You got turned around. No problem."

Above me there was a rustling sound followed by a sudden crack that made me jump and sent my heart pounding. Something above me creaked, like a door in a haunted house slowly opening, or like a branch that was holding too much weight and was slowly giving way.

My thoughts flashed to the too-alive trees that had destroyed the town and retreated to the wood, then to the other words in the history. Other creatures. No detail. No description. Just... other.

And I realized then, in a shocking flash of clarity why the crones went to so much trouble to keep the people of Charm Haven out of the wood. How you could reconcile stories of people disappearing without a trace, with other stories where the crones were, if not benevolent, then a neutral force, like nature itself.

And it was obvious when you thought about it. You saw it in the way the ferns nestled in the roots of the trees, while the moss and lichen clung to its branches. You heard it in the faint far-off chattering of birds in the upper branches, and in the woody chirping of squirrels. If you dug into the loamy soil you would smell it in the petrichor and see it in the dozens of pill bugs and millipedes and pink fleshy worms that squirmed and scurried and dove away.

This was a forest, an ecosystem, an entire world in miniature, and lots of things lived here. And just like the larger world, it was dangerous.

Above me, there was another crack...

47

rack... crack... crack...

I stood still among the massive cedars, heart hammering in my ears, forcing myself not to look up into the branches. The groaning of wood under weight had slowed to single cracking sounds like gunshots, almost far enough apart to blend in with the lazy creaking of the forest as its upper boughs swayed. Almost. But I knew what I had heard.

It had started a rustling, like someone shaking a spruce bough. And the tiny motes of pollen floating in the columns of sunlight had puffed out, moved by a sudden gust of air. It had been followed by the groaning of an overloaded branch that had sounded like a door slowly swinging open.

I didn't look up, but I felt the weight of something above me, something massive, hanging just out of reach. Nothing but something massive could have made the branches of these ancient trees groan like that. Nothing but something huge could displace so much air as to cause its own breeze.

I noticed for the first time that those shafts of sunlight, which sparkled through the high canopy and danced on the spongy forest floor were keeping their distance from me.

They played across enormous ferns, red-brown cedar bark, blankets of needles, saplings growing from nursery trees, wood-ear mushrooms cutting into logs like rusty hatchets. They skittered and danced, and they sometimes moved toward me, but when they got about a dozen feet away they blinked out.

My breath was like a bow saw cutting into a green plank. I felt cold, and not just because of the beads of clammy sweat on my forehead, my cheeks, my upper arms. My thoughts raced so fast they merged into a white blur that might have been no thought at all, then my mind went blank, burned clean as the forest floor after a wildfire. Or maybe my thoughts had stopped because they had reached their final destination. My churning, burning brain had figured out the reason the lights blinked out before they reached me.

I was in shadow.

I was in *something's* shadow.

I swallowed a scream. My vision zoomed in like a camera. I wanted to pan up, to see what was above me, whatever massive creature was above me, big enough to cast a shadow so wide.

Don't look up. Don't look up. Don't look up.

I was supposed to be looking for something, though. My thoughts picked up, slow as molasses. The stream. I was looking for the stream, but not up, and casually as if I was walking through a Sunday garden without a care in the world. But I wasn't walking. I was frozen, still.

I willed my legs to move in the direction they'd been moving just a moment ago, before the sounds and the weight and the shadow. At least I think it was the direction, or, maybe not because the mossy sides of the trees were on my right—but shouldn't they have been on my left? I couldn't remember. I didn't care.

I had to put distance between myself and the weight, and

TANGLED CHARMS | 253

I was already out of the shadow because the dancing lights were here, running up my sneakers and onto my jeans, turning them a searing white, then racing off. I picked up my pace.

But if I was traveling east, that meant I needed to turn around, and that would take me back to the shadow, which was a nonstarter. But east meant I was moving toward the lightning tree, toward the clearing with wide-open land, toward Charm Haven and Gran's house and tea and hot baths.

I had to stop myself from breaking into a run because all I wanted was to get away from the shadow, the rustling, the reeking, to reach the clearing, where nothing could hide above me.

Ahead of me, two enormous tree trunks made a kind of gate. But that was just a trick of my mind. It was only two trees, growing close together, their trunks like ruddy brown posts stuck into the earth, and the passage between them outlined in green moss. *In green... moss...*

But that was impossible. Moss grew on the north sides of trees. I knew it from that stupid book. I knew it because I'd followed the moss north, slightly uphill, away from the port on the south side of the island. But here, the mossy sides of both trees faced each other. They pointed in opposite directions.

And I realized with a rising horror as I scanned left and right that in this part of the forest, none of the mossy sides aligned. I was in a place where none of the rules applied.

I was lost.

Above me I heard a rustling, and a groan from an over-worked branch that sounded like the door of a haunted house opening. The motes of pollen in the air puffed. The dancing light through the canopy blinked out in a circle around me. Suddenly I didn't care if I was lost. I was too busy wondering if the low, slow suspiration above me was what I feared it was. I was too busy wondering if the breeze that tickled the little hairs on the nape of my neck wasn't just a little... too... warm.

I ran.

48

I ran through the forest not caring when way I went. I ran and my heart pounded and I felt bright burning work its way up my lungs. I ran and I heaved moist, mushroomy air, as ferns whipped my legs raw, as branches scraped my neck and upper arms. I ran and I shivered, and a desperate crazy knowledge blossomed.

It was following me.

That rustling sound, and the creaking, and the shadow, and the warm breath were following me, almost lazily, too like the cat I'd once seen catch a spider. The poor spider would run on its tiny legs, and for a while the cat would almost seem to forget about it. But just when the spider thought it had made it to some shady corner, some nook where it could be safe, the cat would bat it with a paw and it would fly to the other side of the room, which might as well have been China.

Had the little spider grown up? Was it following me, swinging itself from tree to tree with sticky webs, lining up to shoot it at me, tangle me, trip me to suck out my life a drop at a time?

I ran as light from the canopy strobed my eyes. I squinted and the world went darker. Ahead I saw a shape on the ground. I jumped. Landed hard. Breathing burned. My legs burned.

I found a mud-brown animal trail. It disappeared into the bushes. I jumped over them. Snagged my foot. Stumbled forward. Caught myself.

A crashing sound came from overhead. A torrent of cedar needles rained down on me and I forced my sore legs faster, but I didn't know how much longer I could take.

I glanced back into the trees. Saw a dark shape twenty feet up. A shape with yellow eyes.

I tripped. Stumbled. Caught myself and saw what I had tripped on. It was a tiny wooden bridge built over a dry stream bed no wider than my hand.

I forced myself forward and felt a crunch under my shoe like a hundred toothpicks snapping, snagging my legs.

My vision swam. My heart beat fast and sticky. I heaved for breath.

The shape in the tree hadn't moved. It watched me, but it hadn't moved.

I stopped and leaned over, supporting my hands on my knees, and panted. I couldn't run anymore. My blurry eyes swam into focus and I saw what I'd tripped on.

Around my feet a miniature city spread across the forest floor, fantastical buildings in silvery wood, all towers and spires and flying buttresses, with vaulted roofs like upturned ships and windows shaped like roses and a steep roofs lined with gargoyles. It was a city of Notre Dame cathedrals, of Versailles palaces, of fairy-tale Bavarian castles, all constructed and carved from the same silvery wood in detail so small I could barely see it. A few dozen feet ahead of me, a fallen tree lay at an angle across the city. At first glance it appeared to be a nursery tree, one of the logs that falls and

TANGLED CHARMS | 257

rots and gathers falling leaves and needles until it has a layer of fresh topsoil from which fresh seedlings can sprout. But there were no seedlings growing on that tree. The city was built right up against it, and onto the rotten part and past it. No, it wasn't rotten. It had been excavated. The tree was the source of the silvery wood from which the city was constructed.

This was whittler work. I'd seen it before, at Gran's house, first when we'd arrived and noticed that the frame around our ancestor Augustus's portrait had been eaten away in places, and in others it had been augmented by ornate miniature woodwork. The farther Hazel and I had gone into the house, the more elaborate the constructions had become, and we'd even found a building not unlike ones around my feet.

The buildings appeared to have been abandoned, but I knew better than that. The whittlers moved too fast for ordinary people to see them. I'd eventually gotten them to leave Gran's house by offering them a drink of fresh cream. I hadn't given much thought to where they'd returned to, but I was starting to suspect it was here. The whittlers had only been at the house for weeks, but this city seemed the work of years. The shadowy forest floor was covered with elaborate wooden architecture as far as I could see.

I picked my way forward, like a giant walking down the Champs-Élysées. But a friendly giant, doing her best not to smash anything.

The dark shape hadn't moved. It was still behind me in the trees. Maybe it was afraid to enter the city. While the whittlers might be tiny, they were so fast they could probably build a cage around their enemy before the enemy took two steps. I hoped they remembered the cream I had given them and wouldn't be too upset about the bridge.

I used to have a geometry teacher who would start each

class by writing a problem on the whiteboard. He would cap his marker, set it on the little tray, turn to the class and say the words that he seemed to take as a kind of mantra: *Stop. Don't panic. You know more than you think.*

I had stopped, and I had panicked, but that tide seemed to roll out and I felt a cool-headed clarity rushing in to replace it.

You know more than you think.

Okay, what did I know? I'd been chased by a large beast. It had followed me here in the trees. I couldn't read its mind but I had to assume it was hunting me.

I stood in a part of the forest filled with elaborate doll-house-sized buildings. It was the work of the whittlers. I couldn't tell if they were nearby, or had built this place then abandoned it. In either case, I didn't need to worry about hurting them because they were so fast. To them I was as slow as the red-brown cedars that surrounded me. If I'd had a bottle of cream handy, I might have been able to ask the whittlers for help, but I didn't, so I was on my own.

I had Vincent's dagger, still in the envelope. I could stand and fight, but the beast was so large I doubted the dagger could do anything but make it mad.

Finding Lucas was out. Finding the crones was on hold. The only thing that mattered now was getting away from that dark shape looming on the edge of the whittler settlement. It jumped sideways to another tree, which rustled and groaned. The dancing light from the canopy raked across it, but little points of light were so bright in the gloom they burned away any sense of color or texture. I still couldn't tell what sort of beast it was.

I noticed something, then, not about the beast, but about the trees it had jumped between. Both were streaked with green on their right sides. The surrounding trees were the same. Whatever strange force had caused the moss to grow on different sides earlier in the forest, didn't seem to be present here. And if the moss pointed north, then I knew which direction would take me out of the wood.

But could I make it?

I was out of shape and out of breath and couldn't run much longer. I had one shot left, one final burst of speed before my legs would become numb stumps and I began to stumble and trip and fall.

But I might not need to run for long. Even though it seemed like the beast had been chasing me for hours, it couldn't have been more than a few minutes. And half of that time had been spent moving parallel to the clearing, not away from it.

And the beast seemed to avoid the whittler city. As long as I was in it I could walk at a normal pace and conserve my energy for my sprint to freedom. I didn't want to turn my back on the looming shadow in the trees, but that was the only way out.

I started walking slowly, picking my way through strange architectural wonderland, hoping that I was right. Hoping that whatever was following me might be afraid of the whittlers, or avoid them naturally, like animals avoid human settlements.

The ground shook. A gust of wind blew thin wisps of my hair into my face. I froze. Muscles tight. Then, with an effort like ripping grass up by the roots I wrenched my neck around to see what had made the noise.

It stood on four legs, just outside the whittler city, black against the red-dark cedars. It was bigger than any grizzly bear, and wider than tree behind it. Its body drifted slowly up and down with its breath as it regarded me with hateful yellow eyes.

It charged.

49

Maybe the whittlers were here after all, because time slowed to a sluggish crawl. I stood, frozen, gripping the envelope with its dagger like I'd been electrocuted. The beast was maybe fifty feet away, and as it bounded toward me, hanging in the air, I saw what it was.

It was wider than a semitruck, and almost as tall, and covered in pitch-black feathers like those of a crow. Its yellow eyes glowed above a sharp black beak that was bigger than my head. But it wasn't a bird. It didn't have wings on its back. It had four enormous paws with shiny black talons, and legs about as big around as my torso.

It made a wild shriek as its front paws landed on the whittler's Notre Dame, and small bits of silvery wood exploded out from under. Its right paw caught on a tower and tore through it with a sound like a thousand twigs being snapped and its steeple flew to the right, hit a tree trunk and exploded.

The crow... bear... beast's back feet landed with a crunch, and I saw the cords of muscle rippling under its oil-black feathers. Its yellow eyes locked on mine and I couldn't look away as it charged me. I watched, as if my death wasn't seconds away, as if it was a show on TV, which it had to be, because it couldn't be real.

The breeze cooled the lingering sweat on my forehead, kicked the small hairs up around my neck into a swirling halo. I breathed in and oily muskiness coated my nostrils and the roof of my mouth.

Whittler wreckage flew by my head, a dazzle of silver-white confetti that smelled like fresh-sawn planks. It peppered my face and arms, and then something larger, a bell tower maybe, hit me with its pointy end right above my eye. A bright clean ray of pain shot down and broke whatever spell had frozen me. My whole body jerked awake with panic. I had to get out of there.

I ran in the direction I'd calculated earlier. My legs were doing better than I expected. My breath was deep and easy. I must have been drawing from some ancient pool of energy that comes to all small creatures before they get eaten.

I leaped over the Taj Mahal, or something like it, and found a great, broad avenue where I could run without being tripped. Behind me it sounded like the world was ending.

The beast was a pool of black in a cloud of splinters. The whittler city wasn't any match for those enormous paws, but the sheer scale of it was slowing him down. Not much. But enough to give me a chance.

I reached the outskirts of the miniature city. I leaped over a log and saw that the forest was getting brighter. The moss hadn't played any tricks on me. The clearing had to be ahead.

My chances might not be any better there, but some force had kept that bizarre creature from leaving the wood and wandering into Charm Haven. Maybe the edge of the wood was a boundary, a barrier, an invisible fence that it couldn't cross. It had to be.

I ran past a dead tree that had fallen against another. It

came crashing down beside me, and the beast let out an angry, Jurassic cry like something from a Godzilla movie.

Light sparkled through the trees up ahead.

My legs felt like fire, but it was good fire now. It filled me with a crazy primal joy. I was in danger, but almost free. I'd been lost but now I was found. My heart and my lungs and my muscles sang an ancient song and the words were: *I'm alive. I'm alive. I'm alive.*

Something hard hit my shoulder.

I stumbled and fell.

I flung my arms out but a knee-high root slammed into my stomach and knocked out my breath.

50

An enormous weight pressed down on my back, driving my face into the spongy ground. Behind me, I could sense the slow rise and fall of the creature's breathing.

My mouth was covered, and my nose was bent, and the weight drove the knee-high tree root deeper against my bottom ribs with urgent singing pain. Breathing was hard and it whistled.

I balled my hands into fists and drove them into the ground. They sank a little, but I couldn't push up.

I twisted my neck back, searching for a way to escape, but I only saw an enormous, black talon. It rubbed against my cheek, cold and hard, and buried itself in the soft earth with a crunch.

I couldn't breathe at all and was feeling lightheaded. Tears filled my eyes and spilled down my cheeks. I didn't want to die. I didn't want to leave my sister with no family. I didn't want her to think I'd abandoned her, or for our last moment to be that awful time in the kitchen when she thought I betrayed her when I was trying to keep her safe.

Safe? What a joke. I was the one about to get eaten by the freakish offspring of a crow, a grizzly bear and an apartment building. *Didn't see that one coming, did you, Holly? Didn't write that one in your Bullet Journal, did you?*

Who was it that said when you were about to die, your life flashes before your eyes? Well, they got it all wrong. I didn't have time to see my sister one last time. I didn't see a glowing door where Mom and Dad were waiting for me with harps and chocolate chip cookies, to greet me and tell me how much they loved me, how proud they were, how everything works in the end even if it might not seem that way.

I only felt a dull sort of blankness. Sadness, fear, panic were all there, but muted, like music from a ship sailing away.

It was over. I was done. The beast was too strong. I couldn't fight it. I stopped trying to press myself up. I let my head rest in the dirt. I unballed my fists and felt the envelope slide through my fingers…

The envelope?

The envelope contained Vincent's dagger.

It wouldn't be big enough to kill the thing, but I didn't need to kill it. Only get it off my back so I could breathe.

I reached for the envelope, found it then shook it until something hard hit the ground with a ringing thud. I grabbed the dagger. Lashed out behind me in blind, awkward strokes.

My arm bent the wrong way but I forced it, and felt the flat of the blade strike something slick and pillowy. But the flat of the blade couldn't bite. I needed a better angle.

If I could only twist the dagger around in my hand, the point would go through the feathers, and into the flesh. I twisted it but the beast shifted. The dagger jolted out of my hand. I tried to catch it, but caught only air and heard that ringing thud as it fell to the ground. The pressure on my back increased. Something sharp prodded the soft flesh of my neck. I couldn't breathe at all.

I groped out blindly searching, not caring if I grabbed the blade, not caring if it cut me because if I didn't breathe soon I'd pass out. I felt prickly dead cedar needles… soft moss… scratchy ferns… dirt… tree roots…

Breath blew against my skin, hot and ripe with the odors of dead things left outside to bake. I could only see an inch of dirt ahead of me, and now even that was filled with black spots that swam across my vision. I had the strangest feeling like I was floating, like the Everest mountain climbers said they felt when they were trapped by a storm and their oxygen tanks ran out, and they felt the cold creep in through their goose-down parkas, through their skin, cooling their blood until they swore that it almost felt as if they were floating without a care in the world in a warm tropical ocean, gently being rolled to sea by the receding tide.

My hand clapped onto cold metal. Sharp pain woke me. I found the dagger's hilt and curled it around it in an overhand grip so the point of the elongated heart would face the beast.

I lashed my arm back. The dagger plunged through the beast's feathers. It pierced the flesh below and sizzled. The beast screamed. The weight lifted.

I took a huge gasping breath and scrambled forward. Turned. Held the dagger in front of me.

The beast had backed up too. Its feathers were ruffled where I had struck it and a stream of white smoke was rising off the wound. I looked at the dagger and its gold and lapis-blue inlay glowed subtly. It wasn't any ordinary dagger.

Oxygen slammed into my brain. I felt giddy, but forced myself to think. The clearing was an unknown distance behind me. If I ran for it, the beast would leap at me again, but I had to put distance between us.

I held the dagger in front of me, the tip pointing up and at an angle to the beast. Tentatively, I reached my right foot back, made sure I was on solid ground, and stepped backward.

The beast cocked its head slightly to the side and looked at me with those yellow eyes. I was more dangerous that it had imagined, but it still thought of me as dinner.

I reached my foot back again. It hit a root or something, but I was able to step over it. Every step toward the clearing was a step toward safety.

The beast stared at me but didn't move.

I reached my foot back again, even farther this time. From the rustling sound and the soft resistance I could tell I'd stepped on a fern, but I figured the fern could take it. I stepped back onto it.

The beast stepped toward me with a huffing sound like a bull. The tendril of smoke rising from its wound was almost gone. Its slick black feathers were no longer mussed there, and I saw the muscle move under them as it tensed and shifted its weight onto its hind legs.

It was going to pounce.

I held the dagger with both hands up, like a porcupine with one quill. The air seemed to ripple and warp, like the air above hot pavement.

The beast leaped, extending both front legs, ten talons against my one, all of them aimed toward my face, my heart, the soft tender parts of which it would make a meal.

It was a struggle to keep the knife up. My body wanted to collapse into a heap, to play possum, to play sick, to play dead.

The beast flew at me and shrieked a sound like a pterodactyl. A sound so loud it filled my world. The last sound I would ever hear.

51

I heard a thud of bodies colliding, and something hit the black-feathered beast. It was another animal, smaller but moving fast enough to knock the beast off course and send it tumbling off to my left.

I swiveled so that it the dagger faced the beast, which was pawing at its face, trying to free itself from the orange, black and white jaguar. The large cat sank its teeth into black feathers and clawed at the yellow eyes.

It must have hit something because the beast let out a cry of shock and pain, and reared back on two legs then whipped its head back and forth. The jaguar flew off and rolled across the spongy ground.

The beast stared at me and seemed to calculate, weighing new danger against the prospect of a meal. The scale must have tipped in my favor, because it snorted, turned, and bounded up a tree. I couldn't see it run away, but heard the rustling and creaking grow more and more distant until finally I couldn't hear it at all.

I let my dagger hand fall and walked over to where the jaguar had landed. Instead of finding a cat there, I found a man. He was tall with messy auburn hair, a tan line on his forearm where he usually rolled up his plaid sleeves. He wasn't wearing a plaid shirt now. He wasn't wearing anything, except the green spruce bough he held over himself like a fig leaf in a painting.

"Thanks, Lucas," I said. I should have been blushing. And in any other circumstance I might have been sneaking glances at his muscular arms and well-defined chest. But I still hadn't shaken the feeling of my imminent death.

"No problem," he said, rubbing the side of his head with his palm, wincing. "Just a completely ordinary day, fighting creatures from a nightmare. What are you doing out here, Holly?"

"Coming to look for you."

I saw the confusion on his face, and then something else. His face seemed to flicker to its animal form, then back to human. It happened so fast I might have thought I was imagining things. Then it happened again and Lucas looked away, embarrassed.

"What was that thing?" I asked.

"I was about to ask you the same question."

"I heard you weren't feeling well."

"Coming to bring me some chicken soup?" *Flicker.*

"Not exactly."

"Then what?" *Flicker.*

"Coming to ask your help."

"I'm the one who needs help." There was a hot, shimmering feeling in the air, and bristly orange fur emerged from his skin. It wasn't just a flicker this time. His face elongated and became that of the jaguar, and his body changed until he was completely in his animal form in front of me. I wondered if I should talk to him. Would he understand me? Would he be able to answer back? An instant later he was back to his old self.

"Something's wrong with me," he said. "I can't stay in one form for long. As soon as I get there, I change back. I... That's why I came to the wood. I didn't want people to see me like this."

I remembered what his brother had said. People are people and even in Charm Haven they can be jerks about those who are different. I could see why Lucas would want his privacy.

"Has it ever happened before?" I asked.

"I've never even heard of something like this. I'm a shifter, not a werewolf. I've always been able to control it."

"When did the problem start?"

"Night before last."

"I was afraid you were going to say that," I said. "It's the magic. It's been going haywire and causing all sorts of crazy things to happen around town. You were there when I released it. It must have done something to your shifting abilities. I'm going to find the crones to ask them to help."

"Why do you think they would be able to help?"

"Because all of this happened before, when people first came to Charm Haven. Magic revolted and trees from the Crone's Wood destroyed the encampment. The founders made a deal to fix the problem. I think the crones might be able to fill us in on the details."

"Makes sense, but they can be hard to find."

"Will you help me?"

He nodded, then cocked his head to one side. "Do you hear that?"

My heart hitched. Could the beast be coming around for another pass at us? But I didn't hear the rustling or the creaking of overloaded branches. I shook my head. "What did you hear?"

"A... humming sound. Or maybe a buzzing? It's hard to describe. Never mind. Follow me."

270 | TABATHA GRAY

I followed him as he led me through the wood. Every few seconds, he would flicker. Every few minutes Lucas would shift more completely from human to jaguar, or back. It slowed us down a little, but not as much as you'd think. I tried not to look, since the constant unpredictable shifting left him naked, but even with the few accidental (and not so) glances I took, I could tell that he was equally comfortable in both forms.

As we walked I filled him in on the murder, on Anwir, my sister, and the haywire magic. He filled me in too. He had been resting at his family temple when a breeze had brought him the scent of the beast. That hot oily musk had been like a trumpet in a quiet room to his animal senses. He'd known at once that the beast was unlike anything he'd seen before, and he'd tracked it not with the intent to kill, but with a curiosity driven by boredom. It had become a much more urgent matter after he picked up my scent. It had only taken him a few minutes to find us, and he had come just in time.

We passed the whittler city. It looked like pictures I've seen of towns in Oklahoma after a tornado rips through. Buildings had collapsed into piles of splintery rubble along the path the beast had taken. But as we passed I heard a strange humming sound, and as I watched, the rubble cleared away, seemingly on its own. The broken bits of buildings vanished. Jagged beams and planks were smoothed. Then they seemed to regrow. It was like watching a time-lapse video of a tree breaking through the soil, reaching tall and swelling, pushing hard green buds from branches then softening them to flowers. Only this wasn't a plant, it was a city. And it wasn't happening on its own, either. It was being done by invisible hands. I imagined that humming was the chatter and the laughter and the singing of countless whittlers happily rebuilding, so fast that they blurred to nothing, while I moved slow as cedars.

Lucas was navigating by smell, by the feel of the forest floor, by the sounds of the birds and squirrels. He would stop and scent a tree, or a patch of moss, or one of the large sunken areas filled with brown spruce needles and cones. Every so often he would stop and gaze into space, sometimes for minutes, before starting off in a new direction, confidently, without hesitation, until something unseen caused him to repeat the process.

We walked like that for at least half an hour, then he stopped.

"The crones' huts are nearby," he said. "I can hear them. I would have found them sooner, but they're usually farther east in the summer since it's cooler over there."

Hear them? I was about to ask what he meant. Then I heard them too.

Boom…

I gripped the dagger and braced against the flood of memory: the weight on my back, suffocation, the hot carrion breath.

Boom…

Lucas looked ahead and to the left, peering into the forest at something I couldn't see. He lifted his arm and pointed.

Boom…

"There," he said.

52

I stood beside Lucas and tried to trace a line from his pointing finger through the trees. I was glad to see that it was brighter in this part of the forest. The trees were farther apart, and the sun came through the canopy in large columns of light, which danced with dazzling motes of dust.

The oily musk of the beast still lingered inside my nostrils, but it was fading. The ring of its Jurassic roar was fading from my ears, and the white-hot panic of the chase already seemed like something that had happened to a stranger long ago.

Far off, a brace of small birds chittered and lifted from the trees into the air, beating their wings. It was the same sound I'd heard yesterday when Hazel had dropped a half slice of sandwich bread to the ground. How long had I been in the forest? I looked up through a break in the branches and watched the birds fly past me overhead. I heard another sound, a distant humming, or maybe buzzing.

Boom...

In the distance, one of the massive cedars lifted itself, roots and all, hung in the air, and came crashing back down.

Boom...

I staggered back and felt like the ground was falling away. It was just like the story Hazel had found. The trees had come alive and marched on the early settlement at Charm Haven. Had they come alive again? The buzzing grew louder.

Boom...

The more I looked, the less likely it seemed I'd seen a tree move. The color was wrong, for one. This was more of an orangish umber, while the trees were ruddy brown. It was thinner than the surrounding trunks. Smoother too. And the roots didn't seem like roots, because there were only four of them. They were short and not caked with dirt like you'd expect. When the tree (or whatever it was) picked itself up again, I noticed it folded forward at the middle in a way that would have splintered any piece of wood. It unfolded itself.

Boom.

This wasn't a tree at all.

It was a leg.

An enormous chicken leg.

I heard myself laugh. That old geometry teacher, the one who always knew more than he thought, was a strange sort of guy. His class had been right after lunch, and he often brought a plate of food back to his desk to munch on while the class worked. He was fond of a particular joke, that I guess wasn't a joke at all, but an odd fact. If birds were the descendants of dinosaurs, he said, then chicken was the closest you could get to eating a T-Rex. *You know more than you think*, he'd said. Sometimes you knew more than you wished you did.

Boom...

I couldn't make myself take a giant chicken as seriously as

a T-Rex. As my eyes traced the legs up into the canopy, I saw that instead of dead-ending into a feathery body, the legs attached to a large platform made of rough-sawn wooden planks. Far above it I saw the outline of a roof and a chimney belching green smoke. It was… a house.

The buzzing was louder. Was the house making the sound? No. It was coming from behind us. Lucas didn't seem to care. He was too focused on the house with legs, and I suppose I couldn't blame him.

"Hello!" Lucas called up.

But still, what was with the buzzing?

A woman leaned over a railing on the side of the platform. "It's about time you showed up."

A bush rustled behind me. I spun around, expecting to see the beast with black feathers glaring with yellow eyes, but it wasn't. It was… some sort of box, or stack of boxes. It had a base with a little slit opening, and a lid that looked like the roof of a house. Around it was a buzzing black cloud of bees. It was a beehive.

It ran toward us, and I just stood there wondering how on earth a beehive was running. It didn't even have legs. It wobbled itself back and forth like you might move a piece of furniture that was too big to pick up. Still, it was surprisingly fast, for a beehive.

I glanced at Lucas, who wore only a puzzled grin and his fig leaf. He should have been a little more concerned, since he was naked and about to be engulfed in a swarm of angry bees.

There was a horizontal seam where the top and bottom boxes of the hive met. It hinged open and flapped up and down like it had something urgent to tell us. Either that or it wanted to swallow us.

The woman above us yelled something, and I heard a strange sound, and the hive stopped moving. Its smooth wooden sides pricked green with shoots that sprouted and unfurled leaves toward the sun. The bottom of the box grew roots that dove into the spongy earth. As the box finally disintegrated, its mouth opened one last time, and something like a contented sigh came out. A sapling was left in its place, along with a bunch of very confused bees.

53

We rose through the canopy and I gripped the porch railing as if sheer unreality might send me toppling. With every inch, the sun grew brighter, the air warmer, until we burst past the treetops like a whale breaching. In the distance water glittered in the sun. The damp, mossy smell of the woods blew away in a stiff salt breeze that carried the sounds of seagulls.

The house behind me looked like it might collapse at any second. At its base was a crude one-room cabin made from dark split timber, like something from pioneer days. But the original cabin had been built up, out, over, then up again, in an impossible way. A tall brick chimney rose up the side of it twenty feet or so, then jogged to the right before continuing up and disappearing in a cloud of green smoke.

It was a witch's house, no doubt about it. Straight from a fairy tale. Which made the sixty-something woman with a leopard print dress and red acrylic nails stand out even more. She looked at Lucas (still naked except for his fig leaf) with such obvious, unbridled lust I worried she might eat him whole.

"Thank you," he said, blushing, "for saving us from the... whatever that was. I wouldn't ever have come here like this if it wasn't an emergency."

"Well, darling, I'll have to make sure you keep having emergencies." It was the first time I'd ever seen a *woman* talk to a *man's* chest.

Her name was Deidre. I'd met her last night with the other crones. Unlike them, she didn't live in the forest, and she didn't wear the stereotypical tattered black dress. But a crone was a crone, I supposed.

"Deidre," I said. "We've come to ask your help."

"Oh, really?" She eyed my dagger. "I am Oz, the Great and Powerful! Who are you?"

"I'm Holly Ni—"

"I know who you are, child. I can see old Augustus's chin on you plain as day, but who is this pretty pound of flesh you've brought me?" She turned to Lucas. "A son of Empusa, is what we used to call your kind. What's your animal nature, darling?"

"A... jaguar," he said. *Flicker.*

"Fascinating." She drew out the words like every syllable was a piece of candy. "Would you like to see my animal nature?" She winked. "Kidding! Only kidding, darling, though I imagine I would make a fine cougar, and you don't need to tell me what kind of help you need. It's written on your face."

She reached out and rested her nails on Lucas's bare chest.

He tensed.

Flicker.

"I don't—" He gasped as the red acrylic nails sank into his sternum like it was Jell-O.

Deidre closed her eyes and frowned. "Who's been cleaning your aura?"

"What do you—"

"You should ask for a refund because it's cobwebs in here, darling. Though it's telling you had to come all the way to me for help. You wouldn't believe what passes for magic these days. Even the people with good intentions and a little bit of the knack don't know what they're doing."

Deidre paused like a cat about to pounce, then bit her lower lip. There was a snapping sound, only it wasn't a sound. It was too real, too clear, too bright, too... too... *everywhere*. Deidre nodded in a satisfied way and removed her fingers from Lucas's chest. She frowned at them for a moment, then wiped them on the side of her dress.

Lucas had stopped flickering. He held up his hands and looked from them to Deidre with awe. "Thank you! How did you—"

"A girl's got to have some secrets, darling. Now, about payment. I have the contract just inside."

"Contract?"

"For your soul." She studied him for a moment, then broke into a smile. "Kidding! Only kidding! Look at you, darling, your checks are so hot I could toast marshmallows on them. I supposed you think I've never seen a naked man before."

His face got redder. "I didn't, uh—"

"Well now you're just embarrassing me." She snapped her fingers with that sound that wasn't sound.

A puff of thick green smoke swallowed Lucas and was whipped away by the salt breeze. Lucas was now wearing tight stone-washed gray jeans and a black mesh shirt that was more hole than fabric. He looked down at the mesh shirt and tight jeans and then glanced at Deidre like a fly looking at a spider.

"Do you have any more normal clothes?" He asked.

She rolled her eyes and snapped her fingers. The mesh top disappeared and was replaced by a white polo shirt.

"There. You're boring. Are you happy now?" She said. "But where are my manners, keeping you out on the porch like this? Come in!"

It was cozy and bright inside. Every wall was covered in display cases. Every shelf was filled with bric-a-brac. Every chair draped with knit doilies (sometimes two or three). Colorful pots of lavender, rosemary, mint clustered around larger pots with orchids, hostas, monsteras and dozens of other plants I didn't recognize. Large windows on two walls looked out above the forest canopy. The sun was a hazy wildfire red, but the air inside smelled of citrus and cinnamon. The strangest thing in the place was the framed photo of Alex Trebek that hung above an ancient console TV.

Deidre led us to a small lace-covered table. "I'll go fetch the tea. I made you a fresh batch."

I watched her disappear through a door and leaned over the table toward Lucas. "You could have told me about the chicken house!"

"But then I wouldn't have gotten to see your face!" He grinned in that way I'd found so endearing when I was younger. "Besides, I wasn't sure if the stories were true. I'd only seen the crone's house once, at a distance, and it wasn't walking around."

"With all the time your family spends here they never saw it?"

"My family is allowed to hunt in the wood, but it's not like we're best friends with the crones."

"You call me a crone again, darling, and you'll find out what happens to little boys who go wandering in the woods looking for gingerbread houses."

She was carrying a golden tray with a tea set made of

280 | TABATHA GRAY

dark-polished wood. She put it on the table, poured, then sat in one of the mismatched chairs and joined us. Lucas looked like a frog about to be dissected.

"Kidding! Only kidding... or am I?" She winked and turned to me. "So, you're here about the magic."

I picked up my tea, and held it below my nose, smelling oranges, spice, and something almost like vanilla. I sipped and it was slightly sweet and the warmth swept through my body.

"How do you know?" I asked.

"Darling, you uncorked a bottle that's been aging for, what, five hundred years? The people around here aren't used to the good stuff. There's bound to be trouble."

I remembered what Tilly had told me after we'd battled with the plants. An old nursery rhyme had popped back into her brain and had nagged at her like an itch until she'd recited it. "It's like the spells are trying to make people cast them."

"Slippery things, spells." She picked up her teacup, took a sip, and sighed. "Tell me, Holly, what do you know about magic?"

"Vincent said magic holds the world together. It stretches between everything and everyone like harp strings."

She raised one eyebrow. "Maybe you're not as hopeless as I thought."

Deidre clapped her hands together, then drew them slowly apart. But there was something in the gap. A sort of blue-white glowing thread that stretched from one hand to the other.

"This is what Vincent was referring to. It's called a line of power. It's like many things, including a harp string. We can pluck it to hear its sound."

The thread of light began to vibrate, slowly at first, then faster until it was a blur. I heard something like a musical note, in that sound that was too clear, too bright, too everywhere to be a sound.

"When you play them, they create the music we call magic. But they're more than that." She wiggled her nose, and the room exploded with blue-white light.

54

I blinked and squinted until my eyes adjusted and I saw where the light had come from. There was no longer only a single thread connecting Deidre's hands, but millions of them, billions of them perhaps, connecting everything in the room to everything else, and near the center of the room the threads seemed to pool and join into something larger, which ran out under the front door. I glanced out the window and saw the blue light attaching to every tree, every branch, every bird in the sky.

"Lines of power," Deidre said, "have an affinity for one another. They flow together, creating massive rivers, which some people call ley lines, but which people like us call the Causeway."

She glanced at an ancient-looking full-length mirror crammed in one corner. The blue-white light made the silver surface shift like liquid mercury.

"Charm Haven is built on a crossroads, where two branches of the Causeway come together. There are other magical places too, which you could reach through that mirror if I showed you how. A week ago you would have had

TANGLED CHARMS | 283

to burn a few thousand dollars' worth of magical ingredients to get enough energy to travel the Causeway. But now that you've released the magic pent up in the locket, it's as easy as snapping your fingers. Easy enough you could do it accidentally."

I considered it for a moment. "You're saying that magic is easier and people are casting spells on accident."

"It's the simplest explanation."

"No it's not," I said. "It doesn't explain why this all happened before to the founders."

Deidre brought her hands together, and the lights went out. "What do you know about the founders?"

The sudden harshness in her tone made me fumble for an answer. "There were... seven houses on seven hills."

She laughed. "My family was the eighth. The inquisitors got our parents, so it was just me and my three sisters who joined Augustus to steal that boat and sail it off to who-knows-where. We were young and hotheaded and the most powerful damned witches anyone had ever seen. When the town made its truce with the wood, the wood demanded hostages to make sure the people didn't try any funny business. My sisters and I were allowed to keep just enough magic to keep themselves alive for thirteen generations, to be around when the locket was unsealed, to make sure that the wood was protected. And they were bound there, too. They couldn't leave."

Her family... her sisters... that would make Deidre over five hundred years old. Anywhere else I wouldn't have believed it, but I was having the conversation inside a house that walked around on chicken legs, and had its very own magic mirror. If ever there was a place to suspend disbelief, it was there.

"Your sisters were bound," I said, "but you weren't?"

"I wasn't around when they made the contract, so certain

parts of it didn't stick to me." A faraway look washed over her. "Oh, those were salad days. I was off chasing a merman I'd seen glittering in the sun on some rocks offshore. Oh, he led me on a chase that lasted a couple of weeks, and in the end he turned out to be a seal, but a year on a boat with no privacy is bound to dive anyone to rut."

"To rut?"

"Now let's see you do it," she said.

"See me... do what exactly?"

"Put your hands together, then show me the line of power between them. It's one of the first exercises they teach you in magic school, back before education went down the commode."

"But I don't have any magic."

"You're a Nightingale aren't you?"

"I gave it all away."

"Stop talking nonsense and put your hands together."

I sighed and clapped my hands together and scowled at Lucas for looking at me. I felt like the biggest fool in the—

She slapped me with a bony hand.

I jerked back and my face stung. "What the hell?"

"What the hell?" Lucas echoed, standing up.

"Simmer down, Lancelot. I could see from the look on her face she didn't have the right attitude."

"And hitting me's going to fix that?" I said.

"Yes, yes it will. Now clap those hands back together and get out of your head. Get into your hands. Feel the tension between them like an electric arc, like magnets held just apart, like lovers about to—"

"I get it!" I sighed and bit my lip and tried to get into my hands, whatever the hell that was supposed to mean. I didn't feel anything but normal hand stuff. The pressure of them pressing together. A small stinging pain from where I'd scraped them while fleeing for my life.

"Now turn on your sixth sense."

A sixth sense? Really? I barely stopped myself from blurting out: *I see dead people.* But I remembered the too-clear, too-bright, too-everywhere sounds. I hadn't heard them with any of my ordinary senses…

I gritted my teeth and tried to feel, or hear (I don't know) something coming from my hands. All I felt were my arms getting tired from holding up my hands, and my right shoulder stiff and sore from forcing it to bend backward during my fight with the beast. It was all so stupid.

I heard the slap and felt a bright pain on my right cheek. I kicked my chair back and stood.

"Why do you keep hitting me!?"

"I'm trying to wake you up, you stupid girl."

"I'm awake! And I'm starting to think that this was a waste of time. I didn't come here to drink tea and get abused. I have to fix this haywire magic before the city council votes. I have to solve a murder to get my sister out of jail! I have to figure out some way to make her forgive me. And then, to top it all off I have figure out how I'm going to protect her in this crazy world where dudes in robes are trying to murder her and people in chicken houses go around slapping me for no reason!"

"Can you hear yourself, darling?"

"With my normal senses or the imaginary ones?"

"I. I. I. Me. Me. Me. Did you ever think it wasn't all about you?"

"All about me?" I walked to the door and grabbed the handle. "My life was literally destroyed last week. I should be on a couch, covered in blankets, eating pint after pint of Ben and Jerry's, watching daytime TV while I try to pull myself together. Instead, I came to this island, and since the moment I arrived, it's been nothing but pressure. Hi welcome home! You're the thirteenth daughter! You have a prophesy! Save the town. Save your sister. Solve a murder. Save magic. Oops! You messed up. Better fix it!"

Deidre let out a sigh. "Oh, child. Don't you realize what a fool you're being?"

"I don't know what you're talking about!"

"You really don't understand, do you?"

"No!"

"Prophesies don't carry quite the same weight when you know the person who made them. And magic doesn't mean you're special, or pure at heart, or any of that bullshit, pardon my French. Magic is a relationship."

"What's your point?"

"You're isolating yourself. You're helping people, sure, but you're cutting yourself off from them at the same time."

"So I'm supposed to just drop everything and let my sister rot in jail so I can get all woo-woo one-with-nature? I won't do that."

"It takes the whole world to make the sun rise, darling. But here you are, squinting and straining, trying to pull the damned thing up all by yourself. You might be the thirteenth daughter. You might be part of the second-most powerful family of witches on the island. But you're not a superhero."

I glanced out the window and looked out across the tree-tops. They stretched like a grassy field into the distance, where they sank into a dazzle of ocean. I didn't know what to think. I felt flustered, back-footed. Deidre had slapped me. Part of me wanted to slap her back. But what if she was right? I'd come into the Crone's Wood thinking I could fix magic and be back in time to see Hazel at visiting hours. I'd been stupid and naive. I could still feel the suffocating weight of the beast with black feathers. I could still smell its carrion breath. The only reason I was still alive was because Vincent had given me a dagger and Lucas had evened the odds. I wasn't a superhero. I couldn't do it all myself.

TANGLED CHARMS | 287

I went back to the table and sat. "Okay," I said. "What do I do?"

"Put your hands together and reach into the *else*, that sixth sense of yours, and try to find the connection between your hands."

I sighed, clapped my hands together and closed my eyes, and tried to be Zen like a monk. But the list of everything I had to do, from saving the town from Anwir, to saving Hazel, kept scrolling in my mind. I remembered a trick I'd read about though, and imagined a cardboard box, then imagined myself putting all my mind's clutter in the box and closing the lid. My body felt lighter, and my breathing was more relaxed.

I felt my hands press together, felt the warmth, the pressure, and then... something else. It was like the moment your heart hitches when you see a long-lost friend at the airport, like the feeling the grass must have toward the sun. A slender thread of connection, a... tugging. No, a *longing*.

"Good," I heard Deidre say. "Now spread your hands apart slowly—slower, don't let the connection break. Now reach out with your mind and pluck the string."

I'm not sure how I did it but the string came to life with a blue-white light, just like it had with Deidre. I felt a lurch of excitement. I glanced to her as the light flickered out.

"There you go," she said, "you're a natural. You'll learn to keep your focus longer with practice."

A warm feeling flooded my body. Was it relief? The little flicker of light I'd made between my hands was proof that magic hadn't abandoned me. I'd just been going about it wrong. And magic hadn't chosen Hazel. It had come to her more naturally because she was naturally more open to the world around her. Still...

"This is all great," I said, "but I need to fix the haywire magic."

"Didn't you hear me? You can't. Not by yourself. The people of Charm Haven have to learn how to use their new power responsibly. My sisters and I will teach them how. It's why we've waited all these years."

"But that will take time."

"Most things do."

"The city council meeting is at four, though. It's too much to explain, but the haywire magic means they might miss an important vote. Is there any way, to, I don't know, stop magic from happening in a certain place?"

"Stop the strings from vibrating? It's easy enough."

"Ummm, Holly," Lucas said. He was glancing at a cuckoo clock on the wall. "You said the meeting is at four?"

"Yeah."

"That's ten minutes from now."

I sucked in a breath. "We'll never make it in time."

Deidre clucked to herself, and grinned so broadly I wondered if she was entirely sane. "This old house has been cooped up in the forest for too long if you ask me. I think it's about time we let it stretch its legs."

55

I looked out from the porch into the wind and watched the beehive sapling disappear into the distance. The house was sprinting through the wood. It moved so fast I'd worried at first that it might shake itself to bits, but the motion from where I stood was as serene as a boat on calm water.

The air rippled and distorted in front of us like a fisheye lens. It made me seasick so I looked away and saw the beast with black feathers stare at us with yellow eyes, then disappear behind. I looked down and saw the silver-gray glint of the whittler city, and one of whittlers themselves raising its hammer in salute. Then they, too, were behind us. The forest grew lighter. We burst into the clearing in a cloud of cedar needles and bark.

Now that it didn't have to navigate the trees, the house sped even faster. The clearing whipped past in an insistent. We reached the rock outcropping and the first scattered industrial buildings on the edge of town. I thought for a moment the house might crash into them, trip and fall and send us flying from the porch, but it didn't. It… jumped.

It landed on the rooftops and kept running, bounding from roof to roof, as light as the wind itself. As the buildings grew closer together, it leaned into the final stretch then made a soaring leap into Charm Haven Square, where it landed, dipping to absorb the impact, and stopped.

I leaned against the porch railing and looked down from the height of a ten-story building at clusters of people staring up at us as if we were invaders from Mars.

"Take us down, girl," Deidre said, stroking the wooden doorframe fondly.

The house responded to her command, dipping low until we were a mere dozen feet off the ground.

"Now comes the fun part," she said, and stepped off the porch into the air. But instead of dropping out of sight she hovered for a moment, then descended gently toward the ground like Mary Poppins floating in on her umbrella.

She looked up at Lucas and me. "Just step down. The house won't let you fall."

I did what she said and she was right. It wasn't like riding the broomstick the other night. That had felt, well, like riding a broomstick. If you kept it up for too long, you'd be waddling from splinters. This felt more like being surrounded by a feather pillow, with just enough pressure to hold you and deposit you safely on the ground.

When my feet touched the cobbles, I wiggled them and stretched a little and looked up at the statue of Augustus. Thank goodness the house didn't also have a chicken's beak. If it tried to eat birdseed from Augustus's hand, he'd probably lose the arm, bronze or not.

"It looks nothing like him," Deidre said. "It completely misses the raw, animal—"

"Come on!" I grabbed Deidre by the arm and dragged her toward city hall. I didn't want her getting distracted and chasing off after any seals.

TANGLED CHARMS | 291

The city hall door stuck like it always did, but I got it open. I felt bad walking by the police office, where Hazel was probably still languishing, but I couldn't do Hazel much good right now.

The meeting room was near the back of the building, on the other side of the post office, and from the shouts and sounds of a gavel banging I could tell it was going like I'd expected.

"I demand decorum!" a gray-whiskered man shouted. He stood at a podium and was banging his gavel. A ball of crackling energy hit him in the chest and pink bunny ears sprouted from his bald head. He blinked and felt around up there, then looked into the room and shouted in an oddly squeaky voice: "Who did that?"

A younger woman with curly hair blew smoke off her fingertips and smiled. "Oh, lighten up, Orimund! You've never looked more huggable!"

"Give me that gavel, Orimund!" Henrietta Thorn shouted. She was holding a stack of papers to her chest so they didn't fall, and a pair of glasses was on top of them. "I'm the chair of the council. Only I get to use the gavel."

"Not for much longer," another woman said. I'd seen her at the fete but didn't know her name. "It's about time you practiced not being in charge, Hattie. You know you're going to lose the chair in the next election, now that you've lost the trust of small business owners."

"You bitch!" The word was a bark and had a trace of that sound that wasn't sound. It blew so strong that the woman's shadow detached from her, whipped out beside her and flapped like a flag in a stiff wind. Then the shadow lost its grip, flew across the room, and slapped onto the wall.

"Can someone please turn me back!" someone else said in a pitiful cooing voice. It was coming from a pigeon, gray and iridescent green, that hopped along the council's table and

292 | TABATHA GRAY

flapped its wings. "Please. Please. Turn me back." It pecked at someone's pencil.

Deidre stepped into the room and shook her head like a teacher entering a rowdy classroom.

"Enough!" Deidre shouted, her voice laced with power. When it faded, the room was quiet.

That sound that wasn't sound was quiet too. All the magic reversed itself. Orimund's bunny ears were gone. The woman had her shadow back. The pigeon turned into an overserious high school boy with thick glasses.

Henrietta Thorn grabbed the gavel from Orimund. She cracked it on the podium. "Now we will move on to new business."

"Wow," I said to Deidre. "She didn't skip a beat."

"Magic can play tricks with memory. Remember that."

I believed it. After all, magic had been used to hide my memories from me for most of my life, and I was still a little salty about it.

"I have new business." It was Vincent. I hadn't seen him before and hoped he hadn't seen me. I was just glad Lucas wasn't naked anymore.

Henrietta Thorn was arguing with Vincent, about some minutia or other, a reason that his anti-Anwir ordinance couldn't be brought up for a vote, but I wasn't paying attention.

My eyes were drawn to the stack of papers she had left on the table and the glasses sitting on top of them. Even from where I stood, I could see that they were horn-rimmed glasses.

"It was you!" I didn't mean to say it as loud as I did. Certainly not loud enough for the entire room to hear me, and turn toward me like that. The shock of the discovery had made it happen.

"This is highly irregular," Henrietta said from the podium.

"You were the woman with the horn-rimmed glasses we saw go into the police station! You were the anonymous informant who told Deputy Sprout that my sister was there at the time of the murder."

"It's none of your business where—"

The doors burst open behind me and slammed into the wall. I turned to see Hazel and Dana and Hector and even Deputy Sprout rush into the room.

"It was you!" Dana said, pointing an accusing finger.

"Is there an echo?" Henrietta said.

She said something else too, but I didn't hear it, because I was too busy looking at Hazel. Her yellow dress was wrinkled and dingy from the night in jail, and it still looked radiant on her. She was still the most beautiful person I'd ever seen. My vision went blurry with tears.

"I'm sorry," I said. "I never should have kept that meeting with Lin from you. I never should have lied about the call. I was being so stupid, trying to fix everything myself like I always do and I didn't stop to think how it would affect you."

"Shut up and give me a hug." She opened her arms.

I looked at her dumbly. Could forgiveness come so easily? Would she give me such a gift? The answer, it seemed, was yes. I rushed to her, hugged her, pressing my head against her shoulder, trying through pressure to communicate everything I wished she knew, all of my guilt, my worry, my fear and the new thing, the feeling of seeing your friend at the airport after a long absence, the cold-hot feeling of magic burning like captured lighting between your hands.

"Look," she said. "It's Dana's big moment."

Dana was in the middle of the room, standing. Everyone looked at her, but she was staring at Henrietta. "... my sources told me that the owner of Anwir Holdings was none other than Joseph Thorn."

The entire room gasped, all except for Henrietta.

"What is this nonsense about my husband? Who cares if he owns some company or other? He's always run our affairs quite efficiently. If you have any questions I'm sure he'll be happy to answer them when he returns from his business trip."

"Your husband was found dead last year in rural Oregon. He had been burned at the stake."

"Nonsense." She laughed, but it wasn't convincing.

"Your late husband did manage your affairs well. He left you a considerable fortune, including Anwir Holdings. When you started to lose the support of the local business community, you came up with an easy solution. You'd buy their shops, and poof, no more pesky business owners."

"Is that true?" A familiar voice said from the other side of the room. It was Tilly. "Were you trying to put a cork in us? What did you think, we'd just move away and forget all about where we're from?"

Henrietta didn't reply.

"I guess I have my answer." She reached into her bag and pulled out the manila envelope I'd given her yesterday—had it been only yesterday? It had contained the paperwork to transfer the deed for her tea shop over to Anwir. She ripped it in half.

"It's over, Hattie," Deputy Sprout said. "Why don't you come on over here and we can avoid making a scene."

"E-even if I were trying to buy property, that's hardly illegal."

"But murder is," Deputy Sprout said. "We have an eyewitness who was working on a scaffold outside the police offices. He saw Hazel Nightingale leave the station, then he saw you. Said he didn't recognize you at first, but then you took off a wig. You're the chair of the city council, so you have the master key to city hall. You used that to disable our

TANGLED CHARMS | 295

surveillance, hide in an unused office, let yourself into the man's jail cell and kill him."

"And what reason would I have to kill a man I'd never met?"

"That's what puzzled me too, until Ms. Dana showed up with her research. Your husband was burned at the stake. Now, what kind of person burns someone at the stake? An inquisitor, that's who. I think you were in league with them. That they helped you knock of your old man, and in return you gave them a warm welcome to our island."

She was silent, barely moving for a dozen heartbeats, then she threw the gavel to the ground. She huffed, and walked stiff-shouldered past me, past the deputy, out of the room. He followed her.

Orimund picked up the gavel with a greedy smile. He stepped over to the podium and cleared his throat. "I would like to propose a motion to make myself, Orimund Withers, temporary chair of the council pending an election!"

A round of ayes went up and the gavel cracked.

"The motion is passed. And now I would like to call a vote on the mayor's ordinance, to prevent Anwir or anyone else from owning more than one parcel in Charm Haven Square. All in favor of the mayor's ordinance?"

Another round of ayes went up and the gavel banged again.

"Now let's see what Hattie left us for business." He went over to the pile of papers and removed the horn-rimmed glasses, setting them off to the side. He flipped through the papers.

"Nothing new here, just minutes, the proposed agenda, and... what's this?" He reached into the pile and came out with an envelope. It was sealed and had nothing written on either its front or back. He slipped a finger under the flap and tore the paper, and took out its contents and frowned at them.

"It's a photocopy of a press clipping. London 1897—Ha! A little before my time, believe it or not. Headline reads: Alderman Slays Wife. And would you look at this, there's an engraving of the alderman and it looks a little like you Mr. Mayor."

Vincent staggered back. He turned and rushed toward the exit, toward me, like an animal running from a burning building. He didn't see me. Then he did and the panic in his eyes turned to howling sadness as Lucas put his arm around my shoulders to protect me.

56

SOMEWHERE IN THE NORTH PACIFIC

Caleb Robinson knuckled the helm of the thirty-foot Zodiac and stared at the flaming trawler. Behind him, twin two-fifties raged like a swarm of angry hornets, thrusting the boat over swell after swell, sending the salt mist up to soak the black robes of the men of his order.

The small craft rode low in the water, its bow cutting through the waves like a knife. The trawler was a hundred yards away, and the heat from the flames was pleasantly warm.

He was leaving with fewer men than had arrived. Nicholas, the abomination had been sacrificed. And Brother Albinus had been struck down before his mortal weakness could threaten his immortal soul. Their contact in Charm Haven had made sure of it.

Now, Brother Kingley, glory be his name, had volunteered to guide the flaming ship and its explosive cargo to its final destination.

Caleb Robinson smiled the serene smile that came to those who had worked hard and done well. Victory was not merely assured. It was already theirs, for they were the Lord's will made manifest. They were His sword of righteousness.

57

*H*azel stood next to me on the crone's porch, looking down with disbelief at the crowd in Charm Haven Square that had come to gawk at the house with chicken legs. The wind had changed and blew the smoke away and a yellow sun hung in the western sky. Not hot, but pleasantly warm.

The door closed behind us, and Deidre stepped beside me.

"Are you sure you don't mind giving us a lift to Gran's place?" I asked.

"Of course not," Deidre said. "This old bird's glad to get out of the coop and stretch her legs a little. But you know it's not your Gran's house anymore. It's yours."

"I guess I'll have to get used to saying that."

"Does your sister's... friend want to join us?"

"Dana?" I shook my head. "She's handing over all her research to Deputy Sprout. We'll pick her up later."

"What about the pretty pound of flesh?" she said.

"I won't stand in the way of true love."

300 | TABATHA GRAY

"Who said anything about love?"

I felt the porch sway gently and the crowd below let up a collective *whoa!* The house moved slowly and carefully at first, so that it didn't squash anyone, then faster on the rooftops, picking up speed and leaping high into the air. I felt the floor press into my legs, just like I'd felt the elevator in city hall, rising to Vincent's office. I don't know what had happened with him. The way he'd looked at me when Lucas put his arm around me made me feel like I'd let him down at a vulnerable moment. Henrietta had tried to blackmail him, and in the end the truth had come out in front of everyone, though I was sure there were more sides to that story.

Hazel grabbed my hand and squeezed and looked at me like she didn't know whether to be whooping with excitement or terror.

We landed gently in front of the gate. It was already open, but that didn't matter, because the crones' house stepped over it, and walked up the garden path to our pink and purple Victorian mansion with the wraparound porch, its turrets and fish-scale shingles.

"You know, I haven't seen the place in years," Deidre said. "Believe it or not, it started out a lot like this house, a simple cabin. But your family seems to have had more conventional taste in architecture than mine."

"Would you like to come in for a tour?" Hazel said. Of course she would offer. My sister was always too empathetic, even after everything she'd experienced. Maybe she could teach me a thing or two.

"I'd love a tour," Deidre said.

But before we could go there was a noise from inside the crone's house.

"That'll be my sisters," Deidre said, opening the door.

I had a good view of that full-length mirror in the corner, and I saw it shimmer, then liquefy into something like a pool of mercury, if mercury could be stood upright without spilling.

The reflection of the inside of the house rippled and distorted, then stilled and it wasn't a reflection of the house anymore. From the shelves, and the way the books were stacked on them, I knew it had to be a bookstore, but not the kind of bookstore I had run, selling new releases in paperback. This was an antiquarian bookstore, and the volumes on the shelves were beautifully bound in leather with gold tooling.

Then someone leaned in from the side. It was a woman, much older looking than Deidre, with a hunch and a wart on her nose, and a black dress that had been worn until it was threadbare. She tapped on the mirror from the other side.

"This thing on?" The words came through the mirror bassy and slurred, as if they had been spoken by a drunk man underwater.

"Of course it's on!" Someone out of sight answered. "Just go! I've got to go powder my nose."

"You haven't worn nose powder in three hundred years!"

"She means she has to pee," a third voice said. "Get on with it!"

"Fine!"

The surface of the mirror rippled and the woman stepped through the mirror as easily as walking through a door.

"Deidre!" the first woman said, looking out the window to the copse of cedar trees that separated Gran's house from the garden. "Now where have you gotten us to?"

"Make way! Make way!" The second crone pushed past me. She ran out of the living area, toward the back, and a moment later I heard a contented sigh. *Ew.*

"Is it the Nightingale house?" The third crone said. "I haven't been there in centuries."

"They're going to give us a tour!" Deidre said.

"Oh, how delightful! And you were right, sister, Paris has changed so much its unrecognizable. Did you know they put up a giant, ugly metal construction right in the middle of the city?"

"It's called the Eiffel tower," Deidre said.

"The Eiffel... Is that what it is? I've heard Trebek talk about it on the television, but I never imagined it would be so large."

"Or so hideous." The crone returned from the bathroom, wiping her hands on her black dress. "Now what's this about a tour?"

We all gathered around the crones' steps. The house squatted, and we all stepped off the side and floated down to Gran's front porch. The front door wasn't locked, so we went in. My nose prickled, and the familiar dirty-tasting wildfire smoke bit into the back of my throat.

The crones followed me inside, and all immediately went quiet.

"Something's wrong," Deidre said. "The house is not alive."

My first reaction was to argue, but hadn't the house kept out the smoke yesterday? Now it had seeped in. My eyes went to the spot by the front door where the magical shoe rack had stood. It was gone.

"Just a second," I said. I left them in the foyer and ran to the kitchen and stepped in. It was cold and quiet. The fire in the stove had gone out. Two shiny foil Pop Tart wrappers still sat on the counter, surrounded by small white crumbs. The house hadn't cleaned up. Something was wrong. My stomach turned.

I walked back to the foyer, knowing my next move, but the crones had beaten me to it. They had taken the portrait of Augustus off the wall and were opening the small iron lock box behind it.

"Well that's the problem right there. Your focus is missing," one of them said.

Focus. The word had been written on the small booklet Uncle Max had taken. That booklet must have powered the house in some way, and I had given it freely to him, and even felt grateful that he'd dropped his lawsuit and let us keep the house.

A loud noise came from the library, like the roar of a freight train, so loud it shook the house.

I rushed in and saw Gran's full-length mirror filled with fire. It was like looking through a furnace window. Then a person appeared, far away at first but getting closer. It was a man, running toward us. He reached the mirror and jumped through.

The sweaty, sooty man stood in Gran's library, doubled over, panting and coughing. He reeked of burning wood and gasoline. After a moment, he looked up. His eyes passed over me, but stopped when they reached Deidre.

"The Inquisition," he said in a voice so ragged and hoarse it might have been a whisper, "has burned Hallowfern Forest."

The tallest of the crones stepped next to me and stared into the fiery mirror. Her eyes covered with swift-moving gray clouds. She spoke:

> *In the holy wood's bright pyre*
> *a prophesy of doom descends.*
> *A hidden power born of fire*
> *casts the bones and bones it mends.*
> *Love, now distant through the haze,*
> *blows like ash upon the wind.*
> *Two souls apart, untethered gaze*
> *across a gulf no love can span.*
> *To shirk your doom, the fates' decree*

a sacrifice to hated Mars.
The sap of ancient Dryad's tears
and whispers caught from dying stars.

EPILOGUE

THE CRONE'S WOOD

Yellow sunlight broke through the canopy of the Crone's Wood. It fell in a long shaft onto the cedar sapling. Around its base lay the shattered remnants of a beehive. Sheets of hexagonal wax filled with golden honey and darker brood, bent and folded and dripped to the forest floor.

Thousands of bees were in the air, but one was not. The queen bee had sensed a certain familiarity in the cedar sapling. She landed in the crook where its two largest branches intersected. Hundreds of her companions joined her and sent out a message, in that mysterious way only known to bees.

They would build a new hive, of wax instead of wood, and when they were finished it would not contain a single straight line.

Also by Tabatha Gray

Gossip Ghost
Buy direct from the author at tabathagray.com

New friends, family ghosts and a riot at the community center.

When Emma, 40, inherits her estranged aunt's psychic shop, she doesn't plan to stay. Back home her career is hanging by a thread. But so is the body she finds in the attic.

Murder spills a lifetime of magical secrets. Decades ago, they destroyed a family and gutted a community. Now they're Emma's only second chance.

Gossip Ghost Chapter 1:

"Are you sure this is where we turn?" Emma scowled and craned her neck to see the next street sign. "I could have sworn we just went through this intersection."

"Turn left."

"Okay, okay, I get it. You're the expert here. I appreciate that. But there's something I appreciate even more than

308 | GOSSIP GHOST

expertise: accountability. So if I find out you're leading me on a wild-goose chase—"

"Turn left."

"—I'm going to throw you out the window." She turned left and gasped. Sunny blue skies reflected off a lake filled with boats. A red-and-white seaplane took to the air, flying past the Space Needle and bending toward a snow-capped Mount Rainier. It was not what she expected.

After listening to hours of her mom's gloom and doom, she'd expected Seattle to be more like a damp anarchist Thunderdome. But it was the most beautiful city she'd ever visited. In the past ten minutes, she'd glimpsed enough scenery to fill a lifetime of postcards.

Was that Lake Union glistening like a jewel? Or Lake Washington? Puget Sound? Elliott Bay? Were those rugged mountains the Cascades or the Olympics? Were those gigantic trees spruce or cedar? Maybe it was better not to know—to just take it all in.

She turned up the stereo. The chorus of "Shake it Off" swelled and made her heart thump with excitement. This was the last song on her playlist titled Jessie! She'd imagined it playing as she pulled into the driveway where her long-lost cousin would be waiting to welcome her back. First, she had to find the place.

"Take the exit on your right."

"Seriously? I'm not even on the highway. How could I possibly exit?" She looked around frantically for anything that might pass for an exit to a GPS on the fritz. "Have you ever thought you might need to go in for a refresher course?"

"Take the exit now."

"Some sort of continuing education for robots?" Emma eyed the window, wondering if she had it in her.

"Take the exit."

"Okay. You're dead." She reached blindly toward the car's

cup holders, finding the smooth hard phone where she expected it. "You too, Taylor—I'm sorry. I still love you."

But before she could shut down the Map and Music apps, the phone slipped from her fingers. It fell through the crack between her seat and the console, landing somewhere below her.

"I guess I should have tossed it out the window after all." The loud music drowned her voice out. She hit the car stereo's Power button, and the world went silent. Decisive action—that's what you needed to get ahead these days. Fortune favored the bold. You made your own luck.

"Make a U-turn, then make another U-turn," the disembodied voice called from beneath her.

"Is that your idea of a joke? You want me to go in circles?" She swerved into the nearest parking spot and slammed on the brakes. "You had one job, GPS lady. You blew it."

She'd been in the city for an hour and was already crazy, yelling to herself in a car. She took a swig of day-old coffee from her travel mug. Dregs. Beneath the seat, her phone chimed, "You have arrived!"

This was all that stupid lawyer's fault…

Buy direct from the author at tabathagray.com

ABOUT THE AUTHOR

Tabatha Gray is a Seattle-based author who loves to explore the supernatural through her cozy mystery novels. She has written several books in the genre, including the popular Undertown series. Tabatha is a lifelong lover of all things spooky, and in her free time, she enjoys exploring the local haunted sites that dot the Seattle area. In her writing, Tabatha aims to bring a sense of comfort and security to her readers while exploring the supernatural. She hopes her stories will inspire readers to embrace the unknown and find solace in life's mysteries.

www.tabathagray.com